Tabitha Locke's Key to Happiness

LIZ DAVIES

CHAPTER 1

Tabitha Locke draped a pristine white tea cloth over the tray and smoothed it flat. The toaster popped and she hurried to fetch the butter from the fridge, glancing at the clock on the wall as she did so. One minute to go before the eggs would be ready to fish out of the boiling water.

She quickly buttered the toast and cut it into soldiers, arranging them on a side plate, then plucked two silver-plated eggcups out of the oak dresser. They weren't in the least bit practical, but Grandad insisted on them. In some ways she couldn't blame him: he had so many lovely things, why shouldn't he use them? On the other hand, *he* wasn't the one who would be cleaning them.

Hastily, she lifted the eggs out of the water and placed them into the eggcups before slicing their tops off. Next, she added a china cup and saucer, a small jug of milk and the teapot, in which Grandad's loose-leaf tea that he had specially blended for him, was brewing.

With the addition of cutlery, she was done.

Oops, not quite! She had almost forgotten the salt and pepper, which would never do, as he would refuse to eat his eggs without a sprinkling of salt.

Carefully she picked up the tray and made her way up the stairs, using her elbow to open the door to Grandad's bedroom. He was awake as usual, and on seeing her, he shuffled up the bed into a sitting position.

Tabitha set the tray down on the cherrywood table at the foot of the bed so she could plump his pillows up, and when he was settled, she smoothed the covers.

'Boiled eggs?' he asked, watching her carry the tray to the bed and position it on his lap.

'Of course.' He always had two boiled eggs for breakfast, two slices of thickly buttered wholemeal toast, and two cups of tea. And ever since the croissant incident, without fail he always asked Tabitha whether she was serving him boiled eggs.

As her grandfather tucked into his breakfast, Tabitha drew the heavy lined drapes and light flooded into the room through the large sash windows.

She peered at the square below. 'It's going to be a nice day for your walk,' she observed.

Every morning, after his ablutions, her grandad ventured into the streets of Bath's city centre. Depending on the weather, the walk would either be a long one or a short one, and always cumulated in a visit to the Georgian Tea Rooms where he met some of his cronies for a cuppa and a natter. The natter, as far as Tabitha could tell, was normally a grumble about all the things wrong with the world, and how they would put things to rights if they were in charge, and whilst Grandad enjoyed his morning, Tabitha would work in the shop, as she did every day except for Sundays.

Although her own breakfast waited for her downstairs, she took a moment to study the scene outside her window.

Abbey Green wasn't a green as such, because it didn't have a grassed central area. It was more reminiscent of an Italian or French square, with its cobbles, quaint shops and cafes. It also boasted a huge tree in its centre, which was famous enough to appear on some of the guided tour routes of the city. The tree provided welcome shade in the summer and was festooned with glorious twinkling lights in the winter. Around its base lay golden-coloured gravel, giving it a regal air and echoing the gorgeous honey-coloured stone that many of the buildings that the green and the historic Bath city centre were constructed out of.

The lights in Embla's Tea Room opposite were on, she noticed. It would be opening shortly to catch people on their way to work, but the rest of the shops around the square wouldn't open until at least nine o'clock.

Locke's Key Emporium opened at nine-thirty on the dot – enough time for Tabitha to eat a leisurely breakfast, tidy up and have a shower in the Victorian-style bathroom (she had begged Grandad to have a shower installed not long after she'd moved in and thankfully he had acquiesced).

Grandad's flat sat above the shop, and the living quarters were laid out over two floors, plus an attic, but that was rarely ventured into. The flat was sumptuously decorated, with period features and antique furniture galore, and to Tabitha, it felt like she was living in a Jane Austen novel. She never tired of it.

Breakfast eaten, she cleaned the kitchen, washing up in the old-fashioned way (by hand in the butler sink) and she swept up the crumbs from the tiled floor using a dustpan and brush because Grandad fussed about the noise the vacuum cleaner made. By the time she had finished tidying up, Grandad was out of the bathroom, so she took her turn, wincing at the cold tiles under her bare feet. The water was lovely and hot though, which more than made up for the lack of underfloor heating; she had also lobbied hard for that, but Grandad had been immovable. He was immovable about a great many things and some of them she agreed with, except when it came to her creature comforts.

Her grandad should have lived in the nineteenth century: he hadn't been too impressed with the twentieth, and the twenty-first was beyond him. It was often beyond Tabitha too, and she must be the only twenty-nine-year-old in Bath to not own a mobile phone. But there was a good reason for that – one she didn't want to think about on this fine Tuesday morning.

There was a landline in the shop, and another in the hall of the flat, but they had no broadband, no website and no online presence, and that was exactly how she and Grandad liked it. Locke's Key Emporium had been here for over a hundred years, all of them without the doubtful benefits of modern technology, and the shop was still thriving. Word of mouth was a powerful tool, and it had served the shop well over the years, so neither Tabitha nor Grandad felt the need for change. They prided themselves on their old-fashioned, olde-worlde service and values, and as the shop only sold antique keys and not modern ones, it seemed rather fitting.

At a quarter-past nine, Tabitha headed downstairs to the shop, contentment flowing through her. It was her favourite place in the world, and she never tired of it. When she was a child, she used to love visiting Grandad and his magical key shop, and used to imagine all the doors those keys unlocked. Castles with pointy turrets and fairy princesses often featured heavily. But she had gradually stopped visiting as often when she became a teenager, as castles were replaced in her mind by exams, boys and a burgeoning social life. University was followed by her first proper job and then she had fallen in love.

And look how badly that had turned out.

Not wanting to let thoughts of her ex darken her good mood, she pushed the memories firmly to the back of her mind. The present was what counted, not the past, and Tabitha's present was quite satisfactory. Gosh – *quite satisfactory?* – she was beginning to sound like Grandad. Not surprising really, considering the two of them had lived in each other's pockets, more or less, for the past three years.

With only fifteen minutes to opening, Tabitha had better get a move on.

The first task was to remove the most valuable keys from the safe in the workroom out the back, one tray at a time, and place them carefully in the display cabinet beneath the counter, which she then locked, using one of the keys hanging from a chain around her waist. She could just as easily have put the keys in her pocket, but she loved the idea of having them hang from her waist as though she were a lady in a great house. The chain was called a chatelaine and it served as a perfect showcase for the antique keys hanging from it, much the way the perfectly made-up face of a sales assistant on a beauty counter in a department store served to advertise the make-up she sold.

The chatelaine went well with the tea dresses Tabitha favoured, but didn't look as nice with jeans, although she could get away with wearing tailored trousers and a nice blouse without the old-fashioned key chain looking too out of place.

There were only a few minutes to go now, so she made sure the card machine was working. Several years back, Grandad had been forced to give in and use a credit card machine after far too many sales had been lost due to his insistence on only accepting cash or cheques. The machine was an old dial-up version, connected via the telephone landline, and Tabitha constantly worried that it was on its last legs.

Seeing with relief that it was still working, her final task before unlocking the door was to check the contents of the antique till, and to place a receipt pad and fountain pen on the counter. Customers loved being given a hand-written receipt, and they were fascinated by the ancient pre-decimalisation till which had pounds, shillings, and pence on its keys. It was a great talking point and added to the shop's charm.

At nine-thirty on the dot, just as the clock on the wall struck the half-hour, Tabitha unlocked the door. Three locks (all of them older than her and with ornate keys) and one bolt later, Locke's Key Emporium was open for business.

Throughout the morning, she had a steady succession of customers. Many came in out of curiosity and to exclaim at the olde-worlde interior, and Tabitha lost count of the number of times she heard people say that stepping into her shop was like stepping back in time a century or two. But she didn't mind, and a couple of people actually bought something.

Tabitha was busy serving a dapper old gentleman who was an avid and discerning collector of keys (although he insisted that she used the correct term of *cagophilist*, instead of *key collector*) when the bell above the door tinkled and a man walked in. This wasn't an unusual occurrence, but what was unusual was the ornate box he carried.

Out of the corner of her eye, she watched him gaze around at the displays, and every so often he would look down at the box in his hands and frown.

Tabitha had seen this kind of behaviour before: the man was looking for a key to fit a lock.

After carefully wrapping her customer's latest purchase – a silver gilt presentation door key with an extremely ornate handle dating from 1880 and still in its original silk-lined box – Tabitha turned her attention to the other customer.

She glanced briefly at him, enough for him to realise that she was at his disposal, but the majority of her focus was on the box.

It was beautiful. Tortoiseshell, she guessed, and the garlands of flowers and leaf inlay that decorated it were possibly mother-of-pearl. It shone and gleamed under the lights, and she couldn't wait to get her hands on it.

Her attention still on the box, she said, 'How can I help?'

'I was hoping you could sell me a key to this.' He put it gently down on the mahogany counter, and as he did so Tabitha's eyes flew to his face.

There was a timbre to his voice that had set her nerves jangling – smooth, melodious, with a faint Welsh lilt. It reminded her of Richard Burton's voice (she and Grandad had watched a lot of films starring Richard Burton). Not as deep perhaps, but then again, that was no surprise as this guy was only about thirty years old.

And starkly good-looking.

Another Richard sprang to mind – Richard Madden. The man standing in front of her had tousled brown hair, blue-grey eyes, a square jaw, and a three- or four-day-old beard.

An unexpected thrill went through her, and she hastily looked down at the box.

Tabitha reached for it. 'May I?'

'Be my guest.'

That voice… it made her go weak at the knees, and her heart was all aflutter.

Concentrate on the box, Tabitha, she told herself. He was just a man. He may be good-looking and have come-to-bed eyes, but he was here for a key, not to be drooled over.

'Is it made out of tortoiseshell?' she asked.

'I believe so. And mother-of-pearl, so my nanna says.'

Tabitha turned it over, examining it from every angle and admiring its beauty, which was far more preferable than staring at her customer and admiring *his* beauty.

Trying to marshal her wayward thoughts, she studied the lock. She was no expert on locks themselves, but by association she knew a fair bit. This was probably a simple two-lever box or cabinet lock.

Risking a glance at him, she asked, 'How old is it, do you know?'

'Early nineteenth century, I believe. My nanna inherited it from her grandmother, who inherited it from *her* granny.'

'It's beautiful.'

'It is.' He was smiling at her, his eyes crinkling at the corners. He had a very nice smile. The kind of smile that begged to be kissed.

It faded, and Tabitha realised she was staring.

She cleared her throat. 'We should have something that will fit. Let me see...'

Over the years, her grandad had amassed a considerable number of old keys which had little or no value. He never threw a key away, and the room out the back, which once used to be a workshop, held boxes of the things, all neatly labelled.

Tabitha picked up a carton of jewellery box keys and returned to the shop floor.

The man was gazing around the walls. 'It's like stepping back in time. Diagon Alley, eat your heart out. Are any of these magical?'

'I wish they were.' She picked up a likely-looking key and offered it up to the lock. The lock was having none of it. She tried another.

It didn't like that either.

'Have you been here long?' he asked.

She glanced up again. He was examining one of the displays.

'Me or the shop?'

He looked over at her and laughed. The eye contact sent a shiver down her spine – a delicious shiver, not an *oh God it's the middle of the night and someone is downstairs* shiver.

It was a long time since she'd felt a shiver like that. But not long enough.

'Both?' he said.

'I've been here three years and all my life,' she replied, enjoying the puzzlement on his face at her cryptic response. 'The shop belongs to my grandfather,' she explained. 'It was his father's before that. My great-grandfather opened it in 1909.'

'It doesn't look as though it's changed much.'

'It hasn't,' she replied proudly.

'Does that thing work?' He gestured to the till.

Tabitha pressed a key and a 1d flag popped up. 'Yes.'

'1d?'

'Old money, pre-decimalisation. 1d means 1 penny.'

'Why the d? Why not a p, like today?'

'No idea.'

'Will I have to pay you in gold doubloons?'

'Why? Are you a pirate?'

He laughed again, then sobered as he saw her try another key without success. 'No luck?'

'Not yet.' Tabitha picked up the box and held it to her eye as she peered into the lock's interior. It wasn't giving anything away.

'Do you have more shopping to do?' she asked. 'This could take a while. On the surface it looks like a straightforward cupboard lock, but I suspect there's more going on inside than it's letting on.'

'Er, not really. I came into town specifically to see you. Not *you* personally—' He stopped and made a face. 'Sorry, that sounded worse than I meant. It is nice seeing you, don't get me wrong, but I meant I came to see the shop.'

Tabitha studied him in amusement. For a handsome chap, he seemed rather awkward and unsure of himself. She liked that. She'd had her fill of suave, self-confident men.

'Most people do,' she replied. 'I don't know anyone who comes to see me *personally*.' She emphasised the last word. Then wished she hadn't replied at all, because it made her sound pathetic and needy. She lowered her head and tried another key.

'Will this take long, do you think?' he asked.

'It might, which was why I asked whether you had any more shopping to do, so you could leave the box with me.' She looked up in time to see a frown sweep across his features. He didn't appear to like that option. 'Or you could wait,' she added.

His eyes narrowed. 'You don't have a website.'

'That's right, we don't.' The abrupt change of subject took her aback.

'You're not on social media either.'

'No, we aren't.'

'Why not?'

Tabitha shrugged. 'We don't need to be.'

'I might never have found you.' His tone was accusing.

'Ah, but you *did* find us.'

'True.' He fell silent for a moment as Tabitha powered through key after key. 'Since 1909, you say?'

'That's right.'

'You're still going to be here in an hour, aren't you?'

'I would have thought so.' She was trying not to laugh. His expression was so serious.

'In that case, I'll pop over the road and have a coffee.'

'Good idea.' Tabitha wasn't fooled. From Embla's Tea Room her customer would be able to see directly into her shop. She slightly resented his lack of trust. The box was worth several hundred pounds, so his concern was understandable but unwarranted. It wasn't as though she was going to steal it.

'If I can't find a key for it, would you like me to pick the lock?' she asked.

He looked surprised. 'You can do that?'

'Yes.' The lock looked straightforward enough, but she had a feeling she might have to do some persuading. The trick was not to damage the box or the lock in the process. 'There isn't a lock made that can't be picked, even if it hasn't been picked *yet*.'

He nodded. 'The same can be said for any operating system.'

'Pardon?'

'Hacking, as opposed to lock picking. It's the same thing, I suppose.'

Tabitha blinked. How had they gotten onto the subject of hacking? 'Er… right.'

'I'll, um, be off,' he said, looking embarrassed. 'Shall I come back in an hour?'

'OK, see you in a bit,' she said, as he headed for the door.

But her customer wasn't done with her yet. 'By the way, my name is Rhisiart. It's the Welsh form of Richard.'

Why wasn't Tabitha surprised?

CHAPTER 2

Tabitha bent her head to the box as he left, but as soon as the bell above the door tinkled, she glanced up from underneath her lashes to watch him saunter across the cobbles.

He had his hands in the pockets of his hoodie, and every couple of steps he tilted his head back to stare into the canopy of the large plane tree that dominated the centre of the square. When he reached the tea room opposite, he paused and glanced over his shoulder.

Tabitha quickly lowered her gaze, not wanting him to see her interest, and by the time she looked up again, he was gone. She could see a figure inside who she guessed might be him, but she wasn't certain, and when her view was obscured by a woman entering her shop, Tabitha tore her gaze away to focus on her customer.

'I want a gift for a dear friend,' the woman said, and Tabitha was soon lost in the intricacies of finding the perfect key. It wasn't easy, as the lady had only a vague idea of what she was looking for, but eventually a purchase was made and Tabitha was able to return to the box and its stubborn lock once more.

Now that she wasn't distracted by a customer, Tabitha had the feeling she was being watched, but when she studied the tea room there was no sign of Rhisiart, so maybe she was imagining it.

She had no sooner selected another key than a second customer demanded her attention, and because Mr Forsythe was a regular and someone to whom she enjoyed showing her latest stock, Tabitha didn't begrudge him a single second of her time.

Mr Forsythe had only been gone a minute or so, when Rhisiart returned.

'I'm so sorry, Rhisiart, I haven't had a chance to look at it,' she said, wincing inwardly at the disappointment on his face.

'Call me Rhys, everyone does.'

'Tabitha,' she replied.

'I did notice you were busy.'

So, he *had* been watching her. She'd thought as much, but she couldn't totally trust her instincts. Not since her life had fallen apart so dramatically had she been able to trust herself. It had taken her a year to stop believing that everyone was staring at her, and even now, three years on, the hairs on her arms stood to attention if a stranger's gaze lingered for too long or if someone gave her a second glance.

Rhisiart was studying her now, but she knew it was only because he was expecting her to say something about the box.

'I'm sorry,' she repeated. 'Can you leave it with me a while longer? Until the end of the day, perhaps?' There was no guarantee that she would have found a key to fit by then, but if the afternoon wasn't busy she would have a fighting chance.

He gazed at the box. 'Um...' A line appeared in the middle of his eyebrows and his lips narrowed. Tabitha guessed he wasn't thrilled with her suggestion.

In the interest of honesty, she said, 'I can't guarantee I'll be able to find a key by then, but if I'm busy, I promise I'll lock it away under the counter. It'll be perfectly safe.'

His lips tightened further and she hoped he didn't think she was accusing him of not trusting her, when all she was attempting to do was to reassure him.

'I'm sure it will be,' he said. 'It's just... Can I call back with it tomorrow?'

'Of course.'

'It's not that I don't trust you.' He patted the box gently. 'It's very valuable. Not to me, to my nan. I mean, it's valuable to me too, but it's even more valuable to her. The contents, that is. Not the box.' He pulled a face. 'The box does have a value, of course. About £600, I believe, but what's inside is priceless.'

Tabitha didn't say anything, hoping he would tell her what it contained without her having to ask.

He picked it up, cradling it to his chest. 'Right then. I'll, er, see you tomorrow.'

'I'll look forward to it,' she replied politely, feeling anything but polite.

What she actually felt was a tingle of pleasure that she would be seeing him again. The tingle worried her. She could do without tingles and good-looking men – that kind of thing brought nothing but trouble. Look how badly it had turned out the last time. It didn't matter how often her grandad or her parents had tried to convince her that men like Austen were the exception, not the rule, she couldn't bring herself to believe it. She would never, ever trust another man again. It was safer that way. Tabitha's life was steady, safe, predictable and uneventful, and that was just the way she liked it.

***

At five-thirty sharp, Tabitha shut the shop. Three keys, three locks, one bolt, plus a turn of the sign hanging from the door from *open* to *closed*. Her final tasks before going upstairs to the flat, was to secure the more valuable keys and the day's takings in the safe, and give the floor a quick sweep. She used an old-fashioned carpet sweeper that was older than her, but it did a decent job of picking up all the bits which had been tracked in to mar the worn Turkish rug and dirty the polished oak floorboards. A quick flick around with a feather duster, and she was done.

'How was your day?' she asked her grandfather when she peered into the parlour.

Grandad was in his usual seat, a wingback chair near the window. It was angled so he could see both the outside world and the TV. A footstool in the same rich ruby-red velvet sat in front of it, and a small table was by its side. On it was the newspaper he'd bought this morning, a cup and saucer, and a substantial hardback. A book on Egyptian tombs, Tabitha saw, as she reached across to pick up the empty cup.

'Good,' he said, tapping his lined cheek for a kiss.

Tabitha's lips brushed against his face and she caught the familiar and comforting scent of his aftershave. He had worn the same fragrance ever since she could remember, tipping some into the palm of his hands and patting it on his face every morning after shaving. When she was little, she had tried to do the same with her mother's Chanel No 5 and had been soundly scolded.

'How was your day?' he asked.

'Come into the kitchen and I'll tell you about it while I cook dinner.' They had the very same conversation at the end of every working day, and Tabitha loved the routine.

With a twinkle in his eye, her grandfather inched his backside to the edge of the chair and levered himself upright. Tabitha tried not to let her concern show. Over the past several months, she had noticed that Grandad was having greater difficulty in getting out of his chair, and she wondered whether she could risk suggesting one of those electric chairs that lifted you out of your seat. Or would she get her head bitten off? Probably the latter. Grandad might be in his early 80s, and he might have more-or-less retired, but he hotly refuted any suggestion that he was getting old. He also refused to admit that he was retired, instead telling people that he was stepping back because Tabitha needed to learn the business, and the best way to learn was to *do*. So she *did*, and her grandfather *didn't*. Although he liked to pretend that he did.

One of their evening rituals was Tabitha reporting on her day in the shop – every tiny detail – whilst she prepared dinner for them both. Grandad would listen intently, ask questions, and offer advice. Sometimes that advice would be a softly worded order.

As usual, Tabitha began her report by telling him how much the shop had taken and, as usual, her grandad made a note of it in his ledger. Tabitha would have already recorded the sale in the book which was kept under the counter, making sure it tallied with the handwritten receipt she gave to each customer. But Grandad liked to keep his own copy. He would then transfer it to the accounts book.

She knew Grandad's accountant despaired whenever he was presented with the big account book and a briefcase full of receipts and invoices, but at least they were all in order and meticulously kept: her grandfather made sure of that.

Next, he wanted to know what keys had been sold and to whom, nodding his head when she told him about Mr Forsythe's purchases.

'I would give my right arm to see his collection,' her grandad said. 'He has bought at least a hundred keys off me over the years, and I suspect that's only the tip of the iceberg. He's been collecting keys since he was a boy. Are you aware he also collects chatelains?'

Tabitha's eyes went to the door leading to the hall. She had removed her chatelain as soon as she'd entered the flat. When she wasn't wearing it, it lived in the drawer of the narrow table. Grandad's keys were kept there too.

When she first came to live with her grandfather, she used to lose her keys constantly until she'd learnt to leave them in the same place. Life was too short to spend it hunting for everyday items. She did the same with her purse, its home being the top drawer of her nightstand.

Besides, Grandad disliked mess, and it was easier to put things away in their rightful places, than have him tell her off, certainly in the beginning, when she had been so fragile.

With practised moves, Tabitha seared two pork chops on both sides, then popped some asparagus into the steamer, in which new potatoes were already cooking gently.

'Five minutes,' she warned.

Her grandad took this as his cue to wash his hands and lay the table.

In the beginning, he used to cook the evening meal, but as time went on he had been happy to relinquish the task to her. And shortly after he'd 'not retired' she had begun bringing him breakfast in bed. He seemed to enjoy the fuss she made of him, and she assumed if he didn't, he would have let her know by now.

Tabitha enjoyed looking after him. It was the least she could do, considering how well he had looked after her, although she would have done it anyway, because she loved him to bits.

When they sat down to eat at the table by the window in the kitchen, Tabitha shook out her linen napkin (they were a nuisance to launder, but they were so much nicer than paper serviettes) and draped it across her lap. Should she mention Rhys and his box? For some reason, she was reluctant to tell her grandfather about him, but she couldn't work out why. Was it her inability to find a key to fit, or was it Rhys himself that she didn't want to discuss?

Tabitha popped a forkful of asparagus into her mouth and chewed. She had lightly seasoned it with salt and pepper and had put a knob of butter over the top. The butter had melted, coating the asparagus spears, and she savoured every bite.

As she ate, she asked herself whether she would be as reluctant to mention him if Rhys was a middle-aged woman with warts on her chin, and she came to the conclusion that she wouldn't. Therefore, it was Rhys himself who she didn't want to mention. Which was ridiculous. He was just a customer. Why wouldn't she tell her grandad about him?

'A man came into the shop this morning. He had an old box with him. It was gorgeous: tortoiseshell, inlaid with mother-of-pearl. About this big.' She indicated the size with her hands.

Her grandad took a sip of water. She always served it in crystal glasses as though it was the finest wine, when in fact, it was just chilled tap water. Grandad had definite views about paying for water in bottles when the same stuff came out of the tap. The only time he didn't object, was if the water was sparkling. Tabitha had rather liked bottled water. There was definitely a difference in the taste. She drank the tap variety readily enough, though.

'Did he want you to open it for him?' her grandad asked.

'He wanted a key.'

Grandad raised his eyebrows. Generally, people who came in with locked items weren't bothered about keys. They merely wanted their lock unlocked. 'Cupboard lock?' he guessed.

Tabitha shook her head. 'A version of. It's a little more complex. Easy enough to pick, but as I said, the customer wants a key for it. I tried a few, but none of them matched.'

'Go fetch it after dinner. I'll take a look, if you like.'

'He took it away with him, but he's coming back tomorrow.'

Grandad chuckled. 'Did he think we'd take a sneaky peek?'

'I think he was more concerned that we might lose it.' Tabitha pursed her lips.

'That is the most ridiculous thing I've ever heard. We do not lose things. Admittedly, I did misplace a bronze interlock steam valve key once, but I found it after a few days.'

She shrugged, equally as baffled as to why Rhys hadn't left the box with her.

'Do you think it particularly valuable?' he asked.

'About £600, he said.'

Grandad waved a hand in the air. 'Pfft. What about the contents?'

'Priceless, to his grandmother, at least. Whether you or I would think the same, remains to be seen.'

'How old is he?'

Tabitha tilted her head to the side, wondering what Rhys's age had to do with anything. 'Thirtyish.'

'Young then. I envisioned someone older.' He put his knife and fork neatly together on the plate and dabbed at his mouth with the napkin. 'That was delicious, my dear. Thank you.'

'Go sit down and I'll bring you a cup of tea.'

'And a biscuit? A wafer would be nice.'

Tabitha smiled at him. 'I'll bring you two wafers, if you like.'

'Let's not be greedy,' he said, patting his stomach. 'I don't want to get portly.'

Tabitha laughed to herself as she boiled the kettle and cleared away the dinner things. Her grandad was so old-fashioned and quaint, and she adored him for it. He was what some people might refer to as 'old school,' many of his habits having been formed in the boarding school he had attended when he was a boy.

Harrow had been followed by Cambridge, his education paid for by a legacy from his own grandfather, Jeremiah Locke – her great-grandfather and the same gentleman who had founded Locke's Key Emporium and had given her grandad his name, albeit Grandad shortened his to Jeremy. From Cambridge, he had gone into the family business and had never left.

Tabitha guessed she would also do the same. She had always loved the old shop but, like her father, she hadn't been remotely interested in taking over the reins – until three years ago, when she had been forced to go into hiding and had fled to Bath and Grandad. And now she couldn't imagine doing anything else, or being anywhere else.

Bath suited her: the history the city boasted was outstanding, and its architecture was some of the best in the world. She adored the secret little alleyways, the cobbled streets, the Roman baths. And although it had its fair share of humdrum high street chains, it also had a diverse range of gorgeous independent shops, which were of far more interest to Tabitha, especially when it came to shopping for clothes. Even as a teenager, when she had so desperately wanted to fit in, she had cultivated her own style, quirky and vintage. And Bath had an abundance of quirky and vintage.

She hadn't been shopping for herself in ages. Maybe she would ask Grandad to mind the shop for a couple of hours later in the week. Not tomorrow, though. She thought it best she be the one to serve Rhys when he returned with his box.

She ignored the voice in her head telling her that her grandfather could probably take one look at the lock and place his hand directly on the key to open it. Rhys was *her* customer, so she would be the one to deal with him.

***

The following morning, whilst Grandad was tucking into his boiled eggs and wholemeal soldiers, Tabitha was standing in front of her open wardrobe and peering at the contents. She had a lovely collection of dresses, but none appealed to her as one by one she dismissed them all. Today she felt more like wearing jeans and a pretty top – but she never wore jeans when she was in the shop. She always wore a dress, low heels, her chatelaine, and maybe a vintage brooch or a string of pearls, or sometimes her gold locket.

But never jeans. Grandad would have a fit if she did. He liked the shop to portray the charm of yesteryear, and that included her. It was the reason customers returned time after time; not for *her*, of course, but for the atmosphere, the ambience. Jeans and a top, no matter how pretty it was, would spoil the effect, a stark reminder that the shop was an illusion and the real world was still out there.

Tabitha resisted her wild impulse and picked out a dress, pale blue with a chiffon skirt and a fitted bodice. Not too fussy, but not pop-to-the-supermarket plain either.

Pearls with this, she thought, and slipped a double string over her head. She had washed her hair this morning and the thick curls bounced around her shoulders.

She stared at her locks critically, wondering whether she should straighten them. If she did, it would be the first time in a while. However, she decided she wouldn't, mainly because she couldn't find her straighteners.

As she was hunting for them, she came across her seldom-used makeup. So she went for that instead; just a swipe of mascara. It was amazing how long and full her lashes were afterwards, and it was also amazing that the tube of mascara hadn't gone gooey or clumpy.

Finally, she was ready. It had taken her longer than usual and when she trotted downstairs it was to find her grandad washing up.

'That's *my* job,' she protested. 'I always wash up the breakfast things.'

'I thought I would give you a helping hand, considering you are running late.'

'I'm not running—' Oh, darn it. She *was* running late. It was twenty past nine.

Grabbing her keys out of the drawer, Tabitha dashed downstairs. She had a shop to open.

But to her disappointment, and although she kept a keen eye out for him all day, Rhys failed to show.

CHAPTER 3

Tabitha adored the spring. New leaves were unfurling, flowers were popping up in gardens, window boxes and planters all over the city, and the days were getting warmer and the evenings were getting longer.

She was about to lock up, her mind on the possibility of going for a stroll after dinner, when a figure appeared at the door just as she reached for the sign.

Her heart thudded when she saw Rhys and she was in two minds to tell him that the shop was closed.

To her mild annoyance, she had been disappointed with his failure to show yesterday. She hadn't wanted to admit that she had been looking forward to seeing him, but the truth was that she had. And she was cross more with herself than with him.

Instead of telling him he was too late and he should come back tomorrow, she treated him the same as she would any other customer who arrived on the cusp of closing time, and she opened the door, stepping to the side to allow him to enter.

'Am I too late?' he asked, sounding out of breath.

'Not at all,' she replied graciously, then said, in direct contradiction, 'Although I'm afraid I won't be able to look at your box right now. I have an appointment, you see. With my hairdresser. Otherwise, I would...' Tabitha trailed off, wondering why she was lying.

'Oh, I see. In that case, I won't keep you. Maybe I could call back another time?' He didn't sound hopeful.

'Maybe you could leave it with me?' she suggested.

He had that look again: the one that told Tabitha he didn't trust her to take care of it. She tapped her foot, her ire growing. Did he think she would hawk it at the first opportunity? Drop it down the stairs? Throw it in the bin?

He must have mistaken her irate foot-tapping for concern that she might miss her appointment, because he said, 'OK, if you insist.'

Tabitha lost patience. 'I don't insist at all. Leave it, or don't leave it. I don't care. You're the one who wants a key for it. I don't need your custom.' She paled, horror-stricken as she realised what she'd said.

Grandad would be appalled if he'd heard. Tabitha had never spoken to a customer like that in her life.

But instead of being offended and taking his business elsewhere, he laughed at her. 'Sorry, did I come across as thinking you were untrustworthy?'

'Just a bit.'

'I didn't mean to be; it's just that this box is special.'

She lifted an eyebrow. He'd told her that already. 'Why? What's in it?' She had already been disrespectful and her customer service so far had been shocking, so she had nothing to lose by asking him out right.

'Letters mostly, and photos. Plus a few mementos. They are memories of my grandfather, and they're incredibly precious to Nanna.'

Tabitha felt awful. Something like that couldn't be replaced by a new-for-old insurance policy. Rhys was right – the contents *were* priceless.

'I promise I'll take good care of it,' she vowed. 'Otherwise, come back tomorrow and I'll see what I can do.'

'Will it take long?'

'About the length of a piece of string.'

'What? Oh, I see! OK then, I will leave it with you. It's just, you don't appear to have an alarm system or any CCTV.'

Tabitha blinked. She hadn't expected that. 'Don't we?' She raised an eyebrow.

The shop *didn't*, but she wasn't about to broadcast that little titbit to the world. Instead, she preferred to let him think that they *did* have those security measures in place, but they were so well hidden he couldn't see them.

As his gaze flickered around the shop, uncertainty flashed across his features. It didn't last more than a second before it was gone. With a shrug, he handed her his grandmother's box.

Tabitha took it from him carefully. 'I'll put it in the safe after I've locked up,' she said, expecting him to leave.

Rhys didn't take the hint. Maybe he wanted to watch her put it in there, to make sure? She decided she would let him stay for a minute. It couldn't do any harm.

Aware of his eyes on her as she switched the sign from open to closed and shot the bolt across (it would do for now, because she'd have to let him back out in a minute), she hurried to open the safe, making sure to shield it with her body. He appeared harmless enough, but she didn't intend allowing him to see the combination.

It swung open heavily and she moved position so he could see her place the box inside. 'There,' she said. 'All done. I'll let you out.'

'Can I give you a lift? I'll feel awful if I make you late.'

Tabitha nearly asked, 'late for what?', but caught herself just in time. 'There's no need. It's within walking distance.' And to add credence to the lie, she explained, 'My hairdresser is in St James's Parade.' Which was true, Tabitha *did* go to that particular hairdresser. She just wasn't going there this evening.

Rhys smiled. 'I'll walk with you. My car's in Avon Road Car Park.'

Tabitha sucked in a breath and let it out slowly. Damn. Hoisted by her own petard. Oh, well, she had been thinking about taking a walk, so this would be it. Grandad wasn't in this evening, as he was going to one of his old boys' meetings, the kind of meeting where men dress up in odd costumes and have strange handshakes, so Tabitha didn't have to rush upstairs to prepare a meal. In fact, she might not bother cooking at all tonight, and would treat herself to a takeaway instead. Grandad hated curry, so she only had it when he wasn't eating with her. Even then, he would complain about the smell. Perhaps she'd have a real treat and eat out? Then again, she didn't fancy sitting in a restaurant on her own, even if she took a book for company.

Rhys was still waiting for a response. 'OK, I'll just finish up here. I won't be long.'

'What time is your appointment?'

'Six-thirty.' She was lifting a tray of keys out of the cabinet as she spoke and she crossed her fingers underneath the tray as she picked it up.

'Is there anything I can do to help?'

'Not really. I've got this down to a fine art. Won't be a sec.' In no time at all, everything that needed to be locked away had been. 'I'll just nip upstairs for my bag and coat.' She would leave a note for Grandad too, although she fully expected to be back long before he returned.

She also took the opportunity to change into jeans and a sweatshirt, then fretted that she had committed the cardinal sin of leaving a total stranger on their own in the unattended shop, so she dashed back downstairs, trying to slip her feet into a pair of ballet pumps at the same time.

To her relief, Rhys was exactly where she had left him. He didn't appear to have moved an inch, but that didn't mean he hadn't. He would have had enough time while she faffed around, to stuff half of the contents of the shop into his pockets, if he had felt inclined.

When Rhys saw her, his eyebrows shot up. Tabitha hoped it was because he liked what he saw (although she might never want another relationship in her life, she wouldn't refuse some male appreciation) but he brought her swiftly down to earth when he said in an incredulous tone, 'You live upstairs?'

'I do. With my grandfather.'

'Handy.'

'Very.'

Her illusions shattered, she was about to leave by the rear exit, when Rhys took a step towards the shop's front door, and she realised she hadn't locked it. The only thing securing it was the bolt.

Good grief! How to look incompetent in one easy lesson! Tabitha decided to style it out.

'Shall we leave by the rear exit?' she suggested. 'I want to pop some rubbish in the bin on the way. Excuse me, while I lock the front door.' Once again, she was conscious that he was watching her every move as she turned the keys in the lock, before leading him through the workroom to the rear door and into the narrow lane beyond.

As they began walking, Tabitha felt self-conscious and more than a little awkward. She had no idea what to say to this man.

Fortunately, he didn't appear to suffer from the same affliction. 'When you're not selling keys, what do you do to relax?'

'I read a lot, watch TV. Documentaries and old films mostly.'

'When you say old, how old do you mean?'

'Thirties, forties, fifties.'

'Black and white?'

Tabitha smiled. 'Many of them are. What about you?'

'Gaming, a bit of RPG.'

'Pardon?'

'Literary Role Play. Very loosely, it's a combination of storytelling and gaming.'

'I see.' Tabitha didn't see at all. Things had clearly moved on since her self-imposed ban on everything to do with the internet. 'Anything else?' she asked.

'I like going to the cinema, watching live bands, eating out.'

Tabitha used to like to do those things too, once upon a time.

'I particularly like Thai food,' he added.

'So do I. Anything Asian, really.'

'There's a fantastic restaurant in Northumberland Place called Koh Lanta. Have you been there?'

'I can't say I have,' Tabitha replied. She definitely hadn't, but that was due to Grandad preferring to go to places where the menus were more traditional.

'You ought to try it,' Rhys enthused.

Tabitha smiled politely, drawing to a halt outside the hairdressing salon. Thankfully Thursday was late night opening, otherwise she would have looked a right idiot. 'This is my stop,' she joked weakly.

'Right. OK. I'll... um... see you tomorrow, then.'

Ah, yes, the box. How could she have forgotten? 'After this, I'll go back and start work on it,' she promised.

She had already tried the more obvious keys, so after her takeaway she would try the less obvious ones. And if necessary, she would use one of the skeleton keys in stock. It wasn't ideal, in that she would prefer to find a key that fitted the lock perfectly, but beggars couldn't be choosers. A skeleton key was better than no key at all, and her customer wouldn't necessarily notice. It was simply a matter of pride that she hadn't used a skeleton key in the first place.

After saying goodbye, Tabitha pushed open the door to the salon as Rhys walked off in the direction of the car park. She had better go inside in case he looked back, so whilst she was here, she may as well make an appointment. Her hair could do with a trim; she hadn't had it cut in nearly six months and it was getting long. Admittedly, not as long as she had worn it three years ago, but she wasn't happy with it getting any longer.

Appointment duly made, she decided to go for a stroll along North Parade and up to Pulteney Weir before making her way to the restaurant she usually favoured when buying a curry to eat out.

Tabitha retraced her steps for some of the way, then her feet took her towards the river and Parade Gardens, with its winding footpaths through landscaped lawns and flower beds. She especially loved the pretty bandstand and the well-maintained borders. It was an oasis of green peacefulness in the heart of the city, and she dawdled to the railings and peered down at the river flowing serenely past. A couple of ducks paddled busily by, quacking to each other, and she smiled. It was little things like this that brought her joy these days. Not parties, or nightclubs, or festivals. This…

She watched the birds until they disappeared from view, then made her way up the sweeping steps leading to the parade, the smell of the river in her nose and its burbling gurgle in her ears, the sound of the water becoming louder as she neared the weir. Shaped like a ship's prow, the three steps of the weir were white with rushing water, and the sound of it masked the noise of the traffic on the road behind as she placed her hands on the stone balustrade and looked over it.

To her left was Pulteney Bridge, the river flowing under its arches, the golden-hued buildings that sat on top of it gleaming in the evening sun.

If Tabitha closed her eyes, she could almost hear the clip of horses' hooves and the trundle of carriage wheels as her imagination transported her to the fictional world of *Persuasion* and *Northanger Abbey*, both of which had been set in the very real city around her.

It was only her tummy rumbling that brought her back to the present day and the need to satisfy her hunger.

Turning away from the river, she plunged into the still-busy streets and headed towards the abbey. Although the magnificent building was closed to visitors at this hour, people were taking photos of the outside, and the area thronged with tourists and locals alike.

Tabitha didn't immerse herself in the city's lively cafe culture or thriving bars (she didn't have anyone to immerse herself with and even if she had, she wouldn't have wanted to) but it was nevertheless nice to see people enjoying themselves. The restaurants and bars were busy, laughter and chatter drifting into the street, along with the tantalising scents of food. Some people were even drinking outside, although it wasn't warm enough for Tabitha's liking.

As she sauntered along, she glanced inside one of the bars, remembering when, many moons ago, she had done the very same thing herself on a Thursday evening, having a laugh and a few drinks with friends, the relief of almost reaching the weekend making her giddy and lighthearted, and the prospect of another day at work made more bearable by the knowledge that tomorrow was Friday and the mood would be lighter.

Her gaze slid across a group of people standing around a tall table, drinks in hand, and an unexpected wistfulness stole over her.

She had been young, her whole life stretching ahead of her, filled with possibilities. She'd had a boyfriend who she shared a flat with, had a great selection of friends, had a job she could tolerate, and she had been having *fun*.

But Austen had blown her world apart and—

Tabitha's gaze flashed back to the group, and her eyes narrowed. Unless she was very much mistaken, the man with one arm slung around a woman's shoulders and a pint raised to his lips, was Rhys.

She froze briefly, then slowly carried on walking, her eyes fixed on him.

He was partly in profile, so she couldn't be entirely certain, but it looked like him from the side, and he was wearing the same colour jacket he had been wearing less than an hour ago when she had said goodbye to him outside the hairdressing salon.

The man turned a fraction, lowering his glass, and in that moment she knew. It *was* him. But he had definitely been going to his car and he had even offered to give her a lift, so what was he doing here?

When Tabitha saw him smiling down at the woman, she knew why he was there, and her heart gave a lurch of disappointment before she told it not to be so silly. He wasn't interested in her (why would he be?) and she certainly wasn't interested in *him*, so there was no reason to feel anything other than mild curiosity.

Tabitha speeded up, and soon the bar was behind her. But when she approached the entrance to the restaurant, she discovered she was no longer hungry.

Despite the enticing aroma wafting into the street, Tabitha's appetite had deserted her.

CHAPTER 4

It was surprising the number of people who came to Locke's Key Emporium for the express purpose of buying a key for an eighteenth or a twenty-first birthday gift, and many of them liked a story to go with that gift. Most of the time, Tabitha was only able to supply the barest of details, such as its approximate age, what metal the key was made of, and what it would have been used to open, but that was generally sufficient.

Tabitha was serving a couple who wanted a special key an eighteenth birthday, when the bell above the door tinkled and she automatically glanced around to check who had entered.

On seeing it was Rhys, her breath caught and she cleared her throat before returning her attention to her customers.

'He can put it on his car key,' the woman was saying. 'His father has bought him a car for his eighteenth, much to his mother's disgust. That man does nothing but throw money at the boy, when what the child needed was a proper father, one who was there for him, not one who bought him the latest electronic gadget and said job done.'

'His mother is our daughter,' the man added. 'We're his grandparents.'

Tabitha had guessed as much. She made a non-committal murmur. 'How about this one?'

As she presented the couple with another key to examine, she glanced at Rhys out of the corner of her eye. He smiled at her, his expression warm. Tabitha gave him a brief smile in return, then looked away. It was only when the sale was complete and the couple left clutching their purchase, did she acknowledge him again.

'Your box is in the safe,' she told him. 'I won't be a moment.' Tabitha used the short amount of time it took to remove the box, to compose herself.

Seeing him again in all his handsome sexiness and hearing his voice, had sent her pulse racing, which in turn made her even grumpier than she was already.

She had gone to bed grumpy last night, despite having found a key to fit the pesky lock and had woken up even grumpier this morning. It hadn't helped matters that her dinner had consisted of a piece of toast, and her mind had been filled with Rhys's smiling face.

She had left the key in the lock, and she watched his face closely as she placed the box carefully on the counter.

He stared at it for a moment, then his eyes lit up. 'May I?'

Tabitha inclined her head. 'Of course.'

Rhys carefully turned the key and the lock clicked open, the lid lifting a smidgeon. He pressed it down without looking at the contents and relocked it. 'That's brilliant. Thank you.'

Taking the key out of the lock, he held the small piece of silver metal in the palm of his hand and examined it closely. The key was quite ornate, despite its size, and in Tabitha's opinion it complemented the box perfectly.

'It's lovely,' he said. 'How much do I owe you?'

Tabitha had taken the liberty of writing out a receipt in anticipation, and she tore it off the pad and pushed it towards him.

Rhys frowned, then he looked at her quizzically.

Tabitha bristled. The price she was charging for the key was more than fair.

'Are you sure this is right?' he asked.

Her tone was frosty when she replied, 'Quite sure.'

'But this doesn't cover your time, surely?'

'Er, no. I haven't charged you for my time.' Perhaps she should have done, but it hadn't occurred to her.

'You were working on this after hours,' he pointed out. 'Your hair looks nice, by the way.'

Self-consciously she put a hand to her head, trying not to smile.

'Have you had it cut?'

'No.'

'Good, that length suits you. Coloured?'

'Um, no.'

'Oh.' He appeared stumped, as though he had exhausted his knowledge of what went on in a hairdressing salon.

'Deep conditioning treatment,' she fibbed. The compliment about the length of her hair lingered in her mind. She had always preferred herself with long hair, until that awful business with Austen had driven her to chop it all off.

'What does that do?' Rhys asked.

'Makes it shiny and soft.'

'It worked,' he said. 'It looks really shiny.'

She thought it was gallant of him, considering her hair looked the same today as it had done yesterday.

He replaced the key in the lock. 'You must let me pay you properly. How long did it take you to find a key?'

'Not long.' It had taken her a couple of hours.

'How long?'

He was persistent, she'd give him that. She stared at him wordlessly.

'You're not going to tell me, are you?'

She shrugged, wishing he would pay and leave.

'I'll just have to take you to dinner then.' He was grinning widely. 'Koh Lanta? Tonight? I'm not leaving until you say yes.'

Tabitha was astounded.

'Go on,' he urged. 'You know you want to.'

'Do I?'

'You said you wanted to try it.'

'Yes, but—'

His face fell. 'Sorry, I didn't think. You've probably got plans, or a boyfriend who wouldn't be too keen on the idea.' His gaze grazed her left hand.

'No plans and no boyfriend, but—'

'Great!' He leapt in before she could finish her sentence, although she wasn't sure what she had been about to say. 'Shall I pick you up at seven?'

Her reply was hesitant. 'OK.'

The smile on his face grew wider. 'Let me have your mobile number, just in case.'

'I don't have one.'

The smile faded. 'You don't have a mobile number?' He clearly thought she was lying and that she didn't want to give it to him.

'I don't own a mobile phone,' she clarified.

'Everyone has a mobile.'

'I'm not everyone.'

His gaze was thoughtful. 'No, you aren't.'

She didn't know how to react to that, so she said nothing.

He seemed to gather himself. 'Shall I come to the back door?'

Tabitha's mind was blank. Her expression must have been, too.

'When I pick you up,' he added.

'Oh, right. Yes please, the back door.'

'I'll call you when I'm outside,' he began, then uttered a rueful laugh. 'Or maybe not.'

'If you're punctual, I'll be waiting.'

'And if I'm not?'

'I won't be.'

'Understood.' He muttered to himself, 'Don't be late, Rhys,' then somewhat louder he said, 'I'll pay for this, then get out of your hair. Did I tell you it looks nice?'

'You did.' She couldn't help the smile.

But after he'd left, her smile faded as she wondered what on earth she had agreed to and what had possessed her to agree to it.

***

Tabitha managed to put the impending dinner with Rhys to the back of her mind until Grandad returned later that afternoon. As usual, he entered through the front of the shop (he always came in that way during opening hours) and when she saw him step inside with his coat folded neatly over his arm and his walking stick (which he didn't need) in his hand, she almost didn't mention it. But she had no way of contacting Rhys to tell him she had changed her mind, and she couldn't face the thought of him waiting in vain outside when she had no intention of showing up.

'Grandad, I'm, um, going out to dinner this evening,' she said.

He faltered and almost stumbled, catching his balance before she was able to hurry forward to steady him. He quickly recovered from his surprise. 'That's nice,' he replied mildly, but Tabitha wasn't fooled.

He was shocked. She hadn't been out to dinner, unless it was with him or her parents since—

Stop thinking about it, she told herself. What was wrong with her? Over the past year or so, she had successfully managed to keep most of the negative thoughts at bay. When they did ambush her, it tended to be late at night when she struggled to get off to sleep, or in the early hours of the morning if she happened to wake up. But rarely during the day, unless something in particular brought that hideous time to the forefront of her mind.

'I'll cook you something before I go,' she assured him.

'No need. I am perfectly capable of fending for myself.'

'But I want to,' she protested. She always made him an evening meal, unless he was out with his cronies.

'I'll be fine,' he insisted. 'Who do you think did the cooking before you came to live with me?'

Tabitha shrugged. *'Fending for himself'* wasn't part of their agreement.

He said, 'Do you mind me asking who with? I take it you're not dining alone.'

'No, I'm not. It's with Rhys, the man with the tortoiseshell box.'

Her grandfather's bushy eyebrows rose.

'It's a thank you for finding a key that fits,' she explained.

'I meant to ask you about that. Which key?'

Tabitha described it and when he nodded she marvelled at his ability to remember every single key in

51

the shop, especially now that he was one step removed from the business. She strongly suspected he remembered every key ever to have passed through his hands.

'A thank you dinner,' he said, giving her an arch look. 'That doesn't happen every day. Would you like me to help you lock up?'

Tabitha glanced at the time, saw that it was five twenty-five and wondered how the day had gone so quickly. 'If you like. It'll give me more time to pop something in the oven. I'd planned on a chicken casserole.'

Her grandad rapped his walking stick on the floor, making her jump. '*I said*, I can make my own dinner. You can spend the extra five minutes making yourself beautiful.' He blanched. 'That came out wrong, my dear; you are already beautiful and no amount of primping and preening will make you any more so. But I know what you ladies are like. Your grandmother used to take an age to get ready.'

He placed his coat on the counter and propped his walking stick against it, before taking his keys out of his pocket and heading towards the door, whilst Tabitha removed the more valuable keys from the display.

'You get off upstairs,' he said, 'and leave that to me.'

Tabitha hesitated. She didn't want to do this. She wasn't ready. She probably never would be. Wishing she had taken Rhys's phone number so she could call it off, she bit her lip, tears close to the surface.

'You're scared,' her grandfather observed correctly. He had locked the door and was gazing at her, his eyes full of sympathy. 'I understand that, but you can't remain in your ivory tower forever. You have to start living again.'

'I *am* living.' Her reply was sharp.

'Are you? Are you *really?* It doesn't appear that way to me. You work, you take care of me, you read, you watch TV. You might even visit the odd gallery or exhibition. But that's not living.'

'What do *you* call it?' she demanded.

'Hiding.'

Tabitha gasped. She wasn't *hiding*. She was being careful. There was no way she was ever going to let anyone do to her what Austen had done. It would break her. She called it self-preservation. It wasn't hiding. OK, she might have been hiding in the beginning, she admitted silently, but who wouldn't have hidden, under the circumstances. The shame had been abominable.

But she wasn't hiding now. How could she when she was customer-facing six days a week? If she had still been hiding, she would have refused to work in the shop at all.

'It's been three years.' Jeremy moved nearer and put a hand on her arm. 'I haven't said anything before now because I realise you needed time, space and a safe place in which to heal, and I hope I've given you that.'

Tabitha nodded vigorously, wishing he would stop talking. 'You have.'

'But now it's time to get back on the horse. You need to start living again.'

She shook his hand off. She didn't want to get back on the horse. She would be perfectly happy never to set eyes on another proverbial bloody horse ever again. And how dare her grandfather tell her what she did or didn't need. She could decide that for herself.

Jeremy snorted. 'I know what you're thinking, but sometimes you're too close to the issue to see it clearly.'

Close was an understatement. She had lived it: it had wrecked her life. *Austen* had wrecked it. If Grandad thought she would ever let anyone get close enough to do something like that to her again, he needed his head examined.

To her utter shame, he had known exactly what had happened; Grandad had witnessed for himself how Austen's vile actions had affected her, yet now he was instructing her to get back in the saddle? No chance.

'You're going to dinner, correct?' he said.

'Yes.' Her voice was tight.

'He's not expecting you to, um, do anything other than dine with him, is he?'

'What?! *No!* Tabitha's face flamed. What an awful thing to say! What had got into him?

'In that case, I don't fully understand your reluctance,' he said.

'Yes, you do,' she shot back. 'You just said I'm scared.'

'Scared of the same thing happening again. But let's be truthful, how likely is that?'

'Not likely in the slightest, because I'm not going to put myself in a position where it *could* happen again.'

'Well, then, just go to dinner and enjoy the meal. If you don't want to, you never have to see him again. Treat it as a trial run.'

'A trial run for what?'

'The rest of your life.'

***

It was all well and good her grandad saying that, but he didn't understand how deeply she had been affected. Having her naked body splashed over the internet for all and sundry to gawk at had almost destroyed her. And it might have done if she hadn't had her grandfather and his flat to bolt to. He had provided comfort, sanctuary, and a steadying presence when she'd thought her life was over at twenty-six.

But not even he knew the full extent of it. She had been careful to keep the worst of the unsavoury details from him, which might have been impossible if he'd had access to the internet. He'd known it was bad. Bad enough to affect her relationship with her parents, who'd had to try to hold their heads up high when their work colleagues, friends, neighbours and acquaintances had probably seen indecent images of her online. And if they hadn't *seen* them, they had been aware of them. The images had been taken down eventually, but not soon enough.

Grandad, bless him, had borne the brunt of her distress and he was aware of the trauma she had suffered, but she had kept the full extent of it from him.

Tabitha got ready on automatic pilot. After a shower she gathered her hair into a bun, not caring how messy it looked or that tendrils were escaping to curl around her face and the back of her neck. She didn't bother with makeup, not wanting to give Rhys the wrong impression, and ignoring the fact that she had worn some the other day when she had been expecting him to return with the tortoiseshell box.

She took a little more care with her clothes, but only because she didn't want to wear jeans to a nice restaurant. Choosing a smart pair of tan trousers, she teamed them with an orange and cream floaty blouse and a pair of heels.

Looking in the mirror, she saw that from the neck down she looked remarkably similar to how she had looked before Austen had turned her world upside down.

Above the neck was markedly different: shorter hair (it had once been waist-length), no makeup (she used to wear the works and had carried lipstick with her everywhere), and her previously open expression had been replaced by the wary pinched face which now stared back at her.

She hardly recognised herself. Which had been her intention when she'd had all her hair chopped off. Not only had she hated herself, but she had also hoped that if *she* didn't recognise herself, no one else would either. So far no one had, but that was undoubtedly due to her avoiding Bristol (the scene of the crime) at all costs, plus not having any online presence whatsoever.

Finally she was ready, or as ready as she ever would be. Taking a deep breath to steady herself, she picked up a bag, flung a butter-soft leather jacket around her shoulders and prepared to have dinner with a man she never wanted to see again after tonight.

CHAPTER 5

'Have you parked your car in Avon Road Car Park?'
Tabitha asked as she fell into step with Rhys, her eyes
skittering towards him.

Gone were the faded jeans, the hoodie and the
trainers. In their place was a smart pair of navy chinos,
an open-neck shirt and desert boots. No jacket, despite
there being a chill in the May evening air.

'I caught the bus in.'

If Tabitha had been expecting him to fall to his
knees and confess that he hadn't returned to his car
yesterday but had gone to a bar instead, she was
disappointed. He was upbeat, his reply natural and
casual. She wanted to pursue her line of questioning, to
determine what he had been playing at by walking her
to her hair appointment when he'd had every intention
of going out for drinks with friends or colleagues, or
whatever; but she hadn't been truthful with him, either.

Besides, it was none of her business what he did. She wouldn't be seeing him again.

The restaurant was within easy walking distance and before she knew it, Rhys was holding the door open for her and gesturing for her to go inside. Grandad would approve; he always did the same for her. Austen had never—

No! This was neither the time nor the place to allow toxic thoughts to invade her mind. Rhys wasn't Austen.

Determined to enjoy the meal, Tabitha studied the restaurant as they waited to be seated. Bright, modern and tastefully decorated, it was a far cry from the places she and Grandad ate at. This reminded her of Bristol, when she often ate out in trendy bars, and was a welcome change from period restaurants. Instead of flock wallpaper and linen tablecloths laid with gleaming crystal, the interior of this restaurant had lime green banquet seating, and bright modern canvasses on the wall. Laughter and chatter filled the air, instead of muted voices and the subdued clink of cutlery on china.

After Tabitha draped her coat over the back of the chair, she slid into the seat. It was difficult not to keep making inadvertent eye contact with Rhys, as he was sitting directly opposite, so she was relieved when their server handed her a menu, and she was able to focus on that instead.

Despite the awkward atmosphere (although maybe only *she* felt it, because Rhys appeared relaxed enough – he was leaning back in his seat, the menu held at arm's length on the table), Tabitha's mouth watered as she scanned the starters.

'Shall we go all out and have three courses?' Rhys asked. 'But if you don't want a starter, that's fine.'

Tabitha did want a starter. She could happily eat several of them; they sounded delicious. 'I'd love one,' she replied.

She was determined to have the works, since she was unlikely to come here again. Maybe they did takeout? She filed the thought away. If the opportunity arose, she would ask discreetly. If not, she would look up their phone number in the (increasingly obsolete) copy of the shop's Yellow Pages. Rarely, if ever now, did she find a telephone number that worked. Grandad stubbornly hung onto his final copy, issued in 2019, but as businesses failed or new ones started up, the old telephone directory was better utilised as a doorstop these days.

'I can't decide either,' Rhys said, and Tabitha realised she was taking a long time to choose. 'How about a sharing platter? We can er...'

'Share?'

'Exactly!'

Tabitha was tempted, but eating food off the same plate as him was rather intimate. However, when she read the selection on offer, greed got the better of her: chicken satay, prawn tempura, crispy duck, prawn toast served with peanut sauce, sweet chilli sauce, and a chilli, carrot and shallot relish.

'Good idea,' she said, making her mind up. Then she turned her attention to the main courses, as their waiter poured them a glass of water.

'Wine?' Rhys asked.

'How about a pint?'

He looked confused. 'Of wine?'

'Never mind.'

'You can have a pint, if you like. Beer or lager?'

'What do you drink?'

'Artisan ales are good, but you can't beat a cold pint of cider on a hot afternoon.'

Had he been drinking ale yesterday evening? She hadn't been able to tell. She had been focusing more on his face. And the company he kept.

'Wine will be fine. White, please.'

'Sparkling, sweet, dry?'

'Crisp.'

Rhys nodded to the hovering waiter, who hurried off to fetch a bottle of something 'crisp'.

'Are we ready to order?' Rhys asked when the waiter returned with the wine.

'Confit duck curry for me, please,' she said.

'And I'll have the pork in tamarind sauce.'

They gave the menus back to the waiter, and once again an awkward silence descended.

Tabitha's gaze swept over the other diners, the decor, the staff bustling in and out of the kitchen, as she fiddled with the stem of her glass. In contrast, Rhys was the epitome of relaxed, as he sprawled in his chair, his fingers idly caressing his own glass. Tabitha's gaze was drawn to them, as the thumb and forefinger of his right hand stroked the stem.

She swallowed and looked away, then glanced back at him to find his lazy gaze lingering on her face, a smile playing about his mouth.

To break the excruciating silence, Tabitha asked, 'Was your grandmother pleased you found a key?'

'You're the one who found it,' he said, picking up his drink and holding the glass aloft. 'Cheers.' She clinked glasses with him. 'I haven't told her yet. I'm seeing her next week, so I'll show it to her then.'

'Does she live far from you?'

'Far enough. She lives in Wales, in a nursing home. She's ninety-three and had a fall last year.'

Tabitha dreaded the same – or worse – happening to her grandad. He would absolutely loathe being in a home. 'Where in Wales are you from?'

'The South Wales Valleys, in a small village in the mountains. How about you? Are you a Bath girl, born and bred?

She might have known this would come up. She had grown up in Bristol but had spent a considerable amount of time in Bath. 'More or less.' Then, to distract him from her deliberately vague answer, she asked, 'What do you do?'

'I work in IT.'

'In Bath?'

'Kind of: I work from home, mostly.'

'Does that get lonely?'

Rhys smiled. 'I've got a lot of online friends.'

And several in the real world, she thought, recalling the easy camaraderie she had briefly witnessed through the window of the bar.

She sensed another awkward silence hovering, but to her relief their starter arrived. It looked delicious and she couldn't wait to tuck in, but she politely held back.

'Ladies first,' he said, pushing the platter closer to her.

She almost quipped that she wasn't a lady, before she caught herself and bit the words back. It would have been too flirty, and besides, it was true. How could she be a lady when half the world had seen intimate photos of her?

Refusing to allow Austen to ruin her first night out in three years with someone other than her immediate family, she picked up her knife and fork and ferried a prawn onto her plate, then added a spoonful of the relish.

'Have more than that,' Rhys urged.

She added a skewer of satay chicken.

He pursed his lips. 'Shall we try this another way?' he suggested, neatly dividing the various dishes into two portions, and dumping one of them onto his plate, along with some of the sauces. 'There you go. The rest is yours.'

'Are you always so...?' She couldn't think of a suitable word.

'Direct? Probably. I see a problem, I solve it.'

'Is that your job? Problem solving?'

'In a way. Mmm, this sauce is wonderful.'

Was it her imagination, or did he not want to talk about what he did for a living? IT was a wide subject, and Tabitha took a punt at narrowing it down.

'Do you work for anyone I might have heard of?'

He chewed for a moment before swallowing. 'Yes, but it's boring. I don't work for a blue-chip company or anyone trendy. I'm in the civil service.'

'Oh, right. That's...'

'Boring?' He smirked.

'Not at all,' she said. 'You just don't seem the type.'

Now he was openly laughing at her. 'What type is that?'

She fluttered a hand at him. 'Stop laughing. I just meant that you seem too trendy.'

Rhys spluttered. 'Trendy? *Me?* I wish! Did you expect civil servants to wear grey suits and carry briefcases?'

Tabitha drew herself up. 'I'm going to stop talking now.'

He was still chuckling. 'I've been called nerdy many times, but never trendy. I'll take that.' He paused, then added, 'I'm not entirely sure you meant it as a compliment, though.'

'Because I look like a middle-aged spinster from the 1930s and I work in a shop selling antique keys?'

Rhys screwed his eyes shut and pressed his lips together. His shoulders shook as he put a hand over his mouth.

Tabitha watched him struggle to hold back his mirth, aggrieved that he was laughing at her.

Finally, he took a deep breath and opened his eyes. They were brimming with merriment. 'That's the funniest thing I've heard in a long time.'

'Clearly.' Her tone was acerbic. She was beginning to regret agreeing to have dinner with him.

'You do not look like a 1930s spinster,' he chuckled. 'You look gorgeous. And if you're middle-aged, I'm positively ancient. How old are you, anyway?'

'Twenty-nine.'

'I'm thirty-one.'

'I guessed early thirties,' she said.

'And I guessed late twenties.'

'Despite the tea dresses and the chatelaine?'

'The what dresses?'

'Tea dresses. Women used to wear them in the first part of the twentieth century to an afternoon or early evening event. They're making a comeback,' she added, somewhat defensively.

'I see.' He clearly didn't. 'And what is a chatel... thing?'

'Chatelaine. It's a key chain that used to be worn by the lady of the house. She would keep the keys about her person at all times to stop the servants from stealing the valuables.'

His face cleared. 'Very in character that you wear one.'

'We think so.'

'We?'

'Grandad and I.'

'Are your parents still around? Excuse me if that's a sensitive subject.'

'They are. What about yours?'

'Mam is, my dad isn't. He buggered off when I was three.'

'That must have been tough.'

'I suppose, but I don't remember him, so I don't know any different.'

'I've never been to the South Wales Valleys.'

'You don't know what you're missing,' he declared and proceeded to tell her about the beauty of his homeland whilst they munched their way through their main courses.

The conversation then turned to travel, and they discussed the places they had been and the things they had seen and experienced.

The evening passed quickly from then on, both of them having got into their stride, and before she knew it Tabitha was cradling a cup of coffee, her tummy delightfully full and the wine she had drunk making life fuzzy around the edges. She was by no means drunk, but she was relaxed, her mood light.

'What made you settle in Bath?' she asked, leaning forward, her elbows on the table as she took a two-handed sip of the hot liquid.

'It's a nice place.'

'Nice? *Nice!* Is that the best you can do?' Tabitha didn't have to feign indignation. 'Bath is beautiful! Just look at the magnificent abbey, the river, the gorgeous buildings, and all the glorious history. The city is a

UNESCO World Heritage Site, for heaven's sake! The Roman Baths, the Royal Crescent and the Jane Austen Centre aren't just *nice*.'

Rhys's expression was sheepish. 'I haven't really been to—' he began, but Tabitha cut him off.

'Are you honestly telling me that you haven't been to the Roman Baths?' She was incredulous, and rather disappointed in him. When he gave her an apologetic smile, she cried, 'Heathen!'

'Ah, now, that's where you're wrong. I can't be a heathen because I've visited the abbey.'

'Walking past it on the way to a bar doesn't count,' she shot back.

His reply was smug. 'I've been inside.'

Slightly mollified, Tabitha said, 'That's something, I suppose. How long have you lived in Bath?'

'Four years.'

'Hmph!'

'I'm sorry.'

'So you should be. All this rich heritage and history on your doorstep, and all you've done is popped into the abbey?'

'I'm ashamed of myself.'

'Good.'

'I promise I'll try to rectify the situation. It's not going to be easy, though.'

'Why not?'

'I don't have anyone to show me around.'

Tabitha's eyebrows shot up and she stared at him in disbelief. 'That's ridiculous. You shouldn't need anyone to show you around your home city. Look it up on the internet, or just go for a walk. You can't move more than a few metres without bumping into something historic.'

'I'd be happier if someone was with me,' he said.

'You're a big boy. I'm sure you can go on your own.' She thought about the group of people she had seen him with last night. He could ask one of them to hold his hand.

'It'll be more fun with someone else,' he insisted.

'Ask your girlfriend.'

He blinked. 'I don't have a girlfriend. If I did, I wouldn't be on a date with you.'

'We're not on a date.'

He gazed at her over the rim of his coffee cup and smiled enigmatically.

'You said this was a thank-you dinner,' she reminded him.

'It is.'

'Then it can't be a date.'

'It can be both.'

Panic filled her, chilling her blood. She didn't want this to be a date. She refused to allow it. He had got her to have dinner with him under false pretences. 'No, it can't,' she replied.

'In that case, this *is* a date.' His retort came with a smile, but his eyes were serious.

Tabitha was shaking her head. 'It can't be.'

'Why not?' he began, then closed his eyes, opening them again to say accusingly, 'You *have* got a boyfriend.'

'I haven't.' Her tone was terse.

'Girlfriend, then?'

'No. I don't have a girlfriend, a wife, or a husband.'

Rhys studied the sugar bowl. 'I see.' He swallowed. 'I'm sorry if I've made you feel uncomfortable. That wasn't my intention. You're right, it's a thank-you dinner, nothing more.'

Damn it, now Tabitha felt bad. 'You haven't made me feel uncomfortable,' she fibbed. 'It's just that... I don't date.'

'Never?'

'Never.'

He thought about that for a moment. 'It's not just because you don't fancy me?'

'Not at all. It's—'

'Ah ha! So you *do* fancy me.' One side of his mouth quirked up at the corner.

'I didn't say that.' Tabitha was cross. 'Stop putting words in my mouth.' He was insufferable. She did *not* fancy him. But even if she did, she wouldn't act on it. She scowled at him.

'Sorry, I couldn't help teasing you. If you don't want this to be a date and you want to keep it as a thank-you dinner, I can do that.' He signalled for the bill, and Tabitha reached for her purse. When he saw what she was doing, he tutted. 'If you insist that this is a thank-you meal, you'll have to let me pay. But if you want to go Dutch, it can't be a thank-you meal, can it? It'll have to be a date.'

'You get ten out of ten for trying,' she grumbled.

'Seriously, I insist on paying. I didn't lure you to this restaurant under false pretences.'

'Glad to hear it.'

'Let me pay the bill, then I'll walk you to your door.'

She noticed he said, 'to your door, 'and not 'walk you home,' the latter having a slightly different connotation, to her at least. 'Walk you to your door,' sounded gentlemanly – like something her grandfather might say.

The bill paid, he helped her on with her jacket, and an inadvertent touch of his finger against the back of her neck sent a tingle right through her. So it was a jolly good thing she *wouldn't* be seeing him again because, despite assuring him that she wasn't attracted to him, she most certainly was.

The stroll back to Abbey Green was a leisurely one, conducted in companionable silence. It seemed that by getting the matter of whether tonight was a date or not out of the way, Rhys had settled into an easy friendship.

Tabitha hadn't achieved that just yet. Knowing what some men could be like and having seen the depths to which they could sink, her concern was that Rhys might expect a kiss after all. He might even expect to come in, but she had made it clear that her grandfather lived in the flat with her, so if he did have an agenda, that might put him off.

Or was she overthinking it? Not all men were like Austen – her grandfather and her father weren't. But wariness and suspicion were ingrained now, and she didn't see that changing.

On the way home, Tabitha pointed out several places of interest. She had hoarded snippets of history the way misers hoarded money, but the difference was that she was happy to share her wealth of knowledge, and Rhys, who appeared to know so little about the city he lived in, was an ideal candidate.

Her knowledge had been acquired by endlessly wandering the streets and lanes of Bath in the early days after she had moved in with Grandad, visiting the places that the tourists frequented. She had often been restless and unsettled in her own skin, and had sought a distraction from the inside of her head. She'd learnt so much and had developed a deep and abiding love of the city because of it.

She was busy telling him about the plane tree in the centre of Abbey Green and dispelling the rumour that it was a thousand years old, when Rhys came to a halt.

Surprised, she also stopped. They might be outside the shop, but this was the main entrance, not the back one.

'How do you know all this?' he asked.

'I visit places, I read.' She smiled. 'And I listen in on the tour guides.'

'Will you show me around the city?'

'You can show yourself.'

'As a friend,' he added. 'No strings. I promise.' He crossed his heart. The gesture was endearing.

'I'll think about it.'

'When is your next day off?'

'Sunday. I never work Sundays.'

'Roman Baths?' He raised his eyebrows, his eyes wide and a hopeful smile on his lips.

'I'll think about it,' she repeated.

'I've enjoyed this evening. It's been fun.'

Grandfather's words floated into Tabitha's head. He reckoned it was time to get back on the horse, that she needed to start living again. She wasn't ready for the kind of living he had been hinting at, but what harm would visiting the Roman Baths with Rhys do? She loved the place and would happily go there again. And it might be fun to share what she knew.

Then she hesitated. Why would a man like Rhys want to spend time with a woman like her? She knew she was an oddity – although she hadn't always been this way. Before Austen, she had been a typical woman for her age, loving parties, shopping, the cinema, chilling with friends, dating... But since Austen, she had aged; not just by three calendar years, but by decades, transported back to another era both by working in the shop and by spending so much time with her grandfather. She had been like a sponge, soaking up his old-fashioned outlook, mannerisms and way of speaking, as though she had been attempting to replace herself with someone new, someone as far removed from her old self as it was possible to get.

'I've enjoyed it too,' she replied slowly, surprised to discover just how much.

'So, will you?'

'Possibly.'

'Will you call me?'

She might. Taking a little notepad and a pen out of her bag, she said, 'Let me have your mobile number.' The resultant smile on his face, gave her a jolt. 'I'm not promising anything,' she warned.

'I know.'

They began walking down the narrow lane leading to the rear entrance of the building. Tabitha came to a stop and fished around for her keys, bringing them out of her bag with a self-conscious flourish, hoping he would take the hint.

He did. 'Sleep tight, Tabitha Locke. I'll see you on Sunday.' Turning on his heel, he strolled away.

'I haven't said yes, yet,' she called after him.

His laughter followed her inside.

Tabitha got ready for bed as quietly as possible, because she didn't want to wake her grandad, and as she changed into her pyjamas she made the decision that she *would* go out with Rhys on Sunday. As a friend. Friends had been lacking in her life these past few years, and without warning a yearning for a friend to confide in hit her in the chest.

Shocked, she realised she was lonely. Tonight had given her a glimpse of what was missing in her life, and memories of what she'd had before rose up, making her eyes sting and the breath catch in her throat.

Almost as though her feet were taking her there of their own volition, Tabitha moved towards the little bureau next to the window and she took out an address book. Running her fingertips across the gold embossed writing, she opened it, flicking through the pages until she found the name she was looking for.

Tabitha stared at it, and the phone number written neatly below, for a long time.

Then she closed the book and got into bed.

If those people who she had once called friends had wanted to remain friends, they had known where to find her. None of them had.

Apart from one: Rosalind. But Tabitha had withdrawn from her and had made it impossible to carry on any kind of friendship.

It was hard to accept that she, Tabitha, was responsible for that. But there was one person at whose feet the blame for her friendless state could be firmly laid – and that was Austen.

As she cried herself to sleep, as she had numerous times before, Tabitha vowed this would be the final time. Although she mightn't be ready to dive back into life again, she had dipped a toe in the water.

It was a start.

CHAPTER 6

'The water is green.'

Tabitha raised her eyebrows and gave Rhys an incredulous look. Two thousand years of history and *this* was what he took from it?

'Algae,' she told him.

He pulled a face. 'Who would want to bathe in that?'

'In Roman times, the bath had a roof on it which would have kept the light out and prevented the algae from growing.'

'Thank God for that! Otherwise, people would have come out grimier than they went in. You would have thought soap would kill algae.'

'The Romans didn't use soap. They covered themselves in scented oils, then use a scraper to remove the oil, along with any dirt.'

Rhys pulled a face again. 'Nice.'

She was tempted to push him in the murky water.

'Hang on,' he said, pointing at an information board. 'I want to hear what it has to say.'

Tabitha waited as he keyed the number on the board into the electronic guide and stuffed his headphones into his ears.

'It's about the statues,' he said, his voice louder than normal.

She could see that for herself: it said so on the board's information panel. Her favourite statue was the one of Julius Caesar.

As they carried on walking along the balcony above the bath, Rhys listening avidly to the voice in his ears, Tabitha watched the expressions flitting across his face. When his eyes widened and he leant over the balustrade, she guessed he had just heard that the water below was rainwater that had fallen on the Mendip Hills around 10,000 years ago, which had then percolated through the rocks and now bubbled up in a spring that fed the baths.

'Wow, 40° Celsius!' he exclaimed, and she smiled, wishing she could dip a toe in the bath to feel its warmth for herself.

Wandering inside, they gazed at the exhibits as he learnt more about its history, and Rhys was particularly taken with the scale model of the baths and the temple. He was also fascinated by the small tablets on which curses had been inscribed before being thrown into the spring. They had been written by the victims of crime or wrongdoing, imploring the goddess Salis Minera to take revenge on their behalf.

'Try some,' she urged, when they reached the area where people could take a drink of the spa water, and she laughed at the slightly disgusted look on his face when he tasted it.

'It's warm,' he declared. 'And tastes metallic. It *is* safe to drink, right?'

'Perfectly. In fact, it's supposed to have healing qualities.'

'Is that so?' He stared at it dubiously.

When they emerged from the baths after two and a half hours, Tabitha having enjoyed the visit immensely, she assumed that was the end of it, but Rhys had another idea.

'How about we have a bite to eat in The Pump Room?' he suggested.

Tabitha nearly fell over laughing. 'You do realise The Pump Room is terrifically expensive, not to mention fully booked. You can't just walk in off the street. Plus, they have specific serving times.'

'Such as?'

Tabitha looked at her watch. 'The next one is 2 p.m., I believe.'

'Let's ask, shall we?'

She trotted doubtfully after him. She had eaten brunch there once, and had thoroughly enjoyed it. Grandad had been with her, and she had loved the way he seemed right at home amid the genteel splendour. Afternoon tea was something she had always wanted to try, but hadn't wanted to do so on her own.

'I'm not dressed for it,' she said.

Her comment brought him up short. 'Why? Is there a dress code?' He looked down at his jeans and trainers.

'Not that I'm aware of.' Tabitha was similarly dressed. 'But if I'm having afternoon tea at The Pump Room, I want to make an occasion of it.'

'You look gorgeous.' He grimaced and his cheeks grew pink. 'I mean, you look fine.'

Heat blossomed in her chest and worked its way up her neck. Gorgeous? Hmm. She didn't know how to respond to that, so she said, 'We'll never get in.'

And she was right, as Rhys discovered when he went to enquire. She had let him go inside on his own, so convinced was she that The Pump Room would be full.

He seemed cheerful enough when he came back outside, though. 'It's full, but that's not a problem as I've booked us in for next Sunday.'

Tabitha couldn't believe the cheek of the man. 'I'm busy next Sunday.'

His good cheer didn't flag. 'Then I'll amend it for the Sunday after.' He turned to go back inside.

'Wait.' She was impressed by his determination. 'I'll change my plans.'

'You don't have to. I can change the booking easily enough.'

'Leave it as it is,' she told him.

'OK. Where shall we go instead? I'm famished.'

Tabitha was hungry, too. By now, if she were at home, she would have eaten a roast lunch, but yesterday, when Grandad had enquired about her evening, she had let slip that Rhys had suggested she show him the sights of Bath, and he hadn't taken any notice of her protestations that she didn't want to play tour guide to a man who had lived in the city long enough to explore it for himself. Neither had Grandad been impressed with her excuse that she had laundry to do and a Sunday roast to cook.

Halfway through yesterday morning he had informed her that the laundry was taken care of and that he was going out on Sunday so she needn't bother cooking lunch because he wouldn't be there to eat it.

Tabitha had initially resented his meddling, but after half an hour of sulking, she remembered that she had vowed to come out of her shell. She also understood that Grandad was only trying to help. Besides, strolling around the Roman Baths wasn't a hardship and Rhys had stressed it would be as friends, so where was the harm in it? And it was preferable to moping about the flat or wandering around the city on her own.

Which was why Tabitha now found herself outside Bath's oldest eatery, Sally Lunn's, her mouth watering at the delicious aromas emanating from the open door.

A sign in the hallway advised them to wait to be seated, and as they waited an elderly couple, the lady in a wheelchair being pushed by her husband, were leaving.

'Do you need any help?' Rhys asked, as the old gent rolled the chair down the narrow hall.

'We're grand, but thanks for the offer.'

Rhys nodded and shuffled closer to Tabitha, tucking himself in so the wheels didn't run over his toes.

He was uncomfortably close. So close that she could smell the soap he used on his clothes, and his thigh was touching hers. She inhaled deeply then blew out her cheeks. Her pulse had sprung into action, letting her know it was fully operational, and every nerve was acutely aware of him.

'Are you OK?' he asked.

'I'm fine.'

He stepped away, and her relief was instantaneous. She didn't relax fully, but at least she didn't feel so crowded. He'd smelt nice, though. He had been close enough that he could have kissed her if he'd been inclined. She was relieved he hadn't. Would he taste as good as he—?

Tabitha growled at the silly inner voice, with its silly unwanted thoughts. 'It dates back to 1480 something,' she blurted, trying to distract herself.

Rhys turned to stare at her. 'What does?' Thankfully he seemed oblivious to her pathetic reaction to his nearness and to her daft musings.

'This building. It's the oldest house in Bath.'

'Table for two, is it?' a woman in a black apron with the name Sally Lunn emblazoned across the front asked.

Rhys answered for both of them. 'Yes, please.'

'We've got a table on the second floor. Are you OK with the stairs?'

They nodded and followed her. The refreshment room (as it was called) was busy, but she led them to a free table by a window. Tabitha was pleased to see it was open, and she welcomed the breeze blowing through it, hoping it would cool her ardour.

She focused her attention on the table to avoid looking at Rhys's face. A clear bottle sat in the middle, containing a sprig of greenery, and salt and pepper pots were next to it, along with a sugar bowl containing coloured cubes, not granules.

The waitress placed two menus on the table. 'I'll give you a few minutes,' she said, 'unless you already know what you want?'

Rhys smiled. 'I think we're going to need those minutes.'

The woman, who was about Tabitha's age, maybe a year or two younger, smiled back.

Tabitha frowned. The waitress's smile had been on the flirty side of friendly.

She left and Tabitha opened her menu.

'It's nice here,' Rhys said, scanning his surroundings.

'Yes.'

'I thought we might have had a bit of a wait.'

'Hmm.'

'What do you fancy?'

'Give me a chance! I haven't had a proper look yet.'

His smile faded and she realised she had been sharp with him. So what if he had flirted back a little? He was entitled to. He didn't owe Tabitha anything. If it had been Rosalind sitting across the table, simpering at a waiter, Tabitha wouldn't have given it a second thought.

'Hangry,' she said, by way of explanation.

'Right.' The smile returned: he got it. 'I'll have to remember to feed you frequently, so it's lucky I've booked us into The Pump Room on Sunday. Where should we go first? There's still a lot of the city to see – the Roman Baths is only a bit of it.'

'A magnificent bit,' she pointed out.

'I agree, but I assume there's more.'

Was he making fun of her?

'Did you have anything in mind?' she asked, throwing the ball firmly back in his side of the court after they had given their order – a smoked salmon savoury toast for her and a steak and mushroom trencher for Rhys.

He said, 'I've been doing some research. I've seen the Circus, so I don't need to see that again, and I've walked along Pulteney Bridge.'

'Have you typed in the top ten places to see in Bath?' she teased, jerking her chin at the mobile he had placed on the table when he had taken his seat.

'You're not a total technophobe, then?'

'I know what a search engine is,' she retorted.

He smirked. 'I was beginning to wonder.'

'I just choose not to use one.'

'Why is that?'

Oh, no, she wasn't going to have that conversation here. Or anywhere. And certainly not with Rhys, so she changed the subject and asked, 'You say you've seen the Circus, how about the Royal Crescent?'

The Circus was a circular street of Georgian townhouses, built in the mid-eighteenth century. It was impressive, but not as impressive as the Royal Crescent. Built slightly later, the Crescent was a sweeping arc of thirty terraced houses.

'Um, no,' he admitted.

'You should,' she enthused. 'It's one of the best examples of Georgian architecture in the UK. As well as houses and flats, there is a museum and a spa hotel.'

'I've never fancied a spa. I'm not a hot-tub kind of guy.'

'It's not compulsory,' she said. She quite liked a spa day, but when a sudden vision of a bare-chested Rhys reclining in a tub of hot water with only a froth of bubbles to cover his modesty slipped into her head, she bit her lip.

He grinned. 'But if you think that's what we should do, then we'll do it.'

'Definitely not.' Her reply was emphatic. Imagining his bare chest was bad enough without seeing it in the flesh. Reeling her wayward thoughts in, she said, 'The museum is worth a visit, though.'

'OK, it's a date.'

Tabitha was about to inform him that it was *not* a date, when she realised that the waitress had returned with their meals, so she turned her attention to the delicious food, and as she ate a feeling of contentment stole over her which lasted until they had almost finished eating.

Rhys blew it out of the water when he said, 'I'm curious – why don't you have a mobile phone?'

Tabitha swallowed her mouthful of savoury toast. He wasn't going to let it lie, was he? 'I don't need one.'

'Have you ever owned one? You're the first person I've met who doesn't have a mobile.'

'Yes. I used to have one.' And it had caused her nothing but grief.

'What happened?' Her eyes were drawn to his mouth as he dabbed it with a serviette. 'Did you drop it down the loo and decide not to bother getting another?' He chuckled at his joke.

'Something like that.' Actually, she had thrown it out of her bedroom window. If the fall hadn't killed it, then being crushed by a lorry on the road outside immediately afterwards had ensured its demise. She had been so relieved to no longer have the temptation of seeing what people had been posting about her online, that she hadn't begrudged paying the monthly fee until the contract expired. Renewing it simply hadn't been an option. The lid on that can of worms was well and truly shut.

In the beginning, she used to wonder what was being said about her, but as time went on her curiosity steadily lessened. The small bit of the world she had inhabited back then had moved on. People had other things to think about, and more recent gossip to exclaim over. She was old news – and she fully intended to stay that way.

Archly she said, 'You ought to try leaving yours at home; it'll do you good.'

An uncomfortable expression flitted across his face. 'I need it for work.'

'On a Sunday?' To be fair, she hadn't noticed him playing with it. Apart from taking a photo or two, he hadn't bothered with it much.

'Yeah.'

'The Civil Service, you said?'

'Er, yeah.'

'Are there many IT emergencies on a Sunday?'

'You'd be surprised.'

His tone and the guarded look in his eye, made her think he was keeping something back. 'You're not a spy, are you?'

His bark of laughter was genuine. 'No.' He pushed his plate away; he had eaten every morsel.

'Do you like cooking?' she asked.

He blinked, the abrupt change of subject catching him off guard. 'Not much.'

'I had a feeling you didn't.'

'What gave it away?'

She gestured to his empty plate. 'You attacked that like you hadn't eaten for a week. You did the same when we had dinner the other evening.'

'Actually, I haven't made myself more than a sandwich or a ready meal since...' He frowned. 'I can't remember. That's bad, isn't it?'

She thought of the roast she would have cooked today if Grandad hadn't encouraged her to go out, and she felt sorry for Rhys. 'Do you eat out much?'

'Not often, unless you class a fast-food burger as eating out. I tend to save my pennies for beer and have a bag of chips on the way home.'

'You sound like a student.'

'I do, don't I?' He glanced at his T-shirt. It had a cartoon dog on the front. 'I dress like one too, most of the time, but I can be a grown-up when I need to be.'

She said, 'I can't imagine you in a suit.' Damn and blast, but she could imagine him *out* of one. Heat crept up her chest and neck, and she willed it not to reach her face. He smiled at her in a way that made her think he could read her mind.

She checked the time, making sure he could see what she was doing. 'I'd better get back,' she said. 'Grandad will be expecting me. He's... um...' She let the sentence hang, for Rhys to make of it what he wanted.

'Of course, I'll get the—'

'No, you won't!' she snapped. 'It's my turn.'

'Are we taking it in turns?'

'No, it's just—'

'Shall we go Dutch?' he suggested.

Her relief was probably written all over her face. 'Yes, please.'

She didn't want to feel beholden or obligated. Friday's meal had been a kind of payment. Today was a late lunch with a friend. Besides, something he had said about saving his pennies made her think he mightn't be able to afford to eat out often, and prices in the tourist hot spots weren't cheap.

They split the bill.

'I'll walk you back,' he offered.

'Where are you parked this time? Or did you catch the bus?'

'I walked, actually.'

'Was it far?'

'It took me about thirty minutes.'

That wasn't what she wanted to know, so she tried again. 'Where do you live?'

'Bear Flats.'

It was an area on the other side of the river to the south. Locke's Key Emporium was just around the corner from Sally Lunn's and was in the right direction for his walk home. She could hardly refuse.

As they began the short stroll to Abbey Green, she asked, 'Why are you walking?'

'I need the exercise.' He patted his flat stomach. 'Too much time spent sitting at a desk.'

'What is it that you do, exactly?' she asked, as they turned into the narrow alley leading to the rear of the shop. IT was a vast field and could cover a wide range of things, and he had dodged the question previously.

'I troubleshoot.'

'Like when someone can't log on or the server crashes?' She intercepted the look he gave her. 'I'm not a total dinosaur.'

'You're too old to be a dinosaur. And too pretty.'

Tabitha dropped her gaze to the ground. And walked slap-bang into her grandfather.

'Tabitha, watch where you're going,' Grandad admonished.

She winced. The last person she wanted to see right now was her grandad, especially having hinted that Grandad needed her at home.

'Sorry,' she muttered.

'Are you all right?' he asked.

'I'm fine.' It was sweet of him to ask, considering she could have knocked him flying. 'Are *you* OK?'

'Never better.' His attention was on Rhys. 'Is this the chap you've been telling me about?'

Tabitha didn't want to do this, but she didn't have any choice. 'Yes. This is Rhys. Rhys, meet my grandfather.'

Grandad extended his hand. 'Jeremiah Lock, but everyone calls me Jeremy.'

'Pleased to meet you, Mr Locke.'

'Jeremy. Tabitha has told me all about you.'

Tabitha wished the ground would open up as Rhys shot her an amused glance. 'Nothing bad, I hope?'

'On the contrary. She has been singing your praises.'

'Grandad!'

'Where are my manners?' Jeremy said. 'Won't you come in?' He removed his keys from a pocket.

'I'm sure Rhys has got things he needs to be doing,' Tabitha said, widening her eyes at Rhys and daring him to contradict her.

He took the hint. 'I'd love to, but I have to shoot off home.'

'Pity. Another time, perhaps?'

'I'll look forward to it. See you next Sunday, Tabitha.'

Tabitha scowled. Rhys's chuckle followed her inside.

'He seems a nice young man,' her grandad said, as he locked up behind them.

'I suppose.'

'Very polite. Handsome, too.'

'I hadn't noticed.'

Jeremy guffawed. 'Do you want me to make you an appointment with my optician?'

'No.'

'He seems quite taken with you.'

'Can we talk about something else?'

'How were the Baths?'

Tabitha stalked into the kitchen, her grandfather close behind. 'Green.'

'Don't be facetious,' he snapped.

She was immediately contrite. He didn't deserve to be spoken to like that. 'Sorry. Tea?'

He nodded. 'You like him.'

Dear lord, he wasn't going to let this drop. 'He's nice enough.'

Jeremy clicked his tongue. 'You can do better than that.'

'Grandad, that's mean. There's nothing wrong with Rhys.'

'I meant, you can give me a better response than *nice enough*. But I'm glad to see you're quick to jump to his defence.'

Tabitha wrinkled her nose. Drat. Now her grandad was going to read more into it.

'Where are you going on Sunday?' he wanted to know.

'The Crescent.'

He inclined his head in approval. 'Will you have lunch in the Hotel?'

She shook her head. 'Too expensive.'

Her grandad's eyes widened. 'I think their lunch menu is rather reasonable.'

'It is, but I get the impression Rhys isn't flush with money.'

'My treat?'

'Thank you, but no. Anyway, he's booked us into The Pump Room for afternoon tea.'

'That's not cheap, either,' Jeremy pointed out. 'You could always bring him here for a late lunch or an early supper instead?'

Good grief, no! What was her grandfather thinking?

But when she saw the twinkle in his eye, she knew exactly what he was thinking and it irked her no end.

Tabitha wasn't ready for romance, and she might never be ready, no matter how much her grandfather wished she was.

CHAPTER 7

Was it only Wednesday? Surely it should be Friday by now? Never had a week seemed to drag more than this one. And it wasn't as though Tabitha didn't have anything to do: the shop was busier than usual due to the unexpected but very welcome trend of buying keys as graduation presents.

Many universities were due to publish their results this month (if they hadn't already) and according to one customer, keys were being bought and framed, or made into pendants to signify that graduating from university was the equivalent of being handed the key to one's future.

Tabitha thought it a lovely sentiment, and not only because it meant increased sales.

She had thought the same once, that her graduation had meant the start of a whole new future; and for a while it had, but life had other ideas. Or should she say,

Austen had. It was ironic to think that it was his name that had been the start of the chain of sorry events that had led to her downfall. If he had been called Jason or Peter, she probably wouldn't have spoken to him: he would have been just an acquaintance of an acquaintance, a face in a crowd. But she had jokingly asked him whether he had been named after Jane Austen (Tabitha had been an English student, so she would make that kind of connection, wouldn't she?) and they'd got talking. One thing had led to another and before she knew it, they were dating and she had fallen in love.

She was thinking about Jane Austen as she served her final customer of the day. The two ladies had just visited the Jane Austen Centre and were gushing over the experience.

'Did you know that Bath holds a Jane Austen Festival in September?' she told them, as they examined the display of chatelaines on sale. 'And there is also a Jane Austen summer ball at the end of this month.'

The women's eyes lit up. 'Do you have to dress up?' They glanced at each other with glee.

'I'm afraid so. Regency costume is mandatory.'

One of the ladies clapped her hands. 'Ooh, goodie! Let's see if we can book into the same hotel. We're staying at The Queensbury and it's fabulous.'

Tabitha smiled as they left, happily chatting about the ball and planning their next visit to the city, then she locked up after them and began her end-of-day routine.

However, there was something under the counter that *wasn't* routine: her address book. She had no idea why she had felt the need to bring it onto the shop floor with her this morning, but she had spied it on the bureau in her bedroom, innocently sitting where she had left it the other evening, and she had grabbed it without thinking too closely about her reason for doing so.

She was thinking about it now though.

Once again she turned the page to Rosalind's name and her hand crept towards the vintage phone on the counter behind her. And once again, she closed the book.

Tabitha dialled her mother's number instead.

'Tabitha! Is something wrong?'

Guilt immediately swept over her as she realised that she rarely made contact first. It was usually her mum who phoned her, not the other way around. 'Nothing's wrong,' she said. 'I just thought I'd ring for a chat.'

The silence on the other end was telling. Eventually her mum said, 'A chat? That's... nice.' A pause. 'So, how are you?'

'I'm fine.'

'Grandad?'

'He's good.'

'A chat, you said?'

'Sorry, someone was peering through the window,' Tabitha fibbed, realising that she wasn't being at all chatty. 'How are you and Dad?'

'Busy, as usual. Your dad thinks his school might be inspected soon.' Tabitha could almost hear her mother's shudder down the phone line. 'He's expecting 'the call' any day now.'

'He'll be fine,' Tabitha said. 'Dad runs a tight ship.'

Her parents were both teachers; her mum taught English at a private school in Bristol, and her dad was the head teacher of a highly regarded and oversubscribed independent boarding school near Chew Magna.

Their profession had made what happened to Tabitha even more appalling. She didn't think she would ever forgive herself for bringing such shame down on them. Thankfully, she hadn't gone down the teaching route herself. Things had been bad enough as it was; imagine if she had been working in a *school?*

It was Tabitha who shuddered now.

'I know he does,' her mum agreed, 'but he's dreading it all the same. How are you fixed for a visit? It's ages since we saw you. We can't do this weekend, but how about the weekend after? Or you could come to us?' Her mum sounded so hopeful it almost broke Tabitha's heart.

'Maybe.' She was being evasive, but despite Bristol being just a half hour drive away from Bath, she had only been back to the city three times in three years, and each time she had hated it, terrified she would bump into someone she knew. Or someone who knew *her*.

Her mum didn't push it and the conversation turned to a less fraught subject as her mother chatted about events at school, and Tabitha told her about her recent visit to the Roman Baths and Sally Lunn's.

'You ought to have shares in that place,' her mum said, laughing. 'How many times have you eaten there?'

'About twenty,' Tabitha admitted. Although, she wouldn't have gone on Sunday if it hadn't been for Rhys.

At the thought of Rhys, Tabitha's heart skipped a beat and a butterfly decided to unfurl its wings in her tummy.

Cross, she dragged her attention back to the conversation, but did a double-take when she heard her mum ask, 'Did Grandad have a trencher?'

'Hmm, yeah, a trencher.'

'Sorry, silly me, I've got my dates mixed up. Grandad was at his club on Sunday, wasn't he?'

'Er, that's right.'

'So he couldn't have been with you. In that case, *who* had the trencher?'

Tabitha scowled. 'You've spoken to Grandad, haven't you?'

Her mum was silent for a moment, before admitting, 'We had a quick chat at the start of the week.'

'He told you about Rhys.' It was a statement, not a question. She might have known her grandad would mention it. After all, it was a big deal.

'He didn't say much,' her mother hastened to assure her. 'Just that you were showing a nice young man – your grandad's words, not mine – some of the tourist spots.'

Tabitha could tell by her mother's tone that Grandad had said considerably more than that. She wished he hadn't said anything at all, but the damage was done now.

In an attempt to ensure that her mother didn't read more into it than was there, Tabitha said, 'He's a customer. I felt obliged.'

Even as the words left her lips, she knew how daft they sounded: the customer would have to be a very special one indeed to coax her out of her ivory tower. And no doubt Grandad would have given her mum a full report.

Anxious to end the conversation, she made the excuse that she needed to cook Grandad his dinner (which was true, but a few minutes more wouldn't have mattered), but before she could say goodbye, her mum added, 'By the way, Rosalind Blacksmith is getting married. I bumped into her mother the other day.'

The air was sucked out of Tabitha's lungs and she hooked the stool behind her with her foot, dragging it nearer and resting her bottom on it, her knees weak. 'Married?' she echoed.

'Yes, and they've got a baby on the way.'

Tabitha swallowed, an ache forming in her chest. 'Married?' she repeated.

It was ridiculous, but whenever Tabitha thought about the people she used to hang out with, some of whom she had known for years, she always imagined them as they had been back then, as though time had stood as still for them as it had done for her. It was a shock to be told that Rosalind had moved on, that she had a life Tabitha knew nothing about.

'She asked after you,' her mum was saying.

Annoyance flashed through her, and Tabitha's tone was ascorbic as she snapped, 'I bet she did.'

There was a deep sigh. 'It wasn't like that,' her mum said. Then more sharply, 'The world doesn't revolve around you, you know. Melanie Blacksmith has more important things on her mind – such as the imminent arrival of a grandchild.'

Tabitha blinked. She was so used to being handled with kid gloves, that her mother's retort stopped her in her tracks.

Tabitha had spent hour after hour, day after day, fretting and lamenting over what those photos had done to her parents, the shame, the embarrassment, and the worry it had caused, that she hadn't considered how her continued seclusion might also be affecting them. Was it possible that her mother actually envied Melanie Blacksmith? Did her mother wish that *she* was the one boasting that she was about to be a grandmother? Did her mother want to be looking forward to *Tabitha's* wedding?

Telling herself she was being silly, Tabitha said, 'When's it due?'

'In about seven weeks, I believe.'

'I'll send a card.'

'Good idea. Must dash, your father and I are going to the theatre this evening. Give my love to your grandad.'

'I will.' Tabitha replaced the receiver thoughtfully, but her hand remained on it and her gaze was once more drawn to her address book.

Should she phone Rosalind and offer her congratulations? She *should* – it was the right thing to do – but she didn't think she could bring herself to. What good would it do either of them? Tabitha was perfectly happy with her life as it was, and Rosalind had moved on. She had probably forgotten all about Tabitha and—

Tabitha sucked in a sharp breath. *Of course* Rosalind hadn't forgotten! It might be a case of out of sight out of mind for her former friend, and possibly for anyone else who had once known her, but the second Tabitha raised her head above the parapet, it would all come flooding back and the gossip would start all over again. Tabitha didn't think she could face it a second time.

So why poke the hornet's nest?

But Rosalind hadn't been a hornet. She had tried to offer Tabitha her support, but she had shunned her.

Tabitha let out an irritated huff, cross with herself for even considering contacting her. Nevertheless, her hand remained on the phone and she continued to stare at the number on the page.

What if her mother was right, and people did have other things to think about? Was she acting like a child, believing the world revolved around her when, in fact, no one had given her a second thought in years? Had she been hiding away all this time for no reason?

Tabitha shook her head. She'd had a perfectly good reason: she had needed time to come to terms with what had happened.

Anger flashed through her and she slapped a hand on the counter, wincing at the sting in her palm. It hadn't *happened*, it had been *done* to her, and for the first time she felt an internal shift as she understood that the person who should be ashamed was Austen, not her.

Without giving herself the opportunity to talk herself out of it, Tabitha lifted the receiver and dialled Rosalind's number.

Taking a shaky breath, she listened to it ring and ring.

She was about to hang up when the call was answered with a tentative, 'Hello?'

'Hi, it's me,' she began, but suddenly it was too much: she couldn't do this. Hastily Tabitha slammed the receiver down and her hand flew to her mouth as she held back the sob that was forming, as the other clutched her chest, her heart hammering frantically against her ribcage.

When the phone rang, startlingly loud in the silence of the shop, Tabitha let out a shriek.

Without considering what she was doing, she lifted the handset and slammed it down again. The ringing ceased abruptly.

Telling herself that it was a coincidence and nothing more, she gathered up the day's takings and, with a shaking hand, she began to tally the money against the receipts, one eye nervously on the phone in case it rang again.

It didn't.

Tabitha wasn't sure whether she was relieved or disappointed.

**

After pushing her meal around her plate whilst Grandad devoured his, then managing to drop a side plate as she was washing up, Tabitha made the excuse that she was tired, and retired to bed. Fully aware she wouldn't be able to sleep (seven-fifteen was too early to even try), she opened her favourite book, *Wuthering Heights*, and attempted to read.

Unsurprisingly, a tale about possessive love, ghosts and jealousy didn't soothe her, so she turned to another. But *Gone with the Wind* wasn't much better for her frame of mind. And neither was the uplifting romance where the happy-ever-after was guaranteed, which she tried next. She simply didn't want to read about love in any shape or form.

Maybe a thriller? She could give it a go.

Grandad was watching a documentary on serial killers when she emerged from her bedroom in the hope of finding something suitable to read on one of the shelves in the parlour, but as she scanned the titles her attention was caught by the images on the screen and she folded herself into a chair and began to watch. This suited her mood perfectly, she decided.

During a commercial break, Jeremy got to his feet. 'Cocoa?'

'I'll make it.' Tabitha made to rise but her grandfather waved her back down.

'You stay there. I'll do it,' he insisted, and before she could object he had scurried out of the room.

When the phone in the hall rang, he must have been right next to it because he picked it up after the first ring.

Tabitha tensed, her heart sinking; she had an awful feeling she knew who would be on the other end.

Ears pricked, she strained to hear the conversation and when she heard Grandad say, 'Yes, she is. I'll just fetch her for you,' she knew she had guessed correctly.

'Tabitha, it's a friend of yours, Rosalind. She says you phoned her earlier but there must have been a problem with the line.' His gaze was unwavering, and she discounted asking him to tell Rosalind that she was in the bath or was having an early night.

Wishing she had stayed in her room, where she could have pretended to be asleep, Tabitha heaved her reluctant body out of the chair. Her mouth dry, she bit her lip.

Injecting a brightness into her voice that she didn't feel, Tabitha picked up the phone and said, 'Hi Rosalind, my mother told me the news. Congratulations! You must be so happy.'

'Tabitha Locke, I never thought I'd hear your voice again. How are you?'

Tabitha swallowed. 'I'm fine. Good, actually. When is the big day?'

Rosalind's familiar laugh made Tabitha's heart constrict with a longing she hadn't been aware of until now. Damn it! She had missed her friend.

'Which one?' Rosalind chuckled. 'The baby will arrive before the wedding, although why I've only given myself three months to get back into shape after the birth, is a total mystery. You must come to the wedding. Please say you will. We haven't seen each other since you left Bristol.'

They hadn't spoken either, although Rosalind had tried. Then Tabitha had destroyed her phone and refused to have any contact with anyone, and that had been that.

'Um, I don't know,' Tabitha hedged.

'I'll send you an invite anyway. It's ages away yet, so you've got plenty of time to decide. You can bring a plus one, if you want.'

Tabitha almost replied that weddings weren't Grandad's thing, but Rhys's face popped into her mind and she imagined him on her arm. 'Thanks,' she muttered. 'I'll let you know.' Obviously she had no intention of going, with or without a plus one.

'We must get together soon,' Rosalind was saying. 'We've got such a lot to catch up on. Are you in touch with any of the old gang?'

'Not really.' Tabitha was in touch with no one. Not even the friends she had made in university, who had moved on after completing their degrees. She didn't know whether any of them had heard what Austen had done, but she hadn't been prepared to find out. Tabitha had cut all ties to everyone, except her parents and her grandad. It had been less painful that way.

'Then we *do* have loads to chat about,' Rosalind said. She lowered her voice. 'I've missed you. I often think about you.'

Tabitha missed Rosalind too. She hadn't realised how much until now.

Rosalind sounded exactly as Tabitha remembered, the voice pricking at her buried memories, and a picture of her friend's face when Rosalind had seen those—

'I'm sorry,' Tabitha blurted. 'I can't do this.' She closed her eyes. 'Goodbye, Rosalind. Be happy.'

Then she gently replaced the receiver on the cradle.

The ensuing silence was excruciating.

When Tabitha opened her eyes again, her cheeks damp with tears, it was to see her grandfather watching her, his face creased with compassion and concern.

Without saying a word, she climbed the stairs to her bedroom with a slow, heavy tread. And once inside, she closed the door firmly and lay down on the coverlet.

It was many hours before she finally fell asleep.

CHAPTER 8

Tabitha gaped when she opened the rear door of the shop the following Sunday morning to see Rhys wearing a suit.

She blinked at him owlishly, then glanced down at herself. She had chosen a pretty dress in teal, turquoise and a splash of pink and white to wear today, and as she had posed in front of the mirror, she had feared she might be overdressed. It seemed that wasn't the case.

'You're, um... looking smart,' she observed.

'And you look beautiful.'

Tabitha winced as his words set her heart fluttering. They also rang a warning bell in her head, and she hoped he didn't consider this to be a date.

He continued, oblivious to her discomfort. 'I didn't think jeans and trainers would be appropriate for afternoon tea at The Pump Room, so I decided to make an effort.' He gazed at her with appreciation. 'I'm glad I did.'

Tabitha silently acknowledged that she had dressed up more than usual, but not by much. Although she had taken more care with her appearance this morning, she wore a minimal amount of make-up and only a quick spray of perfume. Hardly more than she did for a day in the shop.

Tabitha thought it best to change the subject as they began the walk to the Royal Crescent. It would take around fifteen minutes, Tabitha knew, and would take them past the Jane Austen Centre. She wondered whether Rhys had ever visited it, but that wasn't what she asked him now.

'Did you go see your grandmother?'

His face lit up. 'I did. She was thrilled you found a key for her box. She sends her thanks. She also said that one thank-you dinner wasn't payment enough, and that I should take you out again.'

Tabitha ignored the last comment. 'I'm so pleased I was able to help.'

'We spent a lovely afternoon going through the old photos, and she even gave me a couple of the letters to read.' He chortled. 'She vetted them carefully first though, in case they contained anything 'funny'. I think she meant... what's the word?'

'Risqué?'

'Perfect. That's it, risqué. There was lots of talk about how much Grandpa missed her, and how much he loved her. I caught her blushing once or twice.'

'That's so sweet.'

'They were your typical old married couple – squabbled like cat and dog, but loved each other to bits. I hate seeing her in the nursing home, but my mam couldn't cope after Nanna had the stroke, and Nanna seems happy enough though. Hell, she has a better social life than I do!'

Tabitha giggled. The noise surprised her. She hadn't heard that sound come out of her mouth for a very long time.

Clearing her throat, she asked, 'Such as?'

'There is always something going on: bingo, board games, cards, gardening club, boules, ring toss… I could go on. And a hairdresser comes in once a week, plus someone to do their nails, and they're forever going on outings. Not only that, gossip is rife, and there's always a lively discussion when it comes to what to watch on the telly. She's having a ball; much more fun than if she was stuck at home with Mam.'

'What does your social life look like?' she asked. The memory of him smiling at the woman in the bar flitted across her mind.

'Drinks with friends, the odd club, a bit of outdoorsy stuff when I find the time.'

'Such as?' she persisted.

'I've done some rock climbing, paddleboarding, BMXing – although I'm getting a bit old for that as I don't bounce like I used to when I come off my bike. And that's good fun, too,' he said, nodding at one of the buildings they were walking past, and Tabitha realised they were strolling past the Jane Austen Centre.

But when she raised her eyebrows and gave the place a pointed look, she realised he was referring to something else entirely.

Just beyond the entrance to the Jane Austen Centre was a sign saying Gothic House, and as they drew alongside she saw the small print underneath: *'Come in, if you dare.'*

'What is it?' she asked. She had walked this street many times but had never noticed it.

'An escape room.'

'Pardon?'

He gave her a quizzical look. 'It's a kind of adventure game. You're locked in a room, or a series of rooms, and you have sixty minutes to look for clues and solve puzzles in order to get out. Have you never been in one?'

Tabitha shook her head. Now that she came to think of it, she had heard of escape rooms, but she hadn't taken much notice.

'You don't know what you're missing! It's such good fun.'

'I'll take your word for it,' she said.

'You don't have to. You can experience it for yourself.'

'I don't think so.'

'Aren't your friends into that kind of thing?'

Tabitha had no idea what the people who she used to call friends were into – apart from one of them, who was busy making a baby and a whole new life.

To her relief, Tabitha hadn't received any more phone calls, so hopefully Rosalind had got the hint. Tabitha felt bad and she hated herself for brushing her off, but she knew she would feel worse if she allowed herself to resume contact.

Wishing she'd never made that stupid phone call, Tabitha was relieved when they entered Brock Street because it meant they had almost reached their destination. And when they neared the end of it, the road opened up and the magnificent sweep of golden stone appeared overlooking a huge expanse of manicured lawn. They had reached the Royal Crescent, and Tabitha was instantly transported to a bygone age.

Suddenly her tea dress and Rhys's suit didn't look the least bit out of place.

'It's impressive,' Rhys said, as they paused to take in the view.

'Apart from the cars on the streets, I bet it's hardly changed since it was built in 1775,' Tabitha replied, sighing with delight. 'It's magnificent.'

'Go on then, tell me all about it.'

'Do you really want to know?'

'Uh-huh.'

'And you haven't already looked it up?'

'Nuh-uh.'

'OK, then,' she began. 'It was designed by John Wood and there are thirty Grade 1 listed houses altogether. It's 150 metres in length and the front of it has a ha ha that separates the lawn from the pasture and the animals that would have grazed here in the past.'

'A what?' Rhys was looking at her blankly.

Tabitha giggled at his confused expression. Giggling was fast becoming a new habit. 'A ha ha,' she repeated. 'It's a wall with a ditch on the other side. You can't see it from this angle, but that's the beauty of it. The way it's constructed means that the residents have an uninterrupted view without seeing any walls or fences. Clever, isn't it? Come on, let's go inside No 1!'

Tabitha was so focused on the regency museum on the opposite side of the street, that she didn't check the road was clear. As she stepped off the kerb, the blare of a horn made her falter, before she was grasped firmly by the arm and pulled back onto the pavement.

Unbalanced, she fell against Rhys and his arms came around her to steady her.

'Woah, there, you almost got totalled,' he said. 'Are you OK?'

Breathless and trembling, Tabitha managed to utter, 'I'm fine,' and she was grateful to lean against him for a few moments until her heart rate had slowed and she didn't feel quite as shaky.

For several seconds neither of them moved, Tabitha enjoying the feel of Rhys's strong arms as she tried to bring her breathing under control. But the shock of being almost run over by a delivery van was outweighed by the shock of realising that it was having his arms around her that was making her breathless, and she hastily stepped out of his embrace and moved a respectable distance away.

The scent of him lingered in her nose though, and she could still feel his solid warmth on her back where she had been pressed against him.

A respectable distance? Ha! Anyone would think she was the heroine in her own regency romance, Anne Elliot to Rhys's Fredrick Wentworth. But this wasn't Jane Austen's *Persuasion* and there would be no romance between her and Rhys. Tabitha simply wouldn't allow it. Once bitten... Or should she say *savaged*?

But it had felt so good to be held—

Stop it! Her admonishment might have been silent, but something had alerted Rhys and he took a step back. His face was full of concern though, and she felt guilty for overreacting. All he had done was prevent her from getting squashed, and her attraction to him had gone into overdrive. He had only done what anyone else would have done, and she was acting like he had tried to seduce her.

Oh, for goodness' sake! Here I go again. I think I need to get out more. Smiling at him apologetically, Tabitha crossed the road, this time looking both ways before she ventured off the pavement, and soon they were inside the museum, where Tabitha tried to forget she had just had a close encounter with a good-looking man and concentrate on the museum instead.

Being inside No 1, The Royal Crescent, felt like being on a film set, and although Tabitha enjoyed looking around it again, she had more fun watching Rhys's reaction.

He was clearly taken with the attention to details, such as the old spectacles and the coins on the bureau, and he particularly liked the gentleman's retreat with its globe and telescope.

'It's the eighteenth-century equivalent of a man cave,' he chuckled. 'I've got a man-cave, but mine is a fraction of the size of this.'

'Have you got a telescope in yours?'

'No, but I've got a games console or two.'

He was also fascinated by the servant's hall, and the disbelief on his face when he saw the kitchen had her laughing out loud.

'I thought my oven and hob was scary enough, but look at that!' he cried, pointing to the open fireplace where the cooking would have been done.

'I don't think I'd like to cook on that either,' Tabitha agreed, 'and I actually enjoy cooking.'

After the museum, they took a stroll along the length of The Crescent and then wandered through Victoria Park until eventually they were retracing their steps as they made their way towards the abbey and The Pump Room.

'Crikey, this is civilised,' Rhys said as they were shown into the restaurant's incredibly grand dining room with its tall windows, high ceiling and crystal chandelier. Muted conversation filled the air as they took their seats at the white-clothed table.

'I feel like a grown-up,' he joked.

'I don't like to tell you, but at your age you are *definitely* a grown-up.'

'Yeah, but I don't always feel like one. Most of the time I feel like a kid pretending to be an adult. I'm always scared someone will realise and call me out.'

Interesting, Tabitha thought. His words reminded her that she used to feel like a child playing dress-up whenever she had attended meetings at work or had been given additional responsibility. She recalled being worried that one of the team would see through her disguise and escort her from the building.

Now, though, she felt as old as her grandfather, as though she had jumped straight from her twenties to old age, and her body had yet to catch up.

Rhys leant across the table. 'I hope no one asks if we have a responsible adult with us.'

Tabitha pressed her lips together. 'I don't think there's any chance of them asking that. The responsible adult is quite clearly me.'

'Damn it, it's just me that's the big kid, then. I'll try to act my age, and not embarrass you too much.'

'I'm sure you won't. You've been perfectly behaved so far.'

He studied her face and the teasing light faded from his eyes, to be replaced by something altogether more intense. 'I'm not sure I *want* to be perfectly behaved when I'm with you.'

'Oh!' It came out as a squeak, and Tabitha wasn't sure she'd understood him correctly.

Flustered, she picked up the pepper pot and began playing with it, turning it over in her hands. Rhys looked away, and she frowned. Had he expected a reply? But what could she have said in response? *Me, too?* Hardly. *I don't think so?* Stuffy and old maidish. *Not right now?* Er... no.

'Would you like something stronger to go with your pot of tea?' Rhys asked after a short but awkward silence.

'I think I'll have a mocktail,' she said. She desperately wanted a glass of sparkling wine to take the edge off her swiftly unravelling nerves, but she didn't dare. Anyway, the strawberry and elderflower fizz sounded lovely.

Rhys was studying her, his expression inscrutable. Then he smiled, and it was as though the sun had come out. 'I'll have the same.'

Tabitha breathed a relieved sigh. They were going to pretend he had never made that odd comment, which was fine by her. But she couldn't forget he had said it, and she knew she would be picking over the bones of it later.

The arrival of a three-tiered cake stand filled to bursting with a wonderful selection of savoury and sweet items, served as a welcome distraction, and Tabitha's mouth watered as she gazed at the food and wondered what to have first.

She settled for a cream cheese and cucumber sandwich and took a bite. 'Mmm.'

'Nice?'

She nodded enthusiastically. Having afternoon tea here was a rare treat. To eat it in the company of a man she fancied rotten, was even more of a treat. That he appeared to fancy her too (if she had understood him correctly) was a gift. But Rhys was a gift she had no intention of unwrapping and—

Oh dear, a vision of an unwrapped Rhys flashed across her inner eye, and the morsel of sandwich went down the wrong way as she inhaled sharply.

Coughing, Tabitha lifted her napkin to her mouth and waved a hand in the air. After a few moments of spluttering whilst Rhys looked on in concern and one of the waiting staff had brought her a glass of water, Tabitha regained control.

Hot and bothered and with streaming eyes, she took a sip of water and tried to compose herself.

'Are you OK?'

'Went down the wrong way,' she explained needlessly.

He grinned. 'I think it's you who needs the responsible adult today,' he said, and she recalled how he had saved her from a nasty accident earlier.

To go with her watery eyes, her cheeks grew warm, and she guessed she must look a mess.

'I'm not usually this...' She searched for a suitable word but couldn't find one.

Rhys came to her rescue. 'Accident prone?'

She shrugged. Better for him to think she was clumsy, than to realise he unnerved her.

Pre-Austen she would have been intrigued at her reaction. Post-Austen she was scared. Scared of allowing anyone to get too close; scared of an upwelling of a feeling she thought had been buried under an avalanche of shame, guilt, and self-loathing; scared of love and the destruction it could bring.

She had loved Austen, of that there was no doubt. But he hadn't loved her, and there had been no doubt about that either, not at the end, not after how he had treated her.

Rhys wasn't Austen, Tabitha knew that. But the knowledge didn't make any difference. She couldn't bring herself to trust another man again. Neither could she bring herself to trust her own judgement.

Determined that this would be the last time she saw Rhys, she vowed to enjoy the rest of the afternoon for what it was – afternoon tea with a friend.

So why did she feel aggrieved when, after he had walked her to her door, Rhys shoved his hands in his pockets, smiled regretfully, then walked away with nothing more than a 'Bye, Tabi-Cat.'

It sounded so very final.

CHAPTER 9

Tabitha jabbed a fork into one of the potatoes boiling in a saucepan on the hob and nodded. They were almost ready to go in the oven.

'We could have gone out to lunch,' her mother said. 'There was no need for you to go to all this trouble.' She was leaning against the odds-and-sods cupboard, sipping a glass of wine.

Dad and Grandad were in the parlour, enjoying a heated discussion on politics.

'I like cooking,' Tabitha replied.

'Yes, but you do it every day. I would have thought it would be a treat for you to eat out.'

'It's a novelty for her to eat at home these days,' Grandad chuckled.

Tabitha hadn't heard him come in, and she glared at him in irritation. He smiled sweetly back at her.

'Oh, why is that?' Her mum's head tilted to the side as she waited for an explanation.

Jeremy was more than happy to supply his daughter-in-law with one. 'She's been out again with Rhys. The Pump Room, this time. They had afternoon tea on Sunday.'

'Really? That's lovely.'

Tabitha risked a glance at her mother, saw the careful hope in her eyes and hastily looked away, a familiar ache blossoming in her chest.

She wished Grandad hadn't said anything; he was getting Mum's hopes up when there was absolutely nothing to be hopeful about. Especially since Rhys had left her on the doorstep on Sunday without suggesting they see each other again. Tabitha could only assume he'd explored enough of the city, because she hadn't seen or heard from him since. Perhaps if she owned a mobile phone, he would have—?

No, she wasn't going to go there. She had managed perfectly well these past few years without having a mobile in her life, and she would carry on managing.

'When will lunch be ready?' Jeremy asked.

'When it's cooked!' Tabitha's reply was sharper than it should have been but honestly, she was fed up with her family's nosiness.

Her grandad had asked her several times this week when she was going out with Rhys again, and he didn't seem to want to take her 'I'm not,' for an answer. Either that, or his memory was going.

A coil of fear uncurled in her stomach. Was he losing his short-term memory? She racked her brains to think of any other instances, but she couldn't recall any. Twice this week he had forgotten where he'd left his slippers, but that was nothing new – he was often mislaying them – but apart from that he was as sharp as a tack, taking his usual keen interest in the daily running of the shop. Although... she *had* noticed a gradual withdrawal over the past several months. She had assumed it was because he had faith in her, but maybe there was a more sinister reason.

Apart from high blood pressure, which he took tablets for, he appeared to be healthy enough, so was she over-thinking it? She had a tendency to do that since Austen, and she hated that she'd lost all her self-confidence.

Her mum said, 'I thought you might have been otherwise engaged today. I hope you haven't put off a date with Rhys just to cook lunch for your old mum and dad.' She chuckled at referring to herself as 'old'.

'No, I didn't.'

'He hasn't asked her, that's why.' Jeremy shook his head sadly.

'Maybe he's busy?' Mum suggested.

'Can we please change the subject? He doesn't need a tour guide.'

'I don't suppose he does.' Her mother's reply was loaded with meaning.

Tabitha scowled. 'Whatever you think, you are wrong.'

'If he wanted a tour guide, he could have joined one of the tours of the city.' Mum arched a brow. 'He needn't have asked *you*. Or he could have looked it up on the internet. I reckon he must fancy you.'

Tabitha flinched. Her mother couldn't leave it alone, could she? She'd just had to say it, and now Tabitha's irritation had grown into outright annoyance, seasoned with the familiar guilt and an added dollop of sadness. Disappointment was also in there, but she didn't want to examine that too closely. Disappointment wasn't an emotion she wanted to feel, because it indicated she might have been hoping for something more than the friendship that their casual acquaintance would suggest.

'It's nice to see you having a social life again,' her mother continued.

Tabitha gritted her teeth. With jerky movements she drained the potatoes, then tossed them to fluff them up before sprinkling them with a dusting of seasoned flour and placing them in a hot roasting tin. She slammed the tin in the oven and turned up the heat.

'Is there anything I can do to help?' Grandad asked.

'I think you've 'helped' enough,' Tabitha muttered.

Oblivious to Tabitha's sour mood, her mother said, 'I've already offered, but she turned me down.'

Grandad was more attuned to Tabitha's feelings. 'It's his loss,' he said. 'There are plenty more fish in the sea.'

'There are sharks, too,' she snapped. 'I don't want another fish.'

Jeremy peered at her over his spectacles. 'What you need is a friend your own age. Someone to go out and have fun with. Someone like Rosalind. Hmm?'

'Rosalind?' Her mother's ears visibly pricked up.

'She phoned the other week,' Grandad explained.

'She did? You never said.' Her mother gave her an accusing look. 'How is she?'

'Fine'

'Is she excited about the wedding?'

'I expect so.'

'And the baby? Does she know what they are having?'

'No idea.'

Her mum huffed. 'What did she want, if it wasn't to tell you her good news?'

'A chat.'

'You clearly didn't chat about anything important.' She sucked in a breath. 'Or did you?' Her face was full of concern.

'No, we didn't talk about *that*.' Tabitha spat the word out. 'It's not a subject I like to discuss.'

'Of course not, but you haven't spoken to her in years, not since… so I thought you might want to clear the air, mend a few bridges.'

'There is no air to be cleared and no bridges to be mended. We've gone our separate ways, that's all.'

'So why did she phone then?' her mum persisted. 'You must have talked about *something*.'

'No. I was busy.'

'Did she call when the shop—?'

'Mum! I don't want to talk about it, OK?' She was aware that her mum and grandad were exchanging looks behind her back, but she didn't care. She'd had enough of being questioned. 'Lunch will be half an hour,' she announced, 'so you might as well go sit in the parlour for a while and let me get on with cooking it.'

She waited for them to leave, then sagged against the butler sink, the breath whooshing out of her.

Angry with herself, she set about tidying the kitchen, washing any used pots and utensils, making more noise than she needed.

She should never have agreed to play tour guide to Rhys. Her previously nice, ordered, sedate life had been turned upside down since he had come into it. First there had been the totally unwelcome attraction she had felt for him (and still felt, if she was honest), then there had been the enjoyable hours spent in his company which had unsettled her no end, and now her mother was bringing up the past.

Tabitha wished with all her heart that Rhys had never walked into the shop and into her life. But he had, and now she was feeling bereft because he seemed to have walked right back out of it again.

***

Thursday dawned a bright early-summer day. The birds chirped excitedly outside Tabitha's bedroom window, and she could hear the sounds of the city coming alive around her.

She needn't get up yet but she did anyway, because she had been awake for a while and was restless, despite feeling rather tired. She hadn't been sleeping well lately which she blamed on it being light at four-thirty in the morning.

To her surprise her grandad was already up, sitting in his favourite chair, reading.

'I didn't hear you get up,' she said. 'Couldn't you sleep?'

'No, and neither could you.'

Tabitha pulled a face. 'Sorry. I tried to be quiet but I've been awake for ages.'

'You didn't disturb me. When you get to my age, being awake half the night is commonplace.' He closed his book and placed it on the table. 'Shall we go out for breakfast? There's something I want to talk to you about.'

Tabitha's eyes widened and her tummy turned over.

'Don't worry, it's nothing bad,' Jeremy said, noticing her reaction.

Despite her pestering him, Grandad refused to tell Tabitha anything further until they were seated in a cafe, with the smell of coffee and bacon filling the air.

Tabitha sniffed appreciatively. 'Please don't tell me you're going to ask for two boiled eggs?' she joked.

'Not on your life. I'm going to have a full English.'

'Good idea. I'll have one as well. It'll see me through until dinner time. I thought I'd do us some salmon and new potatoes, with a hollandaise sauce.'

'Not for me, thanks. Bertrand Pierce has invited me to the opening of his son's art exhibition. We're having dinner together first, a group of us.'

'Your social life is a positive whirlwind,' she said fondly.

'I wish yours was.'

'Grandad...' Her tone carried a hint of warning.

He held his hands up in mock surrender. 'I'll not say another word.'

'What did you want to talk to me about?'

'The shop.' His expression grew serious and Tabitha's heart dropped to her pretty sandals.

She had kind of been expecting this, but now that she was about to be informed that he was selling up, she realised she wasn't ready. Locke's Key Emporium had been here for well over a hundred years – it couldn't possibly close. But Grandad was way past normal retirement age, and although he was fit and healthy, his advanced years were beginning to show.

He deserved to enjoy himself, and not worry about his business. Tabitha might deal with the daily running of the shop, but it was ultimately her grandfather's responsibility, and she guessed it must weigh heavily.

Would he sell it as a going concern? What about the flat? Would he sell that, too? And what about her? What would she do?

'—sign it over to you. I've made an appointment with Siegfried for Monday morning. You'll be expected to attend.' He looked at her expectantly.

Tabitha squinted at him. 'What?'

'I want you to be there to discuss the conveyancing. The premises will be straightforward, but your taking over of the business will be more complicated. Anyway, Siegfried will advise on how best to go about it.'

Tabitha was only able to focus on a small part of what her grandad had just said. 'Me, take over the business?' The words came out louder and at a higher pitch than she intended, and she swiftly lowered her voice. 'Are you serious?'

Jeremy twinkled at her. 'Deadly.'

Tabitha gasped. 'You're not... you aren't going to...?'

'Eh? Oh, no, nothing like that. But it's about time, don't you think? Tabitha, if you want it, the shop and the flat is yours.'

'But what about Dad? Won't he be upset?'

'Goodness, no. Your father and I have talked about this. Recently, in fact. He doesn't want any part of the shop; he never has. But neither would he like to see it sold. So, if you want it, you can have it. All I ask is that I live out my days in the flat. Or until you find yourself a husband.'

Tabitha leapt out of her chair and threw her arms around him. Unable to hold back her tears, she sobbed into his neck while he patted her back and whispered soothing words in her ear.

'I take it that's a yes,' he said wryly, when she calmed down enough to resume her seat.

Tabitha dabbed her damp cheeks with a tissue. 'It is,' she sniffed, a beaming smile spreading across her face.

With her grandad's generosity, her future was assured. She could carry on exactly as she was, with the dubious added pleasure of doing the accounts. Nothing would change. Her life would continue in the same vein as it had for the last three years. And that was just how she wanted it.

***

The door hadn't opened and the bell above it hadn't let out as much as a tinkle, but a sixth sense informed Tabitha that someone was about to enter the shop. When she saw who that someone was, her heart missed a beat and her mouth went dry.

Rhys was peering through the door's glass panel, then the handle turned and he stepped inside. 'Hi.' His smile was open and sunny. 'I was hoping to catch you before you locked up.'

'Why, do you need another key?'

'No, I need a drink. Care to join me?'

'I don't think so.'

'Aw, go on. It's a glorious evening and I know the perfect place.'

'I bet you do,' she mumbled.

He closed the door firmly and flipped the sign over.

She narrowed her eyes and glared at him.

He made a face. 'Sorry, I assumed you'd be closing, seeing as it's half past five.'

'I am.'

'Toss me your keys and I'll lock the door for you.'

'I can do it myself.'

'I know that.' He laughed softly.

His gentle teasing made her tingle. Why did he have to appear today, when everything had been going so well?

He said, 'Are you cross with me? Sorry I haven't been in touch. I've only just got back.'

'I am not cross,' she replied crossly, then curiosity got the better of her and she asked, 'Where have you been?'

'Cheltenham.'

'Oh.' She had expected somewhere more exotic, or at least further afield than Cheltenham, which was only just over an hour away by car.

'Work,' he added.

She wanted to ask whether he'd had to work on Sunday, but it wasn't any of her business. What he did with his time was up to him. Just because she had spent a couple of Sundays in his company, didn't mean he was obliged to spend any other Sunday with her. Besides, she had made it perfectly clear that they were just friends. He owed her nothing, nor she him. But that didn't prevent her from feeling resentful that he hadn't contacted her for ten days, then breezed in as though nothing was wrong.

Maybe he didn't think anything *was* wrong. And why should he? She was the one whose head was messed up. She had been so used to Austen's controlling behaviour, the way he hadn't been able to go more than an hour without wanting to know where she was, who she was with, what she was doing...

'Keys?' Rhys reminded her.

She threw them to him and he caught them deftly, then she watched to make sure he was doing it right. She knew the snick and click of each lock intimately, and she didn't relax until all the tumblers had turned.

'I take it that means the answer is yes,' he said, sauntering towards the counter, the keys in his hand jangling.

'To what?'

'Coming out for a drink.'

'I haven't eaten yet.'

'We'll grab something later.'

'I'm not sure that drinking alcohol on an empty stomach is a good idea.'

He raised his eyebrows.

Tabitha huffed. 'Yes, I know I sound like your mother, but it's true.'

'We can eat first, if you like.' His tone indicated that it made no difference to him one way or the other. 'We can grab a burger or something.'

'How about salmon and new potatoes?' The words were out of her mouth before she had a chance to think about what she had been about to say.

'Pardon?'

'That's what I was planning to have for dinner.'

'You won't get that at a burger bar. The best I can do is fish and chips from the chippie.'

'I've got enough for two.'

'Are you offering to cook me tea?'

'Dinner, yes.'

He grinned. 'You're on.'

Debating the wisdom of the offer she'd just made, Tabitha completed her evening routine, conscious of Rhys watching her every move, then she led him upstairs to the flat.

When he stepped foot into the hall, she saw him gazing around, open-mouthed. And when he saw the parlour, he let out a low whistle.

'No wonder you like history so much – you're living in it. This is just like No 1, The Crescent.'

'Not quite. Our furniture is a bit of a mishmash of eras and we do have some mod cons.'

'So I see.' He was looking at the TV. Turning to her, he said, 'You've got the best of both worlds – the elegance and atmosphere of the past, with the benefit of modern technology.'

He followed her into the kitchen, his gaze flitting around the room as she reached into the fridge for the salmon steaks. 'It's very you,' he added.

'Old-fashioned?'

'Elegant, classy.'

Tabitha blushed. She had never been called either of those things before and she wasn't sure how she felt about it. If it wasn't for his earnest expression, she might have thought Rhys was taking the mickey.

'Can I help?' he asked, as she plonked a bag of new potatoes on the counter.

'We'll eat in here, rather than in the parlour, so could you lay the table?' She jerked her head towards a drawer.

The formal dining table in the parlour was only used if there were more than two people eating, such as when her parents had visited at the weekend, but seeing as there was only her and Rhys this evening, it seemed silly to eat in there. However, the little table in the kitchen was cosy, to say the least, and she worried that it might be too intimate.

It was also incredibly strange to be in this kitchen with a man who wasn't her grandad or her father. She was aware that her manner was stilted, and she hoped she would relax as the evening wore on. She might feel better after they'd eaten and were out of the flat, in neutral territory so to speak.

The meal didn't take long to prepare, and very shortly she was putting a plate down in front of him.

Rhys raised his eyebrows when she handed him a linen napkin, although he didn't say anything, and she was conscious that her home life was probably quite different to his. Heck, her previous pre-Bath home life had been vastly different to the way she lived now.

Did she miss it? Sometimes. She missed having friends to giggle with, to cry with, to whinge with. She used to love girly shopping days, cafe brunches, the cinema, bars, clubs...

The realisation that she would be going out for a drink shortly hit her, and a fizz of excitement and anticipation surged through her veins. She hadn't had 'just a drink' in a bar or a pub for a very long time.

'Have you got anywhere in particular in mind?' she asked after they'd finished eating. She stood to clear away the empty plates and was pleased to see he had devoured every morsel.

'Huh?'

'For this drink you're so desperate to have. Why is that?'

He pulled a face. 'Work stuff. Been hard at it for days. I need to let my hair down, blow off some steam.'

Tabitha remembered what that was like, the need to forget the working week despite enjoying her job. She used to work to live, now she just... What? Lived to work? But running the shop for Grandad wasn't work, it was a joy, and she loved every minute of it. And now that it was about to become her business, she would be even more devoted to it, if that was possible.

Rhys continued, 'I don't know if you've heard of it – you might even be a regular – but there's a microbrewery that serves some fantastic beers, really unusual flavours.'

'Such as?' Tabitha wasn't a beer person. She preferred gin.

'Coffee, wild berry, peach.'

She wrinkled her nose as she turned on the hot water tap and squirted washing-up liquid into the sink. 'I'm not sure I fancy any of them.'

'Trust me, they're incredible. And if you don't fancy those, there are plenty of other flavours to choose from.'

Unconvinced, Tabitha carried on washing the dishes whilst Rhys dried, but when the task was done she wiped her hands on a towel and said, 'I'd better get changed.' If she was going to a pub with a gorgeous guy, she was determined to make the most of it, and that meant looking the part.

***

Three drinks in and Tabitha was starting to feel tipsy. All of the ales had been delicious – which she was surprised about, considering she had only ever tried beer once before (she'd had a sip of her dad's pale ale) and had hated it. But the artisan ales that this adorable little brewery produced were divine.

She'd actually had a taste of six of them, because Rhys had let her have a mouthful of each of his.

No wonder she was tiddly!

Letting out a contented sigh, she slumped into her chair and gazed around, soaking up the atmosphere. The pub and the seating area outside were full, standing room only, and was so noisy she could hardly hear herself think. Rhys had tried in vain to hold a conversation with her but had eventually given up when she'd kept saying 'Pardon?' and asking him to repeat everything.

Pity – she had rather enjoyed the way he'd leant towards her, his mouth close to her ear, his breath tickling her cheek.

'Ready for another?' he yelled, indicating her nearly empty glass.

Tabitha was tempted, but she had a shop to open in the morning so she thought she'd better not. She would probably have a headache as it was, and she didn't fancy serving customers and trying to appear cheerful when she had a raging hangover.

She shouted back, 'No thanks, I've got work in the morning.'

'That's a shame. I was hoping we could do something together.'

Tabitha's heart skipped a beat and she drew in a sharp breath.

He shrugged. 'No problem. What are you doing Saturday evening?'

'Nothing.' The word was out of her mouth before she had thought about it, and it crossed her mind that she might have sounded too eager, when all she was doing was telling the truth. She didn't want him to think she had nothing better to do than sit around waiting for him to call, but it was too late now.

'Fancy coming to see a band with me?'

'Er, who?'

'The Purple Angels.'

'Who?'

Rhys laughed. 'I'm not surprised you haven't heard of them. They've been going for a while, but they've only recently started doing live gigs.'

'What kind of music do they play?'

'Rock mostly.'

'Where are they playing?'

'The Draconian Bar.'

Tabitha had no idea where that was. 'Um, OK, I'd like that.'

'Great. I'll give you a shout about eight? They're not on until nine.'

To Tabitha, who was unused to going out at night, eight seemed awfully late to start the evening, and once again she mused on how maiden aunt-ish she was becoming. *Had* become. If anyone took a look inside her mind, they would think she was Grandad's age.

She drank the last of her beer and checked her watch. Five to eleven – time to go home.

Rhys walked her to her door once more. Her ears were ringing after the noise of the pub, and she felt a little unsteady. Definitely too much alcohol! She wasn't used to it, and she had a pleasant buzz going on, although she would probably regret it in the morning.

They drew to a halt in the narrow lane at the back of the shop, and Rhys shoved his hands in his pockets as she delved into her bag for her keys.

'Thanks for tea,' he said.

'You're welcome. Thanks for taking me out this evening.'

'My pleasure.' He shifted from foot to foot. 'I had a good time.'

'So did I. Did having a couple of pints work?'
'Eh?'

'You said you needed a drink.'

He stopped shuffling and his gaze locked onto hers. 'I did, but I wanted to see you more.'

Tabitha's mind went blank.

'I like you, Tabi-cat.'

Her numb brain latched onto the nickname. 'Why Tabi-cat?'

'Nine lives. You almost lost one of yours when we were at The Crescent.'

'I can't remember if I thanked you for saving me from getting run over.'

'I don't think you did.' He moved closer, and she swallowed nervously.

'Thank you—' The rest of her sentence ended abruptly as his lips brushed against hers. Then they were gone before she'd had a chance to register what had happened.

'See you on Saturday, Tabi.'

In a daze, Tabitha went inside, closing the door softly behind her, then leant against it, her legs weak. She was trembling from head to foot, and her breathing was ragged as she put a finger to her mouth.

To say she was shocked was an understatement. But what disconcerted her more was that she had enjoyed it. For a fleeting second, she had felt more alive than she had done for years.

And she wanted more.

Damn him, the man was addictive.

CHAPTER 10

It was Saturday morning and Tabitha was sorting out some fresh stock and rearranging one of the displays to accommodate the new keys, when she heard her grandfather plod down the stairs. Assuming he was going out, she was surprised to see that he didn't have his walking stick (he called it a cane, to make it seem less *old man* and more *gentleman*) and neither was there a light-weight coat folded over his arm. No matter what the weather, he always carried a coat with him, just in case: his reasoning being that the British weather couldn't be trusted and that weather forecasters got it wrong more often than not. Jeremy never took any chances, claiming that if 'one was prepared for rain, then one wouldn't be disappointed or inappropriately dressed.'

'I thought I'd give you a hand today,' he announced, scanning the cabinets and nodding to himself when he saw that everything was in order.

'Any particular reason?' Tabitha asked.

'No...'

She narrowed her eyes. Grandad seemed unsure. He was also acting shifty, unable to look her in the eye. She put down the key she was holding and turned to face him.

'You don't have to do this, you know,' she said.

'Do what? Give you a hand now and again? But I like to.'

'Sign the business over to me.'

Bewilderment flitted across his wrinkled features. 'Have you changed your mind?'

'Of course not, but I think you might have.'

'Whatever gave you that idea?'

You, she thought. 'Just making sure.'

Jeremy huffed. 'Can't I help my granddaughter occasionally without her taking it the wrong way?'

'Sorry.' She wasn't sorry at all: he was definitely up to something, and when the clock chimed a quarter to eleven and his eyes shot to the door, she was certain of it.

Wishing she knew what it was, she returned to her task whilst he checked the ledger for any sales so far this morning. A couple of customers had made purchases, and it was shaping up to be a typical Saturday, although there was nothing typical about what was going to happen later. Her skin tingled at the thought of seeing Rhys, and her heart skipped a beat.

If she had owned a mobile phone, she would have spent most of yesterday checking to see if he had messaged her. She hadn't been able to stop thinking about him and the barely-there kiss. He had occupied a significant chunk of the space in her head since, and she was fairly sure it wasn't a good thing, considering she had vowed to leave men well alone.

She had also vowed to not let any man get close enough to hurt her again, and she had vowed that she and Rhys would only be friends.

Tabitha had broken every one of those vows.

The way she felt about him had gone beyond friendship. As well as being attracted to him, she was starting to fall for him romantically. And it felt wonderful.

It was also stupid and terrifying, and she was woefully unprepared.

Since Thursday night, she had seesawed between thinking it best to end it now before they went any further and she became so far out of her depth that she was in danger of drowning, to desperately wanting to see where it could lead.

She thought she had safely locked her heart away in a lead-lined box in her chest, but each time she saw Rhys she could feel the tumblers falling, one by one. Soon, the last of them would give way and the box would click open.

Pandora would have nothing on Tabitha when that happened, and she was so fearful that the idea of risking her heart again had made her toss and turn restlessly for the past two nights. Today she had bags under her eyes larger than a builder's sack full of rubble, and she hoped Rhys wouldn't be put off by her wan, washed-out face.

If he was, her inner voice piped up, then she would be well shot of him, because he wouldn't be the man she hoped he was.

Tabitha was so busy listening to that inner voice that she didn't hear a customer come into the shop. It was only when her grandad stiffened that she realised.

Except... the woman standing hesitantly just inside the doorway wasn't a customer. It was *Rosalind*. Blooming, glowing, heavily pregnant Rosalind, with one hand resting on the mound of her stomach and a question in her eyes.

Tabitha's blood ran cold, and a tremble began in her knees that worked its way up her legs and into her body. With shaking hands, she replaced the key on the hook, and drew in a deep, ragged breath.

'Hi.' Rosalind's smile was tentative and uncertain.

'Hi.' Tabitha forced the greeting out through numb lips, not knowing what to do or what to say. The last person she had expected to see in Locke's Key Emporium was Rosalind Blacksmith. It tugged at her heart and a wave of intense sadness swept over her. She put out a hand to steady herself, her eyes prickling with tears.

Jeremy took charge, hurrying forward. 'Rosalind, isn't it? Nice to meet you.' He shook Rosalind's hand.

Rosalind didn't take her eyes off Tabitha, who could only gaze at her former friend in disbelief.

'I'm Jeremy, Tabitha's grandfather. Can I get you a seat?'

'No thanks, I'm fine for a minute.'

Grandad said, 'Tabitha, why don't you—? *Tabitha!* I'm talking to you.'

Tabitha was jerked out of her immobility and she tore her gaze away from Rosalind to look at her grandfather. 'Pardon?'

'I was trying to say, why don't you and Rosalind go upstairs for a cup of tea and a chat? I can manage here.'

'You planned this,' she accused. She looked from Jeremey to Rosalind, and back again.

'Someone had to do something. Rosalind phoned again and I happened to pick up. The two of you need to talk, don't you think?'

'Please.' Rosalind's tone was pleading, and when Tabitha looked at her, her friend's cheeks were damp and she was rubbing her bump.

Emotional blackmail, that's what this is, Tabitha thought, but she could hardly tell her to leave when she had come all this way to see her.

'If we must,' Tabitha muttered ungraciously, then immediately felt contrite and added, 'Are you OK to go upstairs?'

'I'm pregnant, not ill.' Rosalind wrinkled her nose, an achingly familiar gesture.

'I've not had a great deal of experience with pregnant women,' Tabitha said, indicating that Rosalind should go ahead of her through the door leading to the workroom and the flat above.

'Now's your chance,' Rosalind quipped. 'I can moan about it until the cows come home. Or we can talk about us.'

Tabitha waited until they had climbed the stairs and stepped into the hall before responding. 'What is there to talk about?'

'Me and you, and how you've ghosted me for years.'

'I didn't ghost you.'

'I think you'll find you did. Do you mind if I sit down? My back is killing me, and this little one won't keep still.' Seeing Tabitha's horrified expression, Rosalind added, 'Don't worry, it's completely normal, but it's bloody knackering. She doesn't let me get a wink of sleep.'

'She?'

'We're having a girl.'

'That's wonderful.'

'Isn't it? I wouldn't have minded either, but I'm secretly pleased to be having a daughter.'

'Tea? Or would you prefer a soft drink?' Tabitha remembered how Rosalind rarely drank tea.

'Could I just have a hot water?'

'On its own?'

'Everything else gives me heartburn. See, I told you I can moan about being pregnant, but I realise how lucky I am. Remember Vikki Bradley? She's had three rounds of IVF.' And Rosalind was off, chatting about friends they once had in common, and it was as though the past three years had never happened.

But eventually the subject of Austen came up, as Tabitha knew it would. He was like an elephant in the room, and sooner or later one of them had to acknowledge his presence.

It was Rosalind who mentioned him first. 'I hated what Austen did to you. We all did. It was…' She sighed. 'The man is a total and utter shit.'

'I called him far worse.'

'I bet you did.' Rosalind reached out a hand, laying it on top of Tabitha's, and gave her a squeeze. 'Why did you shut us out?' The hurt in her voice was unmistakable.

'Everyone was talking about me; I was a laughing stock.'

'Yes, we discussed it, we all did. At first, we simply couldn't believe he would do that to you. I mean, *revenge porn?* That's the lowest of the low.'

Tabitha swallowed hard and hung her head. Her cheeks flamed and the far too familiar shame crashed over her. If only she had realised what Austen had been up to – but how could she have possibly known? The camera had been small and well-hidden, and the memory made her feel sick.

Rosalind carried on. 'It wasn't something any of us could ignore, so of course we talked about it. We tried to talk to you too, but you didn't reply to anyone's messages or phone calls. When I went to your place Austen told me you'd gone back to live with your parents, but when I spoke to your mum, she said you'd gone to stay with your grandfather and that you needed some space.'

That was true. Tabitha hadn't wanted to see anyone. She distinctly remembered yelling at her mother, warning her not to let anyone in, her best friend included.

Was that before or after she had smashed her phone? Tabitha couldn't remember. She didn't *want* to remember. It had been a hideous time, a blur of images she wanted to forget, of statements to the police, of knowing looks and pitying, awkward glances.

'I've missed you, Tabs,' Rosalind said, her voice catching.

'I've missed you, too.' Tabitha gulped back tears.

'You can't believe how happy I was when you called. You'd dropped off the face of the earth, and apart from knowing you were here, in Bath with your grandad, I didn't know anything else. Are you happy, Tabs?'

'I… er…' Tabitha blew out her cheeks in a shaky sigh, her eyes raised to the ceiling. 'Not really.'

'Oh, hon, please don't say that. I'd hoped you'd put that horrid business with Austen behind you, and I imagined you having fun, falling in love, learning to trust again.' Tears were trickling freely down Rosalind's face, and Tabitha began to cry in earnest. 'Please don't cry, Tabs, I'm here now. Put the kettle on, let's have another drink and you can tell me all about it.'

So that's what Tabitha did.

***

Rhys took one look at Tabitha's face and said, 'We don't have to go watch a band tonight. We can have a quiet drink somewhere instead. Or we can take a rain check.'

Tabitha summoned up a weak smile and joked, 'I don't look that bad, do I?'

'Oh, no, not at all. Just a bit... um?'

'Washed out? Tired? Look as though I've been crying?'

'Er, yes.'

Tabitha pulled the door closed behind her. 'Can we just go? It'll be a relief not to have to think for a couple of hours.'

'That bad, eh?'

She nodded, expecting him to ask what was wrong, but he didn't. He simply put his arm around her and drew her to his side.

'We'll do whatever you want, whatever you need,' he said.

'Bar. Music. Alcohol.'

'It's a good job I've got tickets for a live band, then,' he teased gently.

Conversation was sparse as they walked through the city centre, but Tabitha didn't feel awkward or uncomfortable. She felt as though Rhys was giving her space, and she sensed he would listen if she wanted to talk, but was just as OK with her not saying anything.

Maybe he reasoned that she would tell him what was troubling her when she was ready, but she wasn't sure she ever would be. Anyway, Rhys didn't need to know. Not yet. Possibly not ever. She liked that he knew nothing about her past apart from those snippets she was willing to share with him. Here, in Bath, Tabitha wasn't that girl who'd had compromising images splashed all over the internet. She was anonymous, and if she wanted to reinvent herself, she could.

As she suspected, the loud beat of the music filled every part of her, resonating in her chest, throbbing in her head and allowing little room for anything else, but now and again, she would recall something Rosalind had said or something she had said to Rosalind, and she smiled.

Tabitha had made Rosalind lunch, although she had been too strung out to eat much herself (Rosalind was eating for two) and Rosalind had only left when her fiancé, who had driven her to Bath this morning, had phoned to ask her how much longer she was going to be because they were supposed to be going to his mother's birthday party later.

Rosalind had left, each of them promising the other that they would stay in touch, and Tabitha had felt as though a weight had been lifted off her chest, her heart less heavy than it had been, her breathing made that little bit easier.

In hindsight, perhaps she had been wrong to run away. Maybe she should have stayed and fought for her dignity and self-respect. Instead, she had left both of those things in Bristol.

By speaking to Rosalind, and later over dinner to her grandfather, Tabitha realised she had actually found them again in the gentle rhythm of her days in the shop. She still had some way to go, but she was on the mend. And seeing Rosalind caressing her baby bump, happiness shining out of her, Tabitha realised she wanted that for herself someday – a man to love her with all his heart, and a child or two. The past was the past, and it was time she looked to the future, and what better way than to begin with the present and the handsome, thoughtful, kind guy standing by her side with one arm around her shoulder and desire in his eyes. *Desire?*

Hmm, one thing at a time, Tabitha, one thing at a time

***

'Music and alcohol worked, I see,' Rhys said a couple of hours later as he took hold of her hand and guided her out of the bar and onto the street. The relative quiet was very welcome.

Tabitha guessed he was referring to her demeanour, and she acknowledged the truth of his words with a grin. This evening she had felt like her old self, the carefree young woman she had once been. A woman who'd had her whole life ahead of her and had been looking forward to it whilst thoroughly enjoying the present.

She wasn't quite there yet, and probably never would be – the events of the past always left their mark, and she would never again be as carefree – but she could be happy. Not that she hadn't been contented these last couple of years (she had) – just not *happy*.

Tonight, though... she'd had a glimpse of what her life could be like once again, if only she was prepared to open her heart to love and friendship.

'I'm hungry,' Rhys announced. 'Shall we grab a bite to eat?'

'Yes, please, I'm starving.' Having not eaten any lunch and having only pushed her dinner around her plate, Tabitha was ravenous.

'Burger?'

'Why not.' Tabitha noticed that Rhys hadn't let go of her hand, and a warm glow spread through her as they walked hand-in-hand in search of a late-night snack.

But when they reached the river and Tabitha saw the full moon reflected in the water, the beauty of the evening took her breath away.

Stuff food, she had something else on her mind, and with that she leant her back against the stone palisade and pulled Rhys towards her.

A momentary look of surprise flashed across his face but was quickly replaced by a sudden and tingle-inducing intensity as he realised what she was about to do.

His lips were firm yet gentle, and there was a faint taste of beer when his tongue found hers.

Tentatively at first, but with growing passion, Tabitha kissed him, his arms holding her in a tight embrace, his hands moving up her back until he buried the fingers of one hand in her hair. His chest was hard as she pressed against him, and his shoulder muscles tensed when she wound her arms around his neck.

Despite the undeniable proof that he wanted her, it was Rhys who pulled away first, ending the clinch with a flurry of light kisses and an incredibly erotic nibble of her bottom lip.

Still holding her, he gazed into her eyes and her lips parted once more. My God, she was so aroused she could drag him off to bed right now, and the naked hunger on his face told her that he shared her desire.

'That was something else,' he murmured.

Tabitha's voice was ragged, along with her breathing. 'It certainly was.'

He held her tight for a few moments longer, his face in her hair, then he slowly released her. 'Let's go.'

Her heart leapt into her mouth. 'Where?' It came out as a squeak.

'We'll either grab that burger I was talking about, or I'll take you home.'

'Er... Grandad will be there.' Despite how much she had enjoyed the kiss and how much she desired Rhys, Tabitha wasn't ready to take things to the next level. And certainly not with Grandad in the next room.

'I know. I suspect he might be waiting up for you.'

'How do you know?'

'I don't, not for certain. But if you were mine, that's what I would be doing. I wouldn't be able to settle until I knew you were home safe.'

Was Rhys, in a subtle way, telling her that he knew that she had been worried he might expect to come in for a coffee (and more) and letting her know that a 'nightcap' hadn't been on his mind at all and that he was content just to kiss her?

Abruptly, she didn't want the night to end. 'Burger, please.'

'I was hoping you'd say that. I could eat a whole cow.' Once again, he'd stepped into that easy, relaxed way of his, and he reached for her hand.

Tabitha had a thought. 'Have you had a proper meal today?'

'Kind of.'

'What did you have?'

'A pasty.'

'Is that all?'

'A slice of toast, and half a packet of biscuits.'

'Have you got anything planned for tomorrow?'

'I'm going paddleboarding. Why?' His face lit up. 'Why don't you come with me? It's great fun.'

'Um...'

'Please? Just try it, and if you don't like it, we'll do something else.'

'OK, on one condition: you let me cook you lunch.'

The way Rhys beamed at her made her heart flutter. But was it because he was happy that she had agreed to go paddleboarding with him, or because he would be eating a home-cooked meal?

Only time, and a Sunday roast, would tell.

CHAPTER 11

Tabitha was nervous. She wasn't sure how Grandad would react when he knew he was going to be sharing his Sunday lunch with a stranger.

Taking extra care with his tray this morning, Tabitha added one of the flowers from the bunch in the hall that she had bought earlier in the week and edged into his bedroom. She placed the tray carefully on the table at the foot of the bed, then drew the curtains before settling Grandad's breakfast across his lap. His sharp eyes noticed a second cup on the tray, and he raised his eyebrows as she perched on the edge of the bed.

'Spit it out, Tabitha.'

'Am I that obvious?'

He picked up a sliver of toast and dipped it into the egg yolk. 'Yes. Did something happen last night?' His voice held little inflexion, but concern lurked in his eyes, and although the toast hovered centimetres from his mouth, he made no move to eat it.

'I've invited Rhys to lunch today,' she blurted.

Jeremy ate his toast soldier. When he'd finished chewing, he said, 'That's nice. What are we having?'

'Beef.'

'My favourite.'

'I know.'

'Are you trying to butter me up?'

'I wouldn't dream of it.' Tabitha poured them a cup of tea.

'I take it you had a good time last night. What was the band like?'

'They were good.' Her mind wasn't on the band: it was on what had happened by the river.

'You like him, don't you?' Jeremy observed.

'Yes, I do.'

'Are you ready for this?'

She lifted a shoulder. 'I think so. I *hope* so.'

'It's nice to see you going out and enjoying yourself.'

Tabitha pulled a face. 'He's taking me paddleboarding after lunch.'

'On the river?'

She nodded. 'He does it quite often, apparently.'

'Have you tried it before?'

'No.' She plucked at a loose thread in the bedspread. 'What if I make a fool of myself?'

'What if you do? Is he the type of person who will make fun of you?'

'He's not like that.' Austen had been, but she refused to think about him. She wasn't going to allow memories of her ex taint this day.

Jeremy smiled. 'There you go, then. You've nothing to fear.'

Tabitha bit back a smile. 'I might drown.'

'You're a strong swimmer. Although…' He gave her a shrewd look. 'You could always pretend to get into difficulties and have him rescue you.'

'Grandad! That's a bit contrived. Besides, I don't need rescuing.'

His gaze was thoughtful. 'No, I don't believe you do. Not anymore.'

***

'What do you do, Rhys?' Jeremy asked, helping himself to a roast potato. He offered Rhys the serving platter. 'Careful, it's hot.'

Rhys took it, and hastily popped it back down on the placemat before spooning a roastie onto his plate.

'Have as many as you want,' Tabitha said. 'I cooked plenty.'

Rhys took two more before answering Jeremy's question. 'I work in IT.'

'Locally?'

'Cheltenham.'

'Say when.' Tabitha had picked up the gravy boat. He hadn't talked about his work much and she was curious too. She began to pour.

'When.' His grateful smile melted her heart, and she had the urge to shovel more food onto his plate.

'That's a bit of a commute,' her grandad said.

'It is, but I mostly work from home, so I only go in now and again.'

'That's the modern way of working, but I'm not sure I'd like to be cooped up in my own house all day every day.'

'It has its advantages,' Rhys said. 'At least I can work in peace without any distractions.'

'What is it you do exactly?' Tabitha asked.

His reply almost made her choke on a slice of carrot. 'I'm a hacker.'

'Is that legal?' she asked when she'd caught her breath.

'It depends on who you're hacking and why.' Rhys had a sheepish expression on his face.

Jeremy balanced his knife and fork on the edge of his plate, and steepled his fingers. 'Cheltenham. Would that be GCHQ, by any chance?'

'It would.'

'He's one of the good guys,' her grandfather told her. 'If Rhys were a cowboy, he would wear a white hat.'

Tabitha, having watched an endless succession of old films with her grandad, knew what he meant. 'In the old Westerns, the goodies always wore white hats, and the baddies wore black ones. You could tell at a glance who was the good guy,' she explained to Rhys.

'Ah, that must be why the good hackers are called white hats and bad guys are called black hats.'

'Why does the civil service employ a hacker?' she asked.

'They employ more than one – there are several of us. My main job is to test for vulnerabilities within systems. If I or my colleagues have difficulty hacking into it, the bad guys will too. No system is wholly secure though, so we're always testing.'

Tabitha was amazed at how far apart Rhys's world was from her own, until Rhys said, 'I suppose it's similar to lock picking, just more advanced.'

Jeremy chuckled. 'I suppose it is, and there isn't a lock made that can't be picked, it just hasn't been picked yet,' he said, at the same time as Rhys cried, 'It just hasn't been hacked yet!'

The two men grinned at each other, and delight spread through Tabitha's chest. She hadn't realised it until now, but she had been worried that her grandfather wouldn't take to Rhys. They existed in such vastly different worlds, or so she had thought. But maybe their worlds weren't as far apart as she had assumed. They both worked with keys in a manner of speaking.

The thought gave her a warm glow throughout the rest of the meal.

***

Tabitha had expected to have to wear a wetsuit (and had assumed one would be provided for her) so she had been surprised when Rhys told her to wear gym gear and bring a change of clothes and a towel.

It had taken her a while to root out her gym top and shorts because she hadn't done much in the way of exercise for years, but she had located a black swimming costume whilst she was scrambling around in the attic, which she decided to wear underneath her Lycra top and shorts.

'Where are we going?' she asked, as she got into Rhys's car.

'There's a hire centre a five-minute drive out of the city. We're meeting everyone there.'

'*Everyone?*' Tabitha was immediately flooded by panic.

'Just a few friends.'

Wait... she hadn't known there would be *others*. The thought hadn't even occurred to her.

'Don't worry, only me and Laurent have done much in the way of paddleboarding. The rest are novices, like you, so you won't be on your own.'

'You're not going to leave me, are you?' Her panic was growing exponentially with each new revelation.

Rhys clipped his seatbelt in, then turned to her. 'I won't leave you, I promise. I'll be by your side the whole time.' His gaze intensified. 'I won't leave unless you ask me to,' he added softly, and she abruptly knew he wasn't just referring to the paddleboarding session.

Her pulse surged and she bit her lip. Then she nodded to show she understood.

He leant across and cupped a hand on her cheek. 'I'll rely on you to tell me when you've had enough, OK?'

'OK,' she whispered, her mouth dry. Then his lips found hers and for a minute she forgot everything except Rhys and the sensations coursing through her.

Once again it was Rhys who ended the kiss. 'We'd better go,' he said. 'The session is booked for three. Ready?'

'Ready,' she echoed, although she was far from ready. She would have liked some warning, but if she had known about it beforehand, she probably wouldn't have come, so perhaps it was for the best that she hadn't. If Rhys wanted her to meet his friends, that was a good thing, wasn't it?

The journey was as short as Rhys promised, and before she knew it the car was pulling up next to a low building with the river to her left, and she could see blue and white boards lined up in a row along the bank.

Other people were there, milling around, chatting, but Tabitha didn't have time to study any of them before Rhys was spotted.

'Rhys, my man!'

She flinched as the roof of the car was slapped by a meaty hand, and the face of the guy who owned the hand peered through the driver's window.

Rhys wound it down. 'Laurent.' The two men bumped fists, then Laurent peered into the car.

Tabitha smiled shyly. Guessing him to be around Rhys's age, he was tall and chunky, and she wondered whether he played rugby because he had the build to be a decent prop-forward. Grey eyes twinkled out of a face topped and tailed by shaggy brown hair and an unkempt beard.

'Who is this?' he bellowed.

'Tabitha, my girlfriend.'

Tabitha tried to hide her gasp of surprise. *Was* she Rhys's girlfriend? Oh, my, she hadn't been expecting *that*.

'Nice to meet you, Tabitha.' Laurent thrust his hand through the window, almost smacking Rhys on the nose.

Tabitha placed her palm in his and he shook it. She hoped he wouldn't pull her arm off.

Rhys chortled. 'As you can see, Laurent is shy and retiring.'

'And Rhys is the life and soul of the party,' Laurent countered with a grin. 'Actually, he's a miserable git, so we were all surprised when he said he was bringing someone with him. We were taking bets on it being either his nan or his mother. Girlfriend, eh? Rhys, you old sod, you're punching above your weight with this one – she's gorgeous.'

'I know. Now, if you've stopped embarrassing her, do you mind letting go of her hand so we can get out of the car.'

'Do I have to?'

'Yes. If you don't, I'll tell Martha.' Rhys turned to Tabitha. 'Martha is his wife.' He directed his next question to Laurent. 'Is she here?'

'She is.'

'Come on, Tabitha, I'll introduce you.'

Bemused and feeling out of her depth, Tabitha climbed out of the car, mouthing, 'Don't you dare leave me,' at Rhys.

He walked around to her side of the car and took her hand. 'I won't, but there's no harm in him. He's like this with everyone – except Martha. He's terrified of *her*.' Rhys leant in close. 'So am I. She might be little, but she's got a fierce temper.'

He led her towards a group of seven people who were standing by the row of boards.

Laurent yelled, 'Lookie here, Rhys has got himself a girlfriend. Play nice, peeps, I think he'd like this one to stick around.'

'This one?' Tabitha hissed out of the corner of her mouth.

Before Rhys could reply, seven pairs of eyes had swivelled in her direction and Tabitha felt the weight of their stares.

A petite, dark-haired woman hurried forward. 'Laurent, shut up. Hi, I'm Martha, his better half. What's your name?'

Laurent leapt in before Tabitha could. 'Tabitha.'

Martha quelled him with a swift glare. 'Nice to meet you, Tabitha. Come say hello to the others.'

A flurry of names and faces later and Tabitha had met the rest of the group, but she knew it would take her a while to remember who is who.

The guy wearing glasses was with a woman with the glossiest hair Tabitha had ever seen, and there were three other men plus a woman who Tabitha recognised as the one she had seen Rhys talking to through the window of the bar a few weeks ago.

Tabitha was on high alert for any signs of jealousy from her, but Kellie seemed just as friendly as the rest. Tabitha would have liked to have had more time to get to know them individually, but a man emerged from the boat house and clapped his hands.

'Right,' he called. 'Shall we get started?' and for the next two hours or so, all Tabitha could do was concentrate on the instructor's advice and try to remain upright on the paddleboard.

She wasn't worried about falling off, because she was a strong swimmer, but it was a matter of pride that she didn't want to spend more time *in* the water, than *on* it.

The instructor made paddleboarding look easy, and it took Tabitha a while to pick up the technique of standing upright on the board without wobbling like a toddler taking its first steps. She had to fight the urge to lean forward and paddle that way, and there was a definite technique to using her core muscles and not just her arms to power the paddle.

'You look cute when you're concentrating,' Rhys said, coming closer.

True to his word, he hadn't left her side, maintaining only enough distance between them so as not to impede her board.

'Stop it,' she said. 'You're putting me off.'

Rhys handled his paddleboard with ease, making it look effortless, but Tabitha was relieved to see that not everyone had his expertise. Aside from Laurent (who was as good as Rhys) and Martha (who had quickly mastered the technique), the others were also novices.

However, it didn't take long before Tabitha got the hang of it, and they were off, paddling serenely down the river. Feeling more secure on the board (although her arms, back, shoulders and legs were already aching), she began to enjoy herself.

Being on the water was remarkably serene, their pace only a little faster than the current. The sun was deliciously warm on her back, the breeze a gentle whisper on her damp skin. The trickle and gurgle of the river was accompanied by the chirping of birds in the trees lining the bank, and the occasional disgusted quack of a disturbed duck.

Peace soaked into Tabitha's soul and contentment filled her. When was the last time she had felt as relaxed as this? She vowed to get out of the city and into nature more often. Although she adored Bath, this was food for the soul, communing with nature, just her, the water, the board beneath her feet and the man paddling by her side. She would have enjoyed the experience without him – but *with* him it was heavenly.

Conscious of his gaze on her, she smiled across at him. The smile Rhys gave her in return was dazzling.

With a contented sigh, Tabitha turned her attention back to the paddle in her hands, feeling at one with the river, and was disappointed when the instructor called to everyone to move to the left bank and pull into the side. Despite her various aches and pains, she wasn't ready to stop, but as soon as she stepped off the board, those aches and pains turned up the volume, and she also became conscious of her wet clothes and bare feet.

'Your towel and change of clothes are in the van,' Rhys said, and she realised she hadn't given any thought as to how they were going to get back to the car.

Thankfully the organisers had, and as she hauled the board onto the sandy bank, she spotted a van parked on the grass, bearing the same logo as the paddleboards.

Martha grabbed hold of her hand. 'Come on, let's get changed. I don't fancy sitting in the back of that in wet clothes.'

Tabitha allowed herself to be dragged towards the vehicle, but baulked when she realised that she was expected to strip off in the back of it with the other women. The last time she had got naked in front of someone he'd—

Backing away, Tabitha shook her head. 'No, it's OK. I'm fine.'

'You're damp,' Martha pointed out.

'I don't mind. I'll soon dry off.'

As though sensing something was wrong, Martha suggested, 'You can get changed first, if you like.'

Tabitha didn't miss the meaningful look which Martha shot Kellie when Kellie opened her mouth to speak.

Kellie closed it and shrugged. 'Go ahead.'

'Seriously, I'm OK,' Tabitha insisted.

Martha put a hand on her arm. 'The offer is there, if you change your mind.'

The men had already grabbed their things and had headed off into the bushes, the instructor included, and the women now clambered into the back of the van, leaving Tabitha standing outside, feeling like an idiot. But no matter how idiotic she felt, she couldn't bring herself to join them.

'It's only a short drive back to the boat house,' Rhys said, making her jump.

She hadn't heard him approach and she put a hand to her chest, her heart thumping.

'They've got toilets, so you can change there,' he added.

'OK, thanks.' She hoped he hadn't noticed the panic on her face.

'Here, take this.' He handed over his towel.

It was damp and when she held it close she could smell a mixture of his cologne, him, and river water.

Tabitha was mightily relieved when they arrived at the boat house and she was able to change into dry clothes. She had felt very self-conscious on the journey back, and she guessed everyone – the women especially – were wondering why she hadn't got changed in the van, and she hoped they were putting it down to her being shy.

When she emerged from the ladies' loos clutching her bag of wet clothes, she heard Laurent ask, 'Fancy a pint? I wouldn't mind a pizza or something, either. I'm hungry.'

'You're always hungry,' Martha teased, her arm around his waist.

'Hey, it takes a lot of fuel to keep this hunk of manhood on the road,' he laughed, slapping his stomach.

Rhys turned and caught Tabitha's eye. She gave him a tiny shake of her head.

'I think we'll give it a miss,' Rhys told his friends and Tabitha blew out a sigh of relief.

'What's up with you?' Laurent cried. 'I've never known you turn down a pint after a session.'

'There's always a first time, and this is it.'

Laurent clapped him on the back and Rhys stumbled forward a step. 'I think our Rhys has got it ba-a-ad.' He drawled out the last word. 'He wants to be alone with his lady.'

Martha took charge. 'Stop it, you oaf. I don't blame him for preferring Tabitha's company to yours. Hell, *I'd* prefer to be with her, rather than with you.' She gave her husband a squeeze, then released him and walked over to Tabitha. 'You go have fun with Rhys. Don't mind us. I vaguely remember what it's like to be in the throes of first love.' She sent Laurent a loving glance that belied her words.

'I'm not—' Tabitha began, then stopped. She had been about to say that she wasn't in love, but she didn't want to embarrass Rhys any more than he was already.

There was a hint of pink in his cheeks, and he couldn't meet her eyes.

Martha was saying to her, 'Let's swap mobile numbers so I can give you advance warning if they plan anything like this again.'

'I... er,' Tabitha began, but Rhys jumped in.

'She's lost her phone and is waiting for a new one.'

Tabitha nodded, grateful to Rhys for coming to her rescue. Although there was absolutely nothing wrong with not owning a mobile, she knew there would be raised eyebrows and questions she didn't want to answer.

It took Rhys a while to extricate them from his friends, but eventually they were in the car and heading back to the city centre.

He was staring straight ahead at the road when he asked, 'Do you want me to take you home?'

Tabitha didn't, but what was the alternative? Another drink in another pub? A coffee in a cafe? 'No…'

He glanced down at her feet. 'How comfy are your trainers?' he asked.

'Fine, why?'

'Let's go for a walk.'

CHAPTER 12

Alexandra Park was an elevated open parkland to the south of Bath, with views across the city. Rhys parked on the road that encircled it, and they began to plod up the slope.

Tabitha had stiffened up in the car, but as she hiked up the hill she slowly loosened up. This was a good idea of Rhys's. If she had gone straight home, she mightn't have been able to move tomorrow.

As they climbed higher, Bath spread out below them, and Tabitha stopped for a moment, ostensibly to take in the view, but in reality it was because she was out of breath. It was a shock to discover just how unfit she was. Casual strolling around her beloved city clearly wasn't enough to maintain her pre-Bath level of fitness. Once upon a time, she had been a regular at the gym, balancing physical activity with days spent behind a desk, and evenings spent out with friends. These days, her only exercise consisted of wandering around the city, looking at the sights.

Neither she nor Rhys spoke much on the way up to the Bath Lookout point, and when they reached it Tabitha sank onto the bench, thankful to be able to sit down. Rhys perched next to her, leaning forward with his forearms on his thighs and his hands clasped together as he gazed over the city, its buildings gleaming a buttery yellow in the late afternoon sun.

'I'm sorry.' Rhys's voice was gruff.

'What for?'

'Inflicting that lot on you.'

'It's OK.'

'You weren't comfortable, and that was remiss of me.'

'Martha seems nice.'

'She is.'

'And Laurent.'

Rhys glanced at her before returning his attention to the vista in front of them. 'Laurent is... Laurent.' He shrugged. 'There's no harm in him. He's got a heart of gold. He's just loud.'

'And big.'

Rhys snorted. 'You can say that again.' He paused. 'I should have warned you they'd be there, and I should have anticipated that Martha would ask for your mobile number.' He sat up and scooted around to face her, his expression sombre. 'You don't need to tell me, but I'm here for you if you ever want to talk.'

Oh, God, he (rightly) suspected there was more to her not owning a mobile than the simple explanation she had given him. Tabitha studied her lap and didn't respond.

Rhys changed the subject. 'Um, about next Sunday, I, er...'

Tabitha froze, her heart thumping. Was she going to go from girlfriend to ex-girlfriend in the space of an afternoon? She didn't blame him: she was damaged goods. The baggage she carried was greater than he could be expected to bear. Maybe it was better if they split up now, before she became any more embroiled in this relationship, because it was bound to end eventually, either when she told him about her past or when he found out. Which he would do, sooner or later. The closer they grew, the greater the chance that he would find out. Someone – her grandad, or her parents if their relationship developed to the point where they met each other's parents – would undoubtedly slip up at some point.

He reached for her hand and wrapped both of his around it.

Here it comes, she thought: the it's-not-me-it's-you speech...

'I promised to visit my nan,' he said. 'My mam and step-dad will be away on holiday, you see, so she'll not have anyone to visit her. Mam goes every Sunday, and I hate to think of Nanna on her own. I mean, I know she won't be on her *own* – there are the other residents and the staff – but she so looks forward to seeing her family. Me and Mam are all she's got since my brother moved to Harrogate.'

'I understand.' And she did. Tabitha didn't fit in with his friends or his lifestyle.

'I wondered if you'd like to come with me,' he added.

'*What?*' He wanted her *to go with him?* To meet his *nan?* Gosh!

'It's not that far, honest. It's less than an hour and a half drive and we can have lunch afterwards, and I thought since I've met your grandad, it was only fair you meet my nan, but you don't have to, of course. I mean, if you've got plans or you think it's too soon for this kind of thing.' He trailed to a halt, his fingers playing nervously with her hand.

Tabitha, shocked and relieved that he wasn't splitting up with her despite only a few seconds ago thinking that it might be for the best, said, 'I'd love to.'

'You would? That's great! She's always saying that she'd like to meet my girlfriends.'

She arched an eyebrow. 'Girlfriends?'

He winced. 'That makes it sound as though I have loads. I don't. I never have had. Just a few. No one serious. Oh, hell.'

Tabitha couldn't help giggling. 'Do you want to put that shovel down, before you dig the hole any deeper?'

He mimed zipping his mouth closed.

She said, 'You don't have to explain. Your past is *your* business.' Just like her past was hers.

It might have been her tone of voice, or it could have been her expression, but something caught his attention and his eyes narrowed a fraction.

Tabitha felt as though his scrutiny lasted ages, but it could only have been for a second, then he said, 'Are you hungry? Would you like a sandwich?'

'Did you bring one with you?'

'No, but I live just over there.' He pointed. 'You could come to mine and I'll make us something to eat, then maybe we could chill in front of the telly?'

Tabitha wasn't going to pass up the chance to spend more time with him, and neither was she going to pass up the opportunity to see where he lived.

'I've got ham, egg or cheese,' he continued, waggling his eyebrows in what he must have thought was an engaging manner, but which just made him look slightly demented.

'How can I resist a ham sandwich?' she joked. 'But I get to decide what we watch.' She was secretly hoping that not a lot of TV watching would take place.

'Deal.' He got to his feet and hauled her upright. 'Race you to the car!'

'Don't you dare—' she began, but he took off down the path, his arms windmilling, and with an outraged shriek Tabitha tore after him.

She suspected he had deliberately let her win when she raced past him and reached the car moments before he did, but she didn't mind – she felt carefree, her heart light – and a big part of it, she realised, was the relief that he hadn't broken up with her after all.

Tabitha, after three years in an emotional wilderness, was falling in love with the most amazing man. And she couldn't have been happier. Or more scared.

***

Tabitha hadn't known what to expect, so when Rhys drove the car into a small private parking area behind a chunky, three-storey, red-brick building, she was burning with curiosity.

'I'm on the top floor,' he said, guiding her inside and up two flights of stairs. 'It's not much, but it's mine.'

He unlocked the door and ushered her into a tiny hall with a door in front of her and a short corridor to her right. At the end of it, she could see a bed, and her breath caught as she imagined him in it.

'Come through,' he said, and showed her into an open plan L-shaped room with a small kitchen at the end nearest the hall, and a living room at the other. French doors revealed a terraced balcony beyond, with views over the city's rooftops. The room was clean, bright and tidy, with a squashy sofa taking up most of one side of the living room and an enormous TV on the opposite wall. A narrow bookcase sat next to it, and in between was a scuffed coffee table.

'Make yourself comfortable,' Rhys said, walking over to the bookcase and popping his mobile phone into a holder. 'I'll put some music on. What would you like? Classical?'

Tabitha glared at him. 'Just because I like history, doesn't mean I don't listen to chart stuff.'

'Oops. Sorry. Will hip-hop do you?'

'Got any Miley Cyrus?'

'It just so happens that I do.' He instructed his phone to play her latest album, then wandered into the kitchen and opened the fridge.

Tabitha strolled around the room, peering at this and examining that, checking out his taste in books, running her fingers across the arm of the sofa.

'Open the patio doors,' he called. 'We can eat out there.'

Tabitha did, venturing outside to gaze at the view. The terrace ran the width of the flat she noticed, as she spied another set of glass doors at the other end, and when she peered through them she saw that they opened onto his bedroom.

A king-sized bed dominated the room, with a chest of drawers in the corner by the patio doors and fitted wardrobes on one wall. Just like the living room, it was neat and clean, and she wondered if his flat was always like this, or whether he had hoped she would come back here with him and had cleaned up in anticipation.

A noise behind alerted her to Rhys stepping onto the terrace, a plate of sandwiches in each hand. 'What would you like to drink? I've got tea, coffee, cordial, or beer.'

'Cordial, please.' She sat at the table and waited for Rhys to return with the drinks.

'Can I get you anything else?' he asked, as she picked up a sandwich.

'No, thanks.' She took a bite, not tasting it. Her mind was still on Rhys's bedroom, and after she had swallowed the morsel of food, she said, 'Your flat is lovely.'

'Not as lovely as yours.'

'Meh.' She waved a hand in the air. 'Antique furniture would look out of place here. Modern suits it.'

'I suppose it does, especially my office. I've converted the second bedroom,' he explained. 'I don't think there's anything in there over three years old. Finish your sandwich and I'll show you.'

Keen to see where he worked, Tabitha popped the last bite into her mouth, then drank the rest of her cordial. Rhys gathered up the plates and Tabitha followed him inside with the empty glasses.

'Put them on the draining board. I'll see to them later,' he said, leading her into the small hallway. 'The bathroom is through there.' He pointed to a door, before pushing open another.

Tabitha's mouth dropped open. The room was filled with banks of monitors, a large black leather chair, several keyboards and lots of menacingly severe black boxes, which she assumed housed equipment of some description. All of the screens were blank, except for one.

The monitor showed a four-way split screen, and she recognised the terrace in one of the video feeds and the front door to Rhys's flat in another.

No wonder he had asked her about the shop's alarm and CCTV cameras. And no wonder he had been surprised when she had told him she didn't own a mobile phone. He had more screens, gadgets and things that flashed, than the flight deck of a jumbo jet.

It was only then that she fully appreciated how different their lives were when it came to technology. He lived and breathed it, whereas Tabitha's only contact was the rather decrepit card machine. Which reminded her, she needed to phone the company she rented it from because it was taking longer and longer for a payment to go through. Maybe she would ask Rhys for his advice. But not this evening. She had other things on her mind.

He was standing so close that she could feel the heat of his body through the thin cotton of her top, and she could smell his intoxicating scent. The air fizzed and crackled between them as he stared deeply into her eyes, his gaze hot and hungry.

Tabitha pushed him against the wall, her arms pinning him to it.

A gentle sigh escaped his lips, and he lowered his mouth to hers.

All thoughts of an evening cuddling in front of the TV were forgotten as she kissed him with a passion she didn't know she had, and when he led her into his bedroom, Tabitha was as eager as he.

***

'I'm sorry.' Tabitha sat up abruptly, pushing Rhys off her. 'I can't do this. I'm sorry,' she repeated, her voice cracking. She was close to tears and she willed herself not to cry.

Yanking her top down, she zipped up her jeans, perched on the edge of the bed and hung her head.

Rhys was breathing heavily, his eyes glinting with desire, and he slumped aside to lie on his back.

Tabitha swiftly averted her gaze, not wanting to see any more evidence of how much he wanted her. She wanted him too, but she simply couldn't bring herself to go through with it.

She took a shuddering breath and repeated, 'I'm sorry.'

Rhys rolled onto his side and propped himself up on his elbow. Reaching up to stroke a wayward strand of hair off her face, he replied, 'That's OK. Please don't apologise. If you're not ready for this, then you're not ready.' His smile was rueful. 'We can wait until you are.'

'What if I'm never ready?'

Even though he didn't move, Tabitha felt Rhys withdraw from her.

'Then you need to tell me. I'm falling for you, Tabi-cat, but if you don't think you could ever feel the same way about me, then please tell me now, before I get hurt.'

Tabitha blinked, not sure she had heard him correctly. Did he honestly think she was reluctant to make love to him because she didn't *like* him enough?

'You've got it wrong,' she said. 'It's not what you think. It's not you, it's me.'

He turned onto his back once more and stared at the ceiling. 'I see.'

'No, no, you don't see. It's... I can't... he...' It was too much, and Tabitha burst into tears. Her head dropped into her hands, and she began to cry with loud, wrenching sobs that shook her whole body.

She wanted to stop bawling, but she couldn't. Grief, anger, and regret welled up from the depths of her soul to cascade through her, and all she could do was wait for the tsunami to be done with her.

Gradually her sobs subsided into coughing, snivelling cries, as she fought to regain control, and she became aware of Rhys's strong arms holding her tight, of her face against his hard chest, and a soft voice murmuring in her ear. He was rocking her gently, like he would a small child in need of comfort, and she relaxed into him, content to remain in the safety of his embrace.

When she finally felt able to move, she pushed herself upright to find that his T-shirt was sodden and he was holding out a bunch of tissues.

She took them gratefully and dabbed at her wet face, then blew her nose. 'I'm sorry,' she repeated, her voice hoarse, her throat scratchy.

'Can I make you a cup of tea? Or would you prefer me to take you home?'

'Tea, please.' Tabitha could *not* go home in this state. Her grandad would take one look at her and have a fit. He would demand to know what had happened, but how could she tell him that she had been about to make love with Rhys and had been all for it, but had then had a meltdown. There were some things she simply didn't share with her grandfather, no matter how deeply she loved him.

Self-consciously, she got to her feet, avoiding her reflection in the mirrored door of the fitted wardrobe, and drifted out of the bedroom.

She found Rhys in the kitchen, his hands on the countertop near the kettle, his head bowed. Tabitha owed him an explanation but she was worried that if she told him, she would lose him, and she really didn't want that.

Leaning against the cupboard, she began to speak. 'When I said it's not you, it's me, I was telling the truth. Something happened in my past. It wasn't nice. It was awful in fact, and I...' Oh, God, this wasn't easy.

Rhys straightened, his expression subdued. 'Tabi, you don't have to tell me. Just answer one question; do you want to carry on seeing me?'

'Yes. Definitely. I want that more than anything.'

When he closed the gap between them and gathered her in his arms, she sank into his embrace and clung onto him, her lifebuoy in a sea of uncertainty.

They stayed that way for a while, Tabitha slowly relaxing as she grew calmer. With her face in his shoulder, she said, 'Are *you* sure you still want to date *me?*'

He huffed out a soft laugh. 'Why wouldn't I?'

'I'm carrying a hefty bag of emotional baggage.'

'One day I hope you'll let me help you carry it,' he said, 'but I don't care if you've got a lorry load, it's *you* I care about, not what happened in the past.'

'But you don't know what it is.'

'Did you kill someone?'

'Gosh, no! Nothing like that. I'd never hurt anyone.'

'I didn't think you would. Then I can wait.'

'I'm worried you may be waiting a long time…'

He kissed her lightly on her forehead. 'Let's take it slow, eh? There's no rush. One day at a time, if needs be. I'm not going anywhere, Tabi – not unless you tell me to. How does that sound?'

It sounded perfect.

Rhys released her and flicked the switch on the kettle. 'Right, let's have that cuppa and then we can snuggle up on the sofa and watch a film. There is one thing,' he said, as he waited for it to boil. 'Will you please, please, please consider getting a mobile phone? While I can't go a whole day without speaking to you, I don't fancy trying to whisper sweet nothings down the phone with your grandad earwigging in the lounge.'

Tabitha hadn't exactly sworn never to have another mobile, but whenever she had thought about it, she had felt a shiver of disquiet.

The shiver was no longer there. In fact, she rather liked the idea of lying in her bed, listening to Rhys's sweet nothings, and an altogether different shiver went through her.

'I might,' she conceded. First though, there was something she had to do. 'Do you mind if I borrow yours for a minute?'

Rhys unlocked it and gave it to her without hesitation. And as he made the tea, Tabitha did something she vowed she would never again do – she typed her own name into the search bar, her thumbs clunky and awkward, and waited to see what came up.

CHAPTER 13

It felt strange not to open the shop on Monday morning, and Tabitha wished that the meeting with the solicitor had been planned for another day, because she needed the familiarity and routine of the shop more than ever as she still felt wrung out and on edge after yesterday, despite how lovely Rhys had been.

He had waited patiently for her to finish with his phone, sipping his tea as she scrolled. They had moved into the lounge, and Rhys had considerately sat far enough away so he couldn't see the screen, and his gaze had been locked on to the TV as he'd searched for a film.

His thoughtfulness had brought tears to her already red eyes, and she'd blinked them away furiously, and not just because her eyesight was blurry and she couldn't see the screen properly.

Poor Rhys – he didn't deserve to have such an emotional wreck for a girlfriend.

Typing her name into the search engine had landed her a couple of hits, but none of them were her. She hadn't had many social media accounts, and the ones she'd had, she remembered deleting, terrified that Austen night tag her.

After three years, the internet appeared to have forgotten she existed, which suited Tabitha just fine. So there was nothing preventing her from buying a mobile, and she was seriously considering it. Not only would she be able to speak to Rhys, but she could also stay in contact with Rosalind.

It was a thought; however, Tabitha didn't intend to rush off and buy one just yet. She would have a think about it first. Events were moving fast enough as it was, without adding another ingredient to the bubbling cauldron that her previously sedate life had now become. In the space of a few days, she had discovered that she was about to become the proud owner of Locke's Key Emporium, she had reconnected with someone she never thought she would see again, and she was now one half of a couple.

Tabitha felt the need to step back, take a breath, and process it all.

However, life had other plans – or rather, Grandad did – and one of those plans was to get the ball rolling on transferring ownership of the business to her.

'Are you sure about this?' she asked for the sixth or seventh time that morning.

She was perched uncomfortably on the edge of a plush upright chair in the solicitor's wood-panelled waiting room. There was a distinctive smell of beeswax and mothballs, and the place reeked of eye-watering hourly rates and hideously expensive contracts.

'Tabitha, I've made up my mind.' Grandad's exasperation was growing each time she asked him the same thing.

'But this is your life's work,' she pointed out.

He tapped his cane on the wool rug in annoyance, the sound echoing dully. 'We can wait until I die or I'm too gaga to wipe my own nose,' he snapped, 'or we can do this now, and I can rest knowing that my business is in good hands. You are more or less running it already; it's time to stop playing in the shallows and wade deeper in, whilst I'm still here to help you stay afloat. It's either this, or you dive into the deep end when I'm gone.'

'Crumbs, Grandad, that's some speech.'

'Your choice. The business will be yours one way or another; I've already left it to you in my will.'

'But are you—?'

'Tabitha Locke, will you stop being so silly! You are trying my patience.'

'Sorry.'

'You need to stop wallowing and start swimming.'

'What's with all the water analogies?'

'I've treated myself to a gym membership.'

'Excuse me? I could have sworn you said you've got a *gym membership?*'

'I have. It's exclusive, for gentlemen of a certain age. They have a pool. I'm going to try it out tomorrow.'

Her grandfather never ceased to amaze her.

'Swimming is good for the joints – low impact, you know. And there's a sauna and various other gubbins.'

'Gubbins?'

'A hot tub and whatnot.'

'I see.' Tabitha had an image of a group of elderly gents sprawled in a hot tub, putting the world to rights before going for a pot of tea and a scone afterwards. That was exactly what would happen she knew, and she was pleased to see him making the most of his later years. 'Good for you,' she said.

'Do you know what else is good for me? Seeing you happy. You're not quite there yet, but you will be, and my transferring the business to you is just another step on the way.'

And as Tabitha sat there, waiting to be shown into the solicitor's office, she realised her grandad was right. She *was* getting there.

***

'Do you want me to come with you?' Rhys asked, a few days later.

Tabitha was perched on the stool behind the counter with the shop's old-fashioned curly-corded phone receiver jammed between her ear and her neck as she unpacked a box of keys bought at a local auction which Grandad had recently attended.

Absently, she wondered how she was going to source new stock whilst manning the shop six days a week. She must make a note to ask Grandad how he had managed it all these years. But right now, she was on the phone with Rhys, who had called for a chat, and he had just asked whether she'd had any more thoughts about getting a mobile.

'Haven't you got work to do?' she asked.

'Loads.'

'Then why aren't you doing it?'

'It's your fault. I can't stop thinking about you.'

Tabitha's tummy did a flip.

'Can I see you tonight?' he continued.

'You saw me last night. And the night before.' She'd been glad to meet him for a drink on Monday evening, wanting to tell him all about the solicitor, and she'd been more than happy to go to the cinema with him yesterday after work, although she hadn't rated the film very highly.

'So? I want to see you tonight, as well. I want to see you *every* night. Every day, too.' His voice was low and husky, making her pulse race.

'What happened to taking it slow?' she wanted to know, and instantly she sensed a change of atmosphere.

'Sorry. I did promise, didn't I? I'll back off a bit.'

'No, don't. I'd like to see you, too.'

'Please tell me if I'm coming on too strong.'

'I will. Now, about this evening... what did you have in mind?'

'Laurent, Martha and a few others are going for a drink. Want to join them? Or you could come to mine and we can have a quiet night in?'

Knowing how much of a social animal Rhys was, she suspected he might prefer the first option. Besides, she'd enjoyed Martha's company and it would be nice to get to know her better. It was about time she had a female friend in Bath, and who better than the wife of Rhys's best mate?

***

'Oh, my, God! I've heard of Locke's Key Emporium!' Martha cried. 'It's been there for yonks, like, for hundreds of years.'

'Not quite; my great-grandfather opened it in 1909.'

'And now *you* own it? Cool.' Martha poked Rhys in the arm. 'Have you told her what *you* do yet?'

'Of course I have.'

'*All* of it?'

'Er…'

'I didn't think so,' Martha chortled, and announced, 'Rhys is a professional hacker.'

'She knows this.' Rhys was looking uncomfortable.

'Ah, but does she know you nearly went to prison?'

'What!?' Tabitha's mouth fell open.

Martha nodded vigorously. 'It's true. He managed to hack into one of the government's super servers. He would have got away with it, too, if—'

'Martha.' Laurent was shaking his head. 'Best not say anymore, eh? Official Secrets Act, and all that?'

Tabitha turned to Rhys. 'Have you signed the Official Secrets Act?'

'Um, yeah.'

'So has Martha,' Laurent said. 'That's how she and Rhys met.' He gently took his wife's drink out of her hand. 'I think you've had enough.'

'Spoilsport.' Martha wrinkled her nose.

Tabitha asked her, 'Do you work for the Civil Service, too?'

'I did, but not anymore. There's more money to be made in the private sector.'

'She works for one of the big banks, keeping our pennies secure.' Laurent slung an arm around his wife's shoulders and planted a kiss on the top of her head.

'What about you, Laurent? Are you a hacker?'

'Not now. I used to be, but I wasn't as good as Rhys here. He's the best.'

Rhys tipped his glass in Laurent's direction, in a silent acknowledgement of the compliment.

'I design video games,' Laurent said. '*Porpoise, The Devil's Chamber, Ted's Treehouse...*' His pleased expression told her that he expected her to know what he was talking about, and when she stared at him blankly, his face fell. 'You must have heard of one of them?'

'No, sorry.'

'You're not a gamer?'

Tabitha shook her head.

'Not even those free game apps that are pre-loaded onto your phone? I mean, *everyone* plays those.'

'I didn't. Don't,' she amended quickly. Rhys squeezed her thigh. His touch reassured her. Out of her depth with so many techie people, she was grateful that Rhys had her back.

'Rhys, man, you've got to get her into gaming. She doesn't know what she's missing.'

'She probably does,' Rhys countered with a laugh. 'You're going to end up having to have that console surgically removed. There's more to life than staring at a screen.'

'So says the sad bugger who stares at a screen ten hours a day for a living,' Laurent shot back.

'More, when there's a threat,' Martha added.

'Threat?' Tabitha's eyes widened.

'Yeah, you know, when a wall has been breached or—'

'Martha, Tabi has no idea what you're on about,' Rhys said. He smiled at Tabitha and carried on, 'Martha means if there is an immediate threat to any of the country's security systems. Then it's all hands on deck until the threat is eliminated.'

Tabitha was shocked. 'Does that happen a lot?'

'Often enough. So if I go AWOL, that's the reason.'

'You'd let me know though, wouldn't you?'

He moved closer and whispered in her ear, 'Of course I would, but it would be easier if I could message you. Do you realise that if someone phones the shop, they can't leave a message?'

Tabitha didn't – it hadn't even occurred to her, and she suddenly wondered how many sales Grandad might have lost, purely because there wasn't any way for a customer to leave a message.

Maybe his reluctance to join the twenty-first century *was* having an impact on the business. She had never really thought about it before, because Grandad had been responsible for everything, but now that it would shortly be hers, could she justify having such an outdated and antiquated system? It was yet one more item to add to the growing list of things she needed to think about, and Tabitha narrowed her eyes as a thought occurred to her – maybe Grandad handing over the reins of the business to her now, rather than her inheriting it after his death, was because he knew deep down that Locke's Key Emporium needed bringing up-to-date and he simply couldn't face it.

Take the other day for instance; he hadn't stopped complaining that he had been expected to fill in an online application form for the gym membership. Reading between the lines, Tabitha gathered that he had made such a fuss, they had printed one off for him to fill in by hand. His continual muttering of 'how do they expect to run a facility for elderly people, when many old folk don't know how to work this modern technology,' had made her smile.

It came to her that she was in the same boat herself. It wasn't that she *couldn't* use it, it was that she didn't *want* to. But whichever way she looked at it, neither she nor Grandad were able to do anything online. The time was drawing near for her to venture back into the modern world again – even if it was just so Rhys could tell her when he was called into work without warning.

***

Computer games were worryingly addictive, Tabitha discovered. It was Friday evening, and rather than go out (she and Rhys had been out every evening so far this week), they had opted to stay in – at his place, naturally, because however wonderful her boyfriend was, she didn't think he would appreciate watching reruns of *Heartbeat* in the parlour with Grandad.

Rhys probably would have been happy to cuddle on the sofa, pretending to watch a film but in reality kissing her every few seconds, but Tabitha had surprised him by asking him to show her his game console. Or should she say *consoles,* because he had more than one.

His face shining, he had carried one of the chairs from his tiny dining table through to the office and plonked it down, insisting she sat in the gaming chair.

As she lowered herself into it, with monitors, keyboards and goodness knows what else in front of her, she said, 'Mother Ship to Earth,' earning an eye roll and a shake of the head.

Rhys had another surprise when he discovered that Tabitha wasn't as bad as she feared, and although she was so far from his level that she could have been on the moon, she hoped she would prove a decent enough opponent, given a great deal of time and an even greater amount of practice.

Halfway through what Tabitha thought might be the last game (her shoulders and neck were aching and her back was stiff), she realised that Rhys was no longer playing.

He was gazing at her with such passion in his eyes that if she hadn't been sitting down, she might have fallen.

Her heart began thumping so fast and so loudly it was a wonder he couldn't hear it, and Tabitha caught her bottom lip between her teeth, the game forgotten.

'God, you're gorgeous,' he breathed, and she blushed furiously. 'I want to carry you off to bed and make love to you until dawn.'

Oh... Her pulse throbbed in her ears and heat flared deep inside, hot and urgent.

Rhys closed his eyes, then opened them again slowly. She noticed how clenched his jaw was, how hooded his eyes. 'I think I'd better take you home.' His voice was gravel-rough, hoarse with desire, and she felt an answering surge of lust.

She was incredibly tempted to stay, to tell him she wanted nothing more than to spend the night with him, but the very real fear that she would freeze reared its head, and she knew she wasn't ready. Not quite yet. But soon...

Wordlessly she slipped her shoes back on, retrieved her bag and followed him out to the car.

When she reached it, she opened her mouth to speak but Rhys pre-empted her. 'Don't apologise,' he warned. 'You have nothing to be sorry for.' He opened the passenger door for her and she got in. He had an uncanny ability to read how she was feeling, because he crouched down next to her and held out his arms. 'Come here, give us a cuddle.'

Tabitha leant forward as his arms came around her, and he wrapped her securely in his embrace.

His mouth was in her hair as he said, 'I'm the one who should be apologising. I didn't mean to make you feel awkward or uncomfortable.'

'You didn't, honestly. I just wish I could...' She trailed off.

'I'm happy just being with you; I don't want anything more,' he assured her.

But he did: she could sense what he wanted with every cell in her body. It was kind of him to fib about it, though.

He pulled back but she didn't want to let him go just yet, so she tilted her chin, her invitation clear.

Rhys took her up on it, but when he groaned she feared he was regretting suggesting that she go home, so she drew away, worried she was sending him the wrong signals with her passionate kiss.

Her lips throbbing, her heart racing, she felt awful when he groaned again. Then he said, 'Tabi, you're going to have to give me a hand to get up. My knee has locked,' and he looked so aggrieved that she burst into giggles.

'No need to laugh,' he grumbled. 'You're the one who'll be walking home if I can't get up.'

Still chuckling, she eased herself out of the passenger seat and took both his hands in hers. 'You're in a worse state than my grandad. How old are you?'

'Eighty-one,' he replied, deadpan. 'Ow.' He flexed his knee with a grimace. 'Rugby,' he explained. 'I dislocated my shoulder playing it, too.'

'Is that why you paddleboard? Less dangerous?'

'Partly. Plus, I'm getting a bit old for rugby now.' He kissed her quickly on the lips, then hobbled around the car to the driver's side.

'If it hurts to drive, I can get a taxi,' she offered.

'You will *not*. I'm going to take you home if it kills me.'

'Shall I ask Grandad if you can borrow his cane?'

'Now you're just being cheeky. I don't need a walking stick just yet.'

Tabitha had a sudden vision of an older Rhys, grey-haired and with lines around his eyes, walking arm-in-arm with her. It was so vivid that it took her breath away. She could imagine spending the rest of her life with this man, growing old with him, loving him through everything life threw at them, the good and the bad.

And in that moment, Tabitha realised she was in love with him. It was both terrifying and wonderful.

CHAPTER 14

Tabitha peered out of the window at the expanse of water hundreds of feet below. They were on the M4 motorway, driving over the bridge that spanned the Severn Estuary which separated England from Wales, and the sun was glinting on the grey water and the exposed sand banks.

It seemed to take an age to get to the other side, but then they were on terra firma again and a *Welcome to Wales* sign appeared.

'How much further?' she asked.

'Half an hour. More if the traffic is bad.'

Tabitha had been to Wales before – a camping trip with the school, a boozy weekend in Cardiff with friends when she was at university, and a vaguely remembered holiday with her parents when she was quite young – but she had never visited the South Wales Valleys before. The only thing she knew about the area was that it was famed for coal mining, but Rhys had informed her that the industry had long since faded away, and the region was now lush and green, with small towns and villages nestled between the mountains.

Soon they had left the motorway and the coast behind and were on a dual carriageway, and then a smaller road, and as the scenery became increasingly rural they passed through towns of terraced houses that clung to the hillsides in long ribbons, and open fields framed by woodland.

What had started as a wide valley, grew increasingly narrower and steeper as the car travelled further into it, and the mountain tops above looked bare and windswept. After a few more twists and turns of the road, a smattering of houses came into view and Rhys announced, 'Almost there.'

The town was small, with narrow streets, most of the shops closed because it was a Sunday, and before long the car was turning off into a side street and trundling up a rather steep hill.

'Here we are,' he said, pulling into a car park with the sign *Foxglove Residential Care Home* at the entrance.

Tabitha clambered out, stiff and ungainly, and she stretched her spine as she looked around. The building was a mixture of grey stone, which appeared to be quite old, meshed with red brick extensions to either side.

She could see several faces peering through the windows, and she wondered whether one of them belonged to Rhys's nan.

'What's her name?' she asked suddenly. She couldn't keep referring to the old lady as *Rhys's nan*.

'Pearl. Ah, there she is!'

A white-haired woman was waving enthusiastically through the window, and Rhys waved back.

Tabitha raised a tentative hand, not wanting to appear rude, and she prayed Pearl would like her. Meeting his grandmother felt like a large step along their relationship road. It wasn't quite as significant as meeting his parents, but it wasn't far off.

Nerves were making her jittery, and Rhys didn't help when he said, 'Don't worry, her bark is worse than her bite.'

They were buzzed into the building and after signing the visitors' book, Rhys was off, hurrying down a hallway, Tabitha following cautiously behind. She wanted to give him space to greet his grandmother first, before she was introduced to her.

However, his grandmother hadn't got the memo: the same woman who Tabitha had seen through the window was coming down the hall from the opposite direction, gripping a walker and shuffling slowly. One leg dragged a little, Tabitha noticed, and she remembered Rhys telling her that his nan had suffered a stroke.

Rhys got to her in a few strides and tried to give her a hug, but Pearl waved him away. 'I want to meet your young lady,' his nan said, and she beckoned Tabitha closer.

Pearl was tiny and frail, and one side of her face drooped slightly, but a light was shining in her eyes which lit up her whole face, and Tabitha recognised the same steely determination that her grandad possessed. Pearl, no doubt, was a force to be reckoned with.

'You must be Tabitha,' she declared. 'My, aren't you a bobby-dazzler.' She turned to Rhys. 'You didn't tell me she was this pretty.' Her tone was accusing.

'I thought I'd let you see for yourself.' Rhys was smiling, and he took hold of Pearl's arm. 'Shall we go sit down and I'll rustle up some tea?'

'I'd prefer a sherry.'

'Nanna, stop it.'

'You're no fun. I've got a bottle in my room. Go fetch some glasses from the dining room.' She scowled. 'They call it a dining room, but it's more like a school canteen.'

'It's not that bad,' Rhys protested, saying to Tabitha, 'It's actually quite nice.'

'You'll have a sherry with me, won't you?' Pearl turned a hopeful gaze on Tabitha. 'He never does because he's driving, and I don't like drinking on my own.'

Tabitha caught Rhys's resigned nod out of the corner of her eye and smiled. 'I'd love to.'

'I'm in number twenty-three. You come with me, Tabitha. Rhys, get the glasses.' Pearl waited until Rhys was out of earshot, then she launched her attack. 'I've seen the way my grandson looks at you. Do you love him?'

'Um...' Good grief! What was she supposed to say to that?!

'You should. He's one of the good ones. Don't get me wrong, he's had his moments, but he's a good boy really. Will you get married, do you think?'

'Er...' Yet another question she wasn't in any position to answer. She knew how she felt about Rhys, but she didn't know whether he felt the same way about *her*.

'Only I don't believe in this living together nonsense,' Pearl was saying. 'No commitment, see? Makes it too easy to walk away. Do you want kiddies?'

'Well, I...'

'Rhys does. How old are you?'

'Twenty-nine.' Finally! A question she *could* answer.

'Good. Not too old. You'd better get a move on, though. Women these days leave it far too late. This is me.' The old lady came to a wobbly halt outside a door. 'And here's Rhys.'

Tabitha had never been so relieved to see someone in her life. She felt as though she had been steamrollered.

'You two will have to sit on the bed,' Pearl instructed. 'There's only one chair and I need that. Rhys, will you pour?'

Tabitha perched on the end of the bed and accepted a glass of pale amber liquid. Pearl downed hers in two gulps and held her glass out to be refilled. Tabitha had yet to take a sip. She lifted the glass to her lips.

'Your young lady has been telling me that she wants to get married and have kiddies,' Pearl announced, and Tabitha spluttered, spraying sherry onto her dress.

She'd worn one of her tea dresses, with a matching cardi and navy pumps, hoping to make a good impression.

Rhys roared with laughter. 'I bet she *didn't*,' he chortled.

Tabitha wanted to disappear into the floor.

'Nan, you are so naughty. No wonder I don't bring anyone with me when I visit. You scare them off.'

'You don't bring anyone because you don't care about them enough to introduce me to them. Except for this one. You care about *her*.'

Rhys sobered. 'I do.'

His admission made Tabitha's head spin.

Pearl gave a satisfied sigh. 'Now that's out of the way, I can tell you my news. Oh, before I do, I'm very grateful to you, Tabitha, for finding a key to my little box. It's got all my treasures in, and I know Rhys could have broken into it but I wanted something I could lock. There are too many nosey parkers in this place, and I'll be damned if I want any of them reading my Stanley's letters, especially the one where he tells me he's going to—' Pearl caught herself. 'Anyway, thank you.' She took another gulp of her sherry. 'Where was I? Oh, yes, my news. You'll never guess what Audrey said to the magician that we had in the other week!' And she was off, chatting non-stop about the goings on in the care home and gradually Tabitha began to relax.

The old lady was a live wire, as Grandad would say, and she was clearly having the time of her life. She also adored her grandson, and when it was time to leave she clung to Rhys for several long seconds, whispering in his ear.

Rhys met Tabitha's gaze over the top of his grandmother's head. The love shining out of his eyes made her want to cry – because she would have given anything for him to look at her in the same way.

***

'Did you grow up near here?' Tabitha asked. She and Rhys were sitting in a pretty pub a five-minute drive away from Pearl's care home, and were about to have a very late lunch.

'I did. We actually drove past the turn-off to the street where my parents still live.'

Tabitha would have liked to have seen it.

'Pearl hinted that you had your moments when you were growing up – her words, not mine. What did she mean?'

Rhys picked up his fork, toying with it as he thought. 'I was always getting into trouble – playing rat-a-tat, kicking balls against the sides of people's houses, tearing around the park on my bike... The neighbours were always complaining. I was the total opposite to my brother: he was a real goodie-two-shoes. He still is.'

'What's rat-a-tat?'

'Where you knock on someone's door and run away.'

Tabitha made a face. 'Why would you do that?'

'For fun, although looking back, it couldn't have been much fun for the people whose doors we banged on.'

'Tell me about your brother.'

'His name is Gareth and we don't get on. We never did, so we don't bother much, except for Christmas, when he visits my parents for a couple of days.'

'How old is he?'

'Thirty-eight.'

'Married?'

'Yep, wife and two kids.'

'You're an uncle? Wow!'

'They're nice kids.' He shrugged, then a slow smile spread across his face. 'Did you really tell Nanna you want children?'

Tabitha winced. 'I did not. She asked me whether I wanted any, but didn't give me the chance to answer.'

'That sounds like her.' Rhys chuckled. 'She's been on at me for years to get married and settle down. She thinks it'll do me good.'

'Will it?'

'Probably. And she thinks you are the woman I should be settling down with.'

Tabitha gasped. 'She doesn't!'

'She does. She reckons you'll keep me out of trouble.'

'Do you get into trouble?'

'Not anymore. I did, once. A lot of trouble.'

Remembering a question Rhys had asked her not so long ago, she said, 'Did you kill anyone?'

He chuckled. 'No. Do you recall Martha mentioning that I hacked into a site I shouldn't have? Well, I got caught.'

'Were you arrested?'

'Not exactly.' Rhys leant forward and lowered his voice. 'I came to the attention of certain people who work for the government. They offered me a job in GCHQ.'

'Flipping heck, that's the kind of thing you read about in a thriller.'

He smirked. 'I'd like to tell you that I'm an international spy, but the truth is I'm just a hacker, and you'd be surprised how often this happens. GCHQ are always on the lookout for talent.' His smile widened. 'They probably need people who can pick locks, too.'

Tabitha stuck her nose in the air. 'Just because I sell keys doesn't mean I know how to pick a lock.'

'I bet Jeremy does.'

'I expect so.' Her reply was wry. What her grandad didn't know about keys would fit on the back of a postage stamp. It was therefore reasonable to assume he knew more about the locks those keys fitted into than he cared to let on. Grandfather definitely hadn't passed on everything he knew to Tabitha, and she would miss his expertise when—

Alarmed, she gave herself a mental shake: she wasn't going to think about that until she had to, because she simply couldn't imagine being without Grandad.

And as she ate a delicious lunch of pan-fried chilli pork, it dawned on her that she couldn't imagine being without Rhys either.

***

After lunch, they drove up a winding road with open moorland on either side, whose gradual incline seemed to go on forever. Sheep were roaming free without fences to keep them in, and once or twice Rhys was forced to slow to a crawling pace because the animals were in the middle of the road, unbothered by the passing traffic. Many had lambs with them, although the babies were quite big, and they nibbled at the grass with the same enthusiasm as their mothers.

They were so cute, but not as cute as the foals. Horses wandered free too, and cows, and Tabitha wondered if she had inadvertently been dropped into a Welsh version of the Serengeti.

Winding the window down, she took a deep breath of fresh, clean air and tilted her face up to the sky. High thin clouds scudded overhead and the sun was warm on her cheek.

Ah, this is the life, she thought – a day out in the wilds of Wales with a gorgeous man: a man who she was falling more deeply in love with every hour she spent in his company. And seeing how tender he had been with his nan, endeared him to her even more. Grandad always said you can tell a lot about a man by the way he treats his family, and Tabitha had seen nothing but love and respect on Rhys's face when he had been with his grandma. Looking back, Austen had been incredibly dismissive when he had spoken about *his* family, and she had got the impression he had been ashamed.

Not that she had met any of them, even though they had also lived in Bristol.

Saying that, Tabitha had never taken him to meet *her* parents, either. She might have done if he had shown an interest... Now, though, she was very glad she hadn't.

This was neither the time nor the place to be letting thoughts of Austen into her mind, and she shoved them away. She wanted to enjoy the rest of the day and focus on the man she was with. He deserved her attention far more than Austen ever had.

A pair of horses play-fighting brought her back to the present, and she craned her neck to watch as the car trundled past. The incline seemed to go on forever and she had just begun to wonder whether it would ever end, when the road abruptly dropped away and a patchwork of fields, mountains and valleys opened up below.

A rough gravelled car park appeared on the left and Rhys aimed the car for it, then cut the engine.

In the relative silence, Tabitha heard the wind sighing through a stand of dried grass and the sound of sheep calling to one another, and she itched to get out.

Rhys was already opening his door and clambering out, and she hurried to join him as they stood side-by-side to admire the view.

'Wow! Just wow!' Tabitha couldn't drag her eyes away from the magnificent scenery spread out before her.

'I knew you'd like it,' he said, putting an arm around her and drawing her close. He pointed to the left. 'Over there is the Brecon Beacon Mountain Range, and you can't quite see it from here, but just over that tump is Pen y Fan, the highest mountain in South Wales. Those bluffs over there are the Black Mountains, and the splash of blue you can see in front of us is Llangorse Lake.'

'It doesn't seem real!' Tabitha cried. 'It's like a film set.'

'Magnificent, isn't it?'

'This is such a beautiful part of the world.'

'It is.' He was looking at her as he said it. 'From where I'm standing it's incredibly beautiful.'

She held her breath as his arms tightened around her and she let it out slowly when his mouth came down on hers. The kiss was deep and intense, and after it finally ended she realised she couldn't wait to return to Bath to continue where they had just left off.

This time she wasn't going to stop at kissing him. This time she wanted him to make love to her. *Tabitha was ready.*

***

The journey back was filled with quiet anticipation – on Tabitha's part, at least. Rhys, bless him, had no idea what was in store.

'Can we go to yours?' she asked as they approached the outskirts of Bath.

'Haven't you had enough of my scintillating company?' His voice was light, and she wondered if he would have been as flippant if he knew what she had in mind.

'I thought we could have a drink on the terrace and watch the sun go down.'

'Aw, that's so romantic.'

Tabitha smiled to herself: if only he knew just how romantic it was about to become…

As soon as they were inside his flat, Tabitha eased off her shoes, her toes sinking into the carpet.

Rhys immediately headed to the kitchen area. 'Cordial? Or would you prefer something fizzy? I've got ginger beer or cloudy lemonade.' With his back to her, he rooted in the cupboard for a couple of glasses.

Tabitha eased the zip of her dress down and slipped out of it, the material puddling at her feet. She had worn her hair in a loose bun today, and while she waited for him to turn around she tugged it free.

He glanced over his shoulder saying, 'Tabi, cordial or—?'

The shock on his face almost made her giggle, but her amusement was swiftly replaced by desire as his gaze raked her body. She shivered with the intensity of it and resisted the urge to cross her arms in front of her chest, wanting her message to be clear; she didn't want him to harbour any doubts that this wasn't what she wanted.

His eyes narrowed, glittering darkly with hunger. His arousal was instant and obvious, and her lips parted as lust coursed through her. Liquid with longing, her heart thundering and her legs barely steady enough to keep her upright, she walked slowly towards him.

He hadn't taken his gaze off her, but now instead of scouring every centimetre of her body, his eyes caught hers. They were filled with an unspoken question.

'Yes,' she breathed. 'I'm sure.' And when he took her to his bed and made slow, wonderful love to her, all her doubts and fears faded, swept away by the force of her passion.

***

It was hard to drag herself out of Rhys's bed, but Tabitha couldn't stay there *all* night.

'Where are you going?' He reached for her to pull her back into his arms.

'I've got to go, Grandad will be worried.'

'You could always phone and tell him you're staying over.'

'It's too late. He'll be in bed. I don't want to give him a heart attack. If I ring him at this time of night, he'll think it's bad news.'

'Will he realise you're not there?'

'He might, if he gets up to go to the loo and sees my bedroom door open and me not in it.'

'Five more minutes?'

'But it won't *be* five minutes, will it?' she pointed out.

'I can make it quick.' He was grinning wickedly.

Tabitha reached for her underwear, and after letting out a despondent sigh, Rhys pushed the duvet aside with a great show of reluctance.

'Stop sulking,' she scolded.

'I can't. I want to spend all night, every night with you. It's your own fault for being so irresistible.'

Tabitha, her modesty now covered by wisps of lace and satin, darted out of the bedroom with a coy look over her shoulder, giggling when she heard him groan.

'You're killing me,' he called after her.

'I might just do that if you don't take me home.'

'Can I see you tomorrow?'

'Yes.'

'And the day after?'

'If you must.'

'How about the day after that?'

'I sense a theme.' Laughing, she shouted, 'Come to dinner tomorrow. We can watch a documentary in the parlour with Grandad.'

'Will he object if I kiss you?'

'Probably. I know I would.'

'You haven't objected before,' he retorted indignantly. 'You *like* me kissing you.'

Tabitha squirmed around to reach the zip on her dress as Rhys emerged from the bedroom fully clothed. She dragged her eyes away from his broad chest and slim hips, scared she might lose her resolve.

'What I meant was,' she said, 'that *I* would object if I was in the same room as a pair of smooching lovebirds'

'Lovebirds?' Rhys sniggered.

'That's what Grandad would call us.'

'It's cute. *You're* cute.' He picked up his keys and turned to her, his expression suddenly sombre. 'No regrets?'

'None whatsoever.'

He searched her face, then nodded. 'I'm glad, because I'd hate for you to wish we hadn't...'

'Made wonderful, beautiful love?'

'Yeah, that.' A slow smile spread across his face. 'It *was* pretty special, wasn't it?'

'Are you fishing for compliments, Rhisiart Flint?'

'Nah, I could tell you were enjoying it.'

Tabitha arched an eyebrow, daring him to continue.

'Oh, Rhys, Rhys,' he cried in a high-pitched, breathy voice. 'Don't stop. Oh, *Rhys!*'

Tabitha burst out laughing and slapped him on the arm. 'I did not sound like that.'

'You did.'

'It was more like...' She lowered her voice and moaned throatily, 'Oh, Rhys, oh, God!' Then dissolved into a fit of giggles as he closed his eyes and shook his head.

'Please don't, not if you want me to be able to drive,' he pleaded, the effect on him obvious.

Tabitha wasn't in the least bit contrite. 'You started it.'

'I'm sorely tempted to make you walk home,' he grumbled, ushering her out of the flat.

'You wouldn't.' She was confident of that. She was also confident that Rhys would never hurt her. Despite having met him only a few weeks ago, she felt as though she had known him forever. So it was with joy in her heart and a lightness in her soul, that she kissed him goodnight and hurried away to her little bed and a deep restful sleep.

CHAPTER 15

Tabitha's lips twitched. 'Jodhpurs, you say?'

Rhys squirmed, tugging at the fabric around his knees where there was extra material stitched onto the inside of the leg, although it wasn't immediately noticeable unless you were looking. However, Tabitha was *most definitely* looking. His thighs were muscly and quite delectable.

The twitch turned into a giggle. *Quite delectable, indeed?!* Not only was she dressed as a Regency lady, but she was also beginning to sound like one in her head. Talk about getting into character!

'You're laughing at me.' Rhys's face fell. 'I knew this was a bad idea.'

'No, no, it's a brilliant idea!' she hastened to reassure him. 'I'm so glad you managed to get tickets. They are normally sold out months in advance.'

When Rhys had told her that he had two tickets for the Jane Austen Summer Ball, Tabitha had been astounded. She had always wanted to go but hadn't had anyone to go with.

Hitching up her dress until her ankles were showing, she did a little jig of joy, and Rhys's expression cleared.

Rhys said, 'As long as you enjoy it, that's the main thing. I'm just praying I don't let you down.' He glanced at his jodhpurs and grimaced.

'You won't. You *don't*. You look like a perfect Regency gentleman.'

He did look rather dashing in his dark navy tail coat, crisp white shirt, and cream and gold waistcoat. A pair of black knee-high boots completed his outfit. The boots weren't what a Regency gentleman would wear to a ball, but they were in keeping with the period, and Tabitha guessed he wouldn't be on his own, and that other men would be sporting boots too.

Tabitha was wearing a mid-blue taffeta gown, empire cut, gathered at the bust and with short, puffed sleeves. The fabric had a gorgeous sheen to it, and several large flowers in the same material were stitched around the hem. A lightweight navy stole, cream elbow-length gloves, a navy silk fan and a single strand of pearls around her neck, completed her outfit.

She had bought the dress a couple of years ago to wear during the Jane Austen Festival which was held every September in the city. Bath's residents embraced it with a passion and many people dressed up for the occasion, shops and businesses included.

The costume Rhys had hired complemented hers perfectly, and with her hair gathered up into a loose chignon, several tendrils artfully teased out to curl around her face, Tabitha felt incredibly glamorous, and she was so excited she thought she might pop.

Grandad appeared in the hall, his face wreathed in smiles. 'The two of you look grand,' he declared. 'Tabitha, my dear, you are beautiful.'

'Thank you.' She kissed his cheek and he pulled her into a hug.

'I am so proud of you,' he whispered, and she felt tears gathering behind her eyes. Blinking them away, she was determined not to cry. This wasn't an evening for tears – it was an evening for dancing and laughter.

Rhys ceremoniously offered her his arm. 'Time to go. Doors open at seven and we don't want to be late.'

The ball was being held in the Guildhall, on the other side of the abbey from the Green, and Tabitha was thankful it was a splendid summer evening because they would be walking to the venue.

As they set off, she was aware of more than one curious glance, and a group of women even asked if they could take a selfie with them. Tabitha and Rhys struck a pose, happy to oblige, although she did feel rather self-conscious. However, as they grew nearer to the Guildhall, they saw other people in Regency costume, and she began to relax and not feel so out of place.

Tabitha loved the Guildhall, especially the Guildhall Market whose entrance was right next door to the more formal part of the building. Like so many other places in Bath, the Guildhall was constructed out of creamy yellow stone, and was ornately decorated with four huge columns on the central facade, and a statue of Justice holding a set of weighing scales in one hand and a sword in the other. A magnificent dome topped the whole thing off.

As they approached the main entrance, Tabitha squeaked with excitement. The doors were open to welcome them and she couldn't believe she was here, about to experience a ball similar to ones which Jane Austen herself would have attended.

'This is going to be so much fun!' she squealed. 'I can't wait for the dancing.'

'I can,' Rhys muttered. 'I've got two left feet, and both of them belong to someone else.'

'You'll be fine,' she assured him. 'Just watch what everyone else is doing and copy them.'

She had her fingers crossed as she said it, having witnessed the intricacies of some of the dances, although she had never participated in any. However, she refused to let their lack of dancing skills put a dampener on the evening, and Grandad had informed her that there would be someone 'calling the dances' – in other words, issuing verbal instructions during each dance, so that should help. Besides, she was sure she and Rhys wouldn't be the only novices.

Tabitha gazed around in pleasure as they entered the magnificent building. It was light and airy inside, with a sweeping staircase of blonde wood and a delicate wrought-iron balustrade leading to the upper floor and the Banqueting Room, where the ball was taking place. A glittering chandelier hung above the stairwell, and the walls were festooned with impressive oil paintings.

As Tabitha and Rhys made their way slowly up the stairs, they fell into step with the other attendees. Tabitha used both hands to lift up the skirt of her dress, so she didn't risk stepping on it, and surreptitiously sneaked glances at the other women, admiring their gowns, and the men who looked resplendent in their tail coats and breeches.

She was relieved to see that Rhys didn't look in the least bit out of place, and when they reached the top of the stairs, she took his arm once more, giving it a squeeze.

'I can't believe I'm here,' she whispered as they shuffled towards the door, waiting to be admitted into the Banqueting Room.

'Neither can I.' Rhys looked nervous, and Tabitha appreciated that he was out of his comfort zone.

'Thank you. I know this isn't your scene.' She smiled up at him and her pulse sang when he smiled back.

'But it is *yours*, and that's what is important.'

His words melted her heart, his thoughtfulness touching her deeply. She was about to tell him so, but just at that moment they reached the door, where a portly gentleman with a staff asked her and Rhys their names and where they were from. With a loud rap of his staff on the floor, he proceeded to announce them to the room in a booming voice. Then they were ushered inside, and Tabitha let out a gasp of pleasure.

The high-ceilinged room was the epitome of elegance: chandeliers hung from the ceiling, tall sash windows ran the length of one wall letting in the evening light, and there were Corinthian columns and guilt-framed paintings everywhere.

Large fireplaces occupied three of the walls, one of them partly obscured by a raised platform where three musicians were playing background music. Large round tables lined the edges of the pale green and gold-highlighted room, leaving the centre free for the dancing which would take place shortly.

'Bloody hell, what century are we in?' Rhys asked, his eyes darting everywhere.

'Early nineteenth,' she said, leading him towards an empty table and laying claim to a couple of seats. The room was filling up fast, and soon the places at their table were filled.

'Isn't this lovely!' a middle-aged woman exclaimed as she sat down. 'I do so adore the Regency Ball.' She opened a fan and wafted her face with it vigorously. 'It gets so frightfully warm in here though, don't you think?'

It was, but then it was the end of June, so Tabitha supposed that was to be expected. She opened her own fan and fluttered it experimentally.

'This is my first time,' she said, 'so I wasn't sure what to expect.' She smoothed her hand over the stole, which she had draped over the back of her chair, and ignored Rhys's snigger as he whispered, 'Frightfully warm,' in her ear.

Sensing that he was on the verge of full-blown laughter, she sent him away to the bar to purchase a couple of drinks.

'Oh, how lovely! I remember my first time – it was simply divine,' the lady declared, and Tabitha feared that she might also laugh, and she bit her lip, not wanting to offend her. Besides, hadn't she been guilty of the same thing herself, earlier?

At seven-thirty on the dot, the Caller welcomed everyone, then announced the first dance. By silent, mutual agreement, Tabitha and Rhys remained in their seats, despite Tabitha itching to give it a go. It was a relief to them both to discover that many people also didn't have a clue, so after watching several dances, Rhys got to his feet and held out his hand.

'Shall we?' he asked.

'Are you sure? We don't have to join in if you don't feel like it.'

'There's no point being here if we don't make the most of it,' he said, and Tabitha fell in love with him even more as he threw himself into the experience with enthusiasm.

Neither she nor Rhys were very good, but it didn't matter; they were having so much fun, the missed steps and hesitations adding to the hilarity.

The music was overlaid by their chatter and laughter, and when supper was called Tabitha was more than ready to return to her seat for some refreshment. She was thirsty and hungry, and she tucked into the two-course meal with enthusiasm.

An hour later, she found herself on her feet again for a cotillion, facing three other couples. Although she and Rhys weren't able to perform the intricate steps of the dance, they managed to hop, skip and twirl in all the right places, and the bit where they galloped around in a circle whilst holding hands had Tabitha in fits of laughter.

It was so much fun, and she was out of breath at the end.

'I thought the ball would be sedate,' Rhys said, collapsing into his seat beside her. 'But it's worse than going to a gym class.'

'My feet hurt,' Tabitha moaned, but she was smiling as she said it. Aching feet was a small price to pay and she couldn't thank Rhys enough for surprising her with the tickets.

'I didn't expect to enjoy myself as much as I am,' he admitted.

Tabitha teased, 'And there isn't a phone or a computer screen in sight.'

'That's not strictly true.' Rhys nodded towards those people who were taking photos or videoing it.

She nudged him with her knee. 'You know what I mean.'

'I do. But technology isn't going to go away. Although this does prove that old and new can co-exist. I do see your point, though. This ball harks back to a simpler time.'

'Not as simple as you might think,' Tabitha told him. 'There were far more social conventions then than there are now, and many more restrictions because of it. For instance, if this really was 1812, then I wouldn't be going home with you this evening.' She edged closer.

'Is that so? I'll have you know I'm a respectable man, not the kind of man who can be taken advantage of.'

'No? Then you won't want me to…' She placed her mouth against his ear and whispered what she wanted to do with him, and had the satisfaction of seeing his eyes widen.

He swallowed hard. 'Really?'

She nodded, catching her bottom lip between her teeth, seduction in her eyes.

'Tabitha Locke, you'll be the death of me,' he growled. 'Two can play at that game,' and when he told her what was in store for her later, she blushed furiously.

'Oh, look at you two,' their table companion cried. 'I remember when Aubrey and I were just as in love.' She fluttered her fan. 'We still are, of course, but gone are the days when we smooched in public like that.'

Tabitha edged back into her seat and smiled politely. Out of the corner of her eye she could see that Rhys was just as embarrassed. Thankfully the woman's attention was caught by someone on the dance floor and she didn't say anything further; because the last thing Tabitha wanted was for Rhys to realise she was in love with him. Having seen the look on his face, she knew he might like her a lot, but he wasn't in love with *her*. And maybe he never would be.

Tabitha couldn't help how she felt though, so she would just have to deal with it, and pray that one day he would love her as much as *she* loved *him*.

CHAPTER 16

Tabitha burst into the flat, almost bent double with laughter, and heard Grandad call, 'Tabitha, is that you?'

'Yes, Grandad, and Rhys is with me.'

Jeremy emerged from the kitchen, wiping his hands on a towel. 'What's so funny?' he asked.

'We've been to an escape room this evening, and I've never laughed so much in all my life.'

'I beg your pardon? You've been to a *what?*'

'An escape room. Rhys, you explain while I make us some supper. Do you want anything, Grandad?'

He handed the towel to her. 'I haven't long made myself a bite to eat,' he said, 'but I'll have a cup of tea if you're making one.'

'I'll pop the kettle on,' she replied and danced into the kitchen.

However, her buoyant mood quickly evaporated when she saw the solitary plate on the draining board, along with a butter knife. The aroma of toast hung in the air.

Was that all he'd had for dinner? A measly slice of *toast*?

Guilt rose up to smack her across the face, because this was her fault; she hadn't cooked a meal this evening. She and Rhys had grabbed a burger as soon as she'd closed the shop for the day and had headed off to have fun.

But her fun seemed to have resulted in Grandad not eating properly, despite her having left a beef and onion pie in the fridge. When she looked inside, she saw that it hadn't been touched, and the vegetables she had prepared for him still sat in the Tupperware box.

There were a couple of portions of homemade lentil and vegetable soup in the freezer which wouldn't take long to defrost in the microwave. She would get those out for supper, and at least he would have something nutritious in his stomach to go to bed with.

'I'm going to heat some soup. Can I tempt you with a bowl, Grandad?' she asked, poking her head around the parlour door. Rhys and her grandfather were watching snooker. 'There's too much for me and Rhys and it will only go to waste otherwise,' she added, knowing how much Grandad hated throwing away food.

'I suppose I could manage a small portion,' he said.

Rhys's attention was fixed on the screen and she glared at him, willing him to look at her. When he eventually did, she jerked her head in the direction of the kitchen, her eyes wide.

Frowning, he got to his feet. 'I'll be back in a sec,' he told Jeremy, who lifted a hand in acknowledgement.

As soon as he entered the kitchen, Rhys asked. 'What's up?' He kept his voice low, and she was grateful he had realised she needed his discretion.

'It's Grandad. He's not eating. I left a pie in the fridge for him for his dinner, but he's not touched it.'

'Is that the reason we're having soup for supper? I was imagining a fish finger sandwich.'

Tabitha shuddered. She wasn't particularly keen on fish fingers at the best of times, but in a *sandwich?* Yuck. 'He's got to eat properly. If he doesn't, he might get ill.'

She worried at her bottom lip with her teeth as she rooted around in the freezer for the soup. There was a packet of wholemeal rolls in there somewhere, too.

After prising the lid off the container of soup and placing it in the microwave, she pulled the kitchen door closed before she poked at the digital display. With any luck, Grandad wouldn't realise that she was heating his supper in it.

When she had bought the microwave, Grandad had played his face for a week, grumbling that they weren't to be trusted. A 'mod con' he'd called it and although she had argued until she was blue in the face that this particular mod con had been around for well over half a century, her words had fallen on stubbornly deaf ears.

What irked her the most was that he thoroughly enjoyed watching TV and had a very modern one indeed in the parlour. And neither did he object to the iron, the fridge or the kettle. Go figure! Her grandfather was an enigma, wrapped in a conundrum, as Mum put it. Tabitha thought he was better described as stubborn, ornery and set in his ways.

Rhys waited until the container of soup was turning slowly, the timer counting down, before he drew Tabitha into a hug. 'In future, we'll eat here first before we go out, shall we?' he suggested.

'But it's not always practical, is it?'

'We'll make it work,' he promised, holding her tight. 'Jeremy's wellbeing is more important than us going out gallivanting.'

Tabitha had to smile: gallivanting was one of her grandad's words. She wasn't entirely sure what it meant, but it seemed to imply going out and enjoying oneself.

Rhys was so thoughtful and considerate, putting her grandad's needs before his. It was one of the things she loved about him.

Rhys began nibbling her ear, making her squirm with desire, and she wondered whether she should spend yet another night at his place. She had stayed over at his for the last five nights out of seven, and it was only a desperate need for sleep (because, let's face it, when she spent the night with Rhys not much sleeping took place) that made her say, 'Rhys, I think I'd better stay here tonight. I've been neglecting him lately.'

'How about if I promise to bring you back by seven a.m., so you can make him his breakfast?'

'OK, but it would be more logical for *you* to stay here,' she pointed out. 'But I'm not quite ready to share my bed with you, not when Grandad is in the next room.'

'I know what you mean,' he replied with a grimace.

'It would be so much easier if I had a car, then I wouldn't have to drag you halfway across the city.'

'It's something to think about,' he agreed.

Tabitha checked the display on the microwave, and when she saw it had only five seconds to go, she hurried to intercept it before it pinged.

As she dished up the soup, she ran the idea of buying a car through her mind. It would certainly make dashing between Abbey Green and Bear Flats easier, but what would she use it for otherwise? She would have to have a serious think about it, weigh up the pros and cons. It was a costly decision, and one that she didn't want to make lightly.

Putting it on the back burner (along with getting a mobile phone, because she hadn't made a final decision about that yet, either) Tabitha looked forward to slipping off to Rhys's place later, just as soon as Grandad took himself off to bed. She would be back first thing in the morning, and hopefully he wouldn't even notice she had gone.

***

Shrill tinny music pierced her consciousness, and Tabitha groaned as she struggled to open her eyes.

'What?' Rhys muttered, groping for his phone.

Tabitha groaned again, picked up a pillow and plonked it over her head. 'Is it time to get up?' she croaked. Surely not: she'd only just gone to sleep, or so it felt.

'Tabi, it's only ten past two.' His voice was muffled by the pillow over her head, but she heard his worry; phone calls in the middle of the night were never good news.

Tabitha pushed the pillow aside and sat up to find him peering blearily at the screen. Wordlessly, he held up the phone so she could see the number.

It was her own. Or rather, it was the shop's number.

Tabitha froze. Why was the—? *Grandad!*

Rhys answered. 'Hello, Jeremy?... Yes, she is. Do you want to...? *What?* When?... Are you all right?'

Tabitha pulled on Rhys's arm, frantic with worry. 'What's wrong? What's happened?'

Rhys raised a hand. 'Have you phoned the police?... Right, OK... Don't touch anything. We'll be there as soon as we can.'

Tabitha was already dragging on her jeans as Rhys ended the call, and she turned stricken eyes to him. Her heart constricted in fear and she felt sick.

Before she could ask, Rhys said, 'There's been a break-in. Don't worry, your grandad is fine.'

'Oh, God!' She yanked her top over her head and darted into the hall to find her trainers.

Rhys was hot on her heels, zipping up his jeans, his T-shirt in one hand as he hooked his keys off the kitchen counter.

They were out of the flat in seconds, racing down two flights of stairs, Tabitha in the lead. Rhys caught hold of her arm when they reached the communal lobby.

'He's fine,' he repeated. 'Shocked, but unhurt. The police are on their way, so I'm not going to drive like an idiot, OK?'

Tabitha nodded through the tears welling in her eyes and beginning to spill over.

Despite Rhys saying that he wasn't going to drive like an idiot, he drove faster than usual, pulling into Abbey Green in record time, and Tabitha was out of the car almost before it had come to a halt. She raced to the rear of the building, her only thought was getting to her grandfather and seeing for herself that he was unharmed.

She heard Rhys yell, 'Tabitha! Wait!' and it was only when she skidded to a halt at the sight of the shop's open rear door that she realised the police had yet to arrive. What if the intruder was still in there?

Tabitha didn't care. God help him if he was, because she would flatten the sod. And if he'd hurt Grandad, she wouldn't be responsible for her actions.

Not bothering to check the shop floor itself, she barrelled inside and charged up the stairs, taking them two at a time.

Rhys was behind her, his feet pounding up the stairs as she burst into the flat.

'Grandad? Grandad! Where are you?'

A glance showed her there was no one in the kitchen and she carried on, running down the short hallway to slam into the parlour door as she pushed it open. That room was also empty.

Whirling around, she caught sight of Rhys disappearing up the stairs to the bedrooms, and she pelted after him.

'Empty!' he called, after pushing the first door open and poking his head around it.

Tabitha guessed it might be, considering that was her room, not Grandad's.

There was no one in the bathroom either, the door ajar enough for Rhys to check without having to go in, but Tabitha, having caught up with him, had a quick look to make sure. Which only left her grandfather's room. A light was on and his door was open, but it wasn't possible to see all the way inside.

She made to push past Rhys, but he put out an arm to stop her. 'Let me look first, just in case,' he begged.

Whilst she appreciated the sentiment, Tabitha had to see for herself. If her grandfather wasn't OK, it was better that she knew now, rather than in a couple of minutes. She glared at Rhys and he moved aside to let her pass.

With bated breath, Tabitha stepped inside, calling, 'Grandad?'

He didn't answer, because he wasn't there.

Tabitha gasped, clapping a hand to her mouth, then felt Rhys's arms around her. 'Where is he?' she cried.

I don't know,' he began.

They had the same thought at the same time. 'The shop!' they yelled in unison and whirled around as one, to jostle their way along the landing and down the stairs, where they found Jeremy waiting for them at the foot, his walking stick raised and a grim expression on his face.

'Oh, it's you,' he declared. 'I thought the blighters had come back and were chancing their arm upstairs. I was going to let them have it.' He banged his walking stick on the newel post, making Tabitha jump.

'Are you all right?' she demanded, her gaze travelling over him, searching for injuries.

'No, I am not! I'm furious!' he yelled.

Tabitha sagged with relief. He was unharmed – physically at least.

'What happened?' The adrenalin was starting to fade, and she felt weak and a little nauseous.

It was typical of Rhys to notice. 'Tabitha, sit down before you fall down. You too, Jeremy. Are you sure you're OK?'

'Stop bloody fussing. I'm fine. Where are the police? They should be here by now.' The fact that her grandfather had uttered a swear word proved to Tabitha that he wasn't fine at all.

He might be angry but he was also scared, she realised. This had badly shaken him. It had shaken her too, and she hadn't even been here. But she *should have been*. If she hadn't gone to Rhys's place, the break-in might never have happened. And even if it had, Grandad wouldn't have had to deal with it on his own. He was eighty-one, for God's sake! She should have been here for him, looking after him the way he had looked after her when she'd needed it.

She felt so guilty she wasn't able to look him in the eye when she took his arm and led him to the chair. Then she knelt beside him, wrapped her arms around his waist and buried her head in his lap.

She could feel him trembling, the tremor in his hand evident when he lifted it to stroke her hair.

'I'm so sorry, Grandad. I should have been here.'

'Tabitha, I—' But whatever her grandad had been about to say was cut off by the arrival of the police.

She would apologise to him again later, but for now there were questions to answer and fingerprints to be dusted for.

***

Two hours later, the police were gone, the shop's rear door had been made secure, albeit a temporary measure, and Tabitha, Grandad and Rhys were in the kitchen nursing cups of tea and rehashing the events.

For about the sixth time, Jeremy said, 'It was sheer luck I heard them. I was in the kitchen, getting a glass of water and I heard the door go.'

Tabitha studied him anxiously: the lines on his face had deepened, his cheeks had a sunken look, and his skin a grey pallor. He looked ill, old, and scared.

Seeing him like this made her heart ache.

He continued, 'I thought it was youths, banging on the door for a laugh, but there was a breeze you see, coming up the stairs.'

Tabitha knew what he meant. When the rear door to the building opened, it seemed to create a kind of updraft, made worse the windier it was outside. There had been a breeze tonight but hardly a hurricane, so the disturbance in the air would only have been noticeable to anyone familiar with the building.

He continued, 'I shouted, 'who's there?' Then I yelled, 'phone the police, Tabitha', because I didn't want them to think I was here on my own.' He turned apologetic eyes to her, and Tabitha's chin wobbled.

'You shouldn't have been on your own,' she said. '*I* should have been here.'

'Nonsense. You're young, you've got your own life to lead.'

'But—'

'No buts. Anyway, I'm thankful you *weren't* here. By the time I got down the stairs, they'd gone. You would have been much quicker than I, and I dread to think what might have happened if you had confronted them. I saw him, you know. One of them. Dressed in black. Well, his legs, at least. I couldn't see the rest of him. I told that younger officer I would recognise the blighter's shoes anywhere.' He lifted his cup to his lips using both hands. 'He didn't get anything,' he repeated for the umpteenth time.

However, Tabitha wasn't as sure; she would do a complete inventory in the morning. At first glance though, nothing appeared to be missing. They'd got off lightly. But they might not be so lucky a second time, she thought, remembering the police officers' incredulity that the shop didn't have an alarm system fitted.

'Do you think they'll catch who did it?' Tabitha asked, directing her question to Rhys.

He hadn't said a great deal, but she was thankful for his solid, calm presence. He was the one who had made the rear door secure, although it couldn't be used in its current state, so they would have to go in and out through the shop's main entrance for the time being.

Not that Tabitha had any intention of going anywhere. She was still racked with guilt that Grandad had had to face this alone. The shock could have given him a heart attack.

'They might,' Rhys said. 'The CSI officer said the burglar had been wearing gloves, but they're going to check any CCTV footage in the area in the morning. Maybe they'll get something useful from that.' He pursed his lips. 'You should think about installing some cameras, one at the front and another at the back.'

'I know,' she sighed, realising he hadn't been fooled when she'd attempted to mislead him when they'd first met. He had clearly realised the shop's security hadn't left the dark ages. But it was high time it did. Grandad's aversion to mod cons had to be put aside. If Tabitha hadn't been so terrified of using the internet after what had happened with Austen, she would have insisted he get an alarm system. Or she would have at least tried to talk him into it.

It was yet another thing to feel guilty about. She bet her parents weren't aware that the shop didn't have an alarm, so no doubt she and Grandad were due a lecture from her dad. And quite rightly, too.

Abruptly Tabitha felt shattered, and she could see that her grandad was exhausted. 'Get yourself off to bed,' she told him, fully expecting him to argue, so she was concerned when he shuffled off without a murmur.

'He'll be fine,' Rhys said, studying her face as she watched Grandad leave the room. 'He's had a bit of a shock, that's all.'

'You should get off, too,' she said.

'I don't want to leave you on your own.'

'You're going to have to. You can't stay here indefinitely: you've got work in the morning.' She glanced at the clock. '*This* morning,' she amended. It was nearing five a.m. and it had been light for a while.

'I'll go, but only because I want to research CCTV cameras and it's easier on a computer than my phone.' He put his mug in the sink, then drew her into a hug. 'Try to get some sleep, Tabi-cat.'

'You too,' she murmured.

She desperately wanted him to stay, but she didn't think it a good idea. Grandad disliked change of any kind, and he was very set in his ways. Finding Rhys here in the morning would probably upset him, even if he didn't show it.

Tabitha saw Rhys to the door and locked it behind him, then she leant against it, too weary to move. And as the emotions of the last few hours caught up with her, she began to tremble.

It was several minutes before she was able to find the energy to climb the stairs, and considerably longer before she collapsed into bed.

Her mind was whirling, as she suspected it would be, but surprisingly her thoughts weren't on the break-in or her grandfather. They were on Rhys and how deeply she was in love with him. But her feelings were irrelevant; she had a grandfather who needed her much more than she had appreciated. How could she abandon him to follow her heart? She couldn't be that selfish.

CHAPTER 17

Grandad emerged from his room just after midday, looking less frail and more like his old self, although Tabitha thought the trauma had aged him. His eyes were sunken, he hadn't shaved (which was unheard of), and a tremor remained in his hand, although it wasn't as pronounced.

She half-expected Rhys to turn up at closing time, but he didn't, so she assumed he was busy. Or asleep. After all, he had been up most of the night, the same as her.

The meal had been cooked and eaten and the washing up done, and Tabitha had given up on seeing Rhys today when the phone rang.

Grandad gave her a worried look as she hurried into the hall to answer it.

'It's me,' Rhys said. 'I'm outside. Can you let me in?'

Jeremy subsided into his chair when she told him who it was, and she left him to finish watching the news as she trotted down the stairs. Giving the rear door a nervous glance on the way (someone was coming to give her a quote tomorrow to replace it), she scurried into the shop, her heart melting when she saw Rhys's familiar figure through the glass.

'What's all this?' she asked as he stepped inside with two large carrier bags. He also had another bag slung over his shoulder. 'If I'd known you were stopping by, I would have kept some dinner back. Come on up.'

'Can I have a word first?'

'OK...' Tabitha worried at her lip, hoping it wasn't going to be more bad news.

Stepping around her, Rhys went into the workroom and hoisted the carrier bags onto the bench. The shoulder bag quickly followed, and when he opened his arms, she fell into them, relishing being held.

'I've missed you,' he murmured after kissing her thoroughly.

'I've missed you too. It's been a long day.'

'You can say that again. I'm ready for bed.'

'Um, about that – I can't leave Grandad on his own.'

'It's OK, Tabi, I don't expect you to.'

She bit her lip again, and continued, 'I also don't think it's a good idea for you to sleep *here*. It wouldn't feel right.'

'I agree.' He kissed her hair.

'I don't know what to suggest,' she admitted.

'Neither do I, but we'll work something out. Let's get this place sorted first, then we'll think about it, yeah?'

Tabitha was grateful for his understanding. Right now, she was too tired to think straight. She wanted nothing more than to slip into bed next to him and fall asleep in his arms. That bloody burglar! If she ever got her hands on him, she would—

Oh, hell; the intruder wasn't solely to blame for the predicament she found herself in (although he was 100 per cent to blame for breaking into the shop). Sooner or later Tabitha would have had to face the fact that travelling back and forth to Rhys's place every day wasn't ideal, not with Grandad growing older with each passing month. She had been so remiss in her duty to him lately, that she was ashamed of herself. When she had moved in with him, she had taken it upon herself to do all the cooking and the household chores – mainly out of gratitude and a sense of responsibility, but also because keeping busy had held the dark memories at bay. But since Rhys had come along, she'd hardly given Grandad a second thought.

Rhys held her for a couple more minutes, then said, 'Let me show you what I've been up to today.' Releasing her, he opened the nearest bag and took out a box. It had a picture of a sleek white camera on the front. 'I've got you two external cameras and four internal ones,' he said. 'As soon as you've got broadband sorted, I'll install them for you.'

Seeing them sent a cold shiver down Tabitha's back. The external cameras she could handle, but the thought of having a camera watching her every move in the shop made her feel sick, and bile rose up in her chest, burning her from the inside out. It didn't burn as hot as her remembered shame, but it was darned uncomfortable all the same.

As Rhys outlined where he thought the internal cameras should be located (one at the front of the shop above the door, a second one behind the counter, the third would cover the workroom and the safe, and the fourth would be halfway up the stairs and trained on the rear door) Tabitha fought hard not to let her discomfort show. The last thing she wanted was for Rhys to start asking questions. But dear God, she couldn't shake the horror she felt. She had come to Bath and her grandfather's house to escape from cameras, and here she was about to knowingly have them installed in the very place she should feel safe.

It made her skin crawl. But she had to think of her grandad's welfare and the shop's security. Being the victim of a break-in was a violation, even if nothing had been taken, and she was determined to be better prepared next time. With a new door, more modern locks (her heart was heavy as she thought of those vintage locks being relegated to a shelf in the workroom), an alarm system and cameras covering every centimetre of the ground floor, she would have the satisfaction of knowing she had done everything she could. She was aware she couldn't prevent a determined criminal from getting in, but she would be damned if she was going to make it easy for them.

So yes, she was extremely grateful to Rhys for offering to install the cameras, even if she loathed the very thought of them. And for him to do that, she knew the shop had to have broadband. Contacting a reputable provider was another job to add to her to-do list…

The irony was, that without connection to the internet, it wasn't easy to find the phone numbers of those companies she needed to call.

As though sensing her frustration, Rhys said, 'Shall I come over in the morning? I can at least help you get the ball rolling.'

'Yes please, and I've decided it's time I had a mobile phone.'

Rhys threw his hands up in the air. 'Hallelujah!' Then his expression became more serious. 'How is Jeremy?'

'Better, but he's not going to like having an alarm system, or CCTV. But unfortunately, our insurance company insists on it, and on more secure locks.' She rolled her eyes. 'Yeah, I know, ironic, isn't it?'

'He's not going to like what *I've* been doing then,' Rhys stated.

Tabitha tilted her head to one side. 'Go on.'

'Hang on a sec, let me set this up.'

She watched curiously as he removed a laptop from the shoulder bag, opened the lid and began typing and clicking.

'Voila!' he exclaimed, just as she was about to lose patience. 'Look at this.' He angled the screen so she could see it, and Tabitha leant in for a closer look.

'Why am I looking at a website selling keys?' she asked, bewildered. She had a shop full of the blasted things: she wanted to sell what she had, not buy more. Or certainly not until Grandad handed over the buying reins to her and let her in on his purchasing secrets.

'Because it's *your* website,' Rhys informed her. 'Or it will be, if you want it.'

Tabitha sucked in a breath. She had been too intent on the pictures of the keys on the screen, that she hadn't noticed the header with Locke's Key Emporium emblazoned across the top of the page. 'You've made me a website?' Her tone was incredulous.

'It's a bit basic and it's not connected to a domain, but I just wanted to give you an idea of what it might look like.' He clicked on one of the pages, and the screen was filled with a close-up of a key.

'That's not one of ours,' she said, her eyes narrowing.

'It's just a random holding image I got off the internet. You would insert a picture of your own stock in its place. There's still a huge amount of work to be done on it – assuming you want to go ahead – even if it's just a *this is who we are and this is what we are about* kind of site. It can be as easy or as complicated as you are comfortable with. I suggest keeping the front end fairly simple, but building lots of features into the back end ready for when you decide you need them.'

'You can do all that?' Rhys cocked an eyebrow and she added hastily, 'Of course you can. Silly me.'

A fizz of excitement broke through her exhaustion. The shop was currently doing OK financially, but having a website would open up a plethora of opportunities – selling direct being one of them.

'I've checked and *lockeskeys.com* is available, so is *lockeskeyemporium.com* but *lockes.com* isn't, which is a shame because—'

Tabitha was shaking her head. 'No, *lockes.com* is no good – it's got to have the word *key* in it, so people know what it's about. I like the full title. It's a bit of a mouthful, but I think it's perfect.' She peered at the screen again and wrinkled her nose. 'The colour scheme is a bit... modern?' She was going to say garish, but as Rhys had chosen it, she didn't want to hurt his feelings.

'You can have whatever colour scheme you like,' he said, grinning. 'Might I suggest using the same colours that are in the sign outside? That will tie it all together, and you really must keep the old-worlde ambience and—'

'You planned this, didn't you?' Tabitha broke in. 'You deliberately made the website look icky, knowing that I wouldn't be able to resist making it better.'

'Would I do such a thing?'

'Yes.' She wound her arms around his neck and slid onto his lap. 'Thank you.'

'You're welcome. It was fun, actually – I don't get to do this kind of thing as a rule.'

'I'm going to have to buy a computer, aren't I?' she said, in between kisses.

'I know where you can pick up a refurbished one for a good price,' he told her. 'Mmm, that's nice. I could stay here all night.'

She could too, but just then her grandad called down the stairs, 'What are you doing down there, Tabitha? Is Rhys here?'

Rhys shook his head and pointed at the door, then mimed walking with his fingers.

'He is,' she called back, 'but he's just leaving. He only wanted to drop something off.'

'I'll see you tomorrow,' Rhys promised. 'And maybe we could pop back to mine for an hour or two after dinner?'

'You just want to have your wicked way with me,' she teased.

'Yep.' And when he gathered her closer for a final kiss and whispered just how wicked he wanted to be, Tabitha almost melted into a puddle of desire on the floor.

He was right, they would *have* to figure out a way to make this work.

***

Three days later, Tabitha was the slightly reluctant owner of a shiny mobile phone, a laptop, and a website. The shop had received an overhaul too, in that it now sported a new back door, more substantial locks on the front, an alarm system that scared the life out of her, and a CCTV system which she had mixed feelings about.

Broadband had also been installed, so she had an internet connection too, although Grandad didn't want anything to do with it. He flatly refused to take any part in the setting up of the website and scowled heavily whenever it was mentioned. So Tabitha had taken to not discussing it when he was in earshot.

As well as all this, she and Grandad had revisited Siegfried's office to sign the contracts and the transfer documents that had been drawn up and filed, which meant that Tabitha was now officially the proud owner of Locke's Key Emporium.

After so much excitement all she wanted was to spend a quiet evening with Rhys, preferably in bed. However, Grandad, for some reason known only to himself, had decided that it was time he took an interest in this *'internet thing'*, and had demanded to see the website.

Out of the corner of her eye, Tabitha could see Rhys struggling not to laugh as she tried to explain what she wanted to achieve.

'Why is there a photo of you?' Grandad wanted to know.

'Because you refused to let me put a photo of *you* on the website,' Tabitha retorted. Rhys had suggested that the *About Us* page depicted the history of the shop over the decades, and she had managed to unearth an old photo from the 1920s and one from the 1950s. She had wanted to include Grandad in the story, but aside from his name, she hadn't written much about him.

She had however, informed anyone who landed on the page, that Locke's Key Emporium was now in her capable hands as she carried on the family business. Tabitha would have preferred to have had Grandad's face staring out of the screen rather than hers, because she thought his was more in keeping with the age and gravitas of the shop, as well as the image it portrayed.

Instead, she had made sure to wear a string of pearls (fake) and a jewelled brooch (also fake), and ensured the chatelaine was in shot. She had her hands demurely clasped in front of her and was wearing a dress that harked back to times gone by, and Tabitha sincerely hoped she was portraying an air of quiet confidence and expert knowledge.

She hoped nobody realised it was all smoke and mirrors! She was scared witless by the new responsibility of owning the business, and she was convinced that even if she lived to be a hundred, she still wouldn't know half of what her grandfather knew.

Tabitha flicked through the webpages, making sure that everything looked just so, and she was satisfied with what she saw. Rhys had created several hidden pages for her to populate at her leisure with the keys she had for sale, but she wasn't entirely confident with online selling yet, so that would come later. Right now, she just wanted to get the website up and running, and for the shop to have a presence on the internet.

'What do you think?' she asked her grandad.

Jeremy screwed up his face. 'It looks like you know what you're doing.'

Tabitha laughed. 'I think you'll find it is *Rhys* who knows what he's doing.'

'Don't put yourself down,' Rhys told her. 'You're doing fine. Apart from setting it up, I've not done much.'

'Not true! You've held my hand every step of the way.'

'You've done most of it. I'm just here for the ride, and because I like holding your hand.'

Tabitha batted her eyelashes at him. She loved how he was so supportive of her, and how he bolstered her confidence at every opportunity. They both knew there wouldn't be a website without him. In fact, she didn't know what she would have done without him these past few days.

'Thank you,' she mouthed over the top of Grandad's head.

'You're welcome,' he mouthed back.

'Can anyone see this website?' Grandad asked.

'Not yet. It's not live at the moment. Only Rhys and I can see it.'

'What's the point of that?' Jeremy wanted to know. 'I thought the whole idea was that people could see it.'

'It is.'

'Then why can't they? It's a damn waste of time and money, if you ask me.'

'As I said, it's not live yet.'

'Why not? Do you have to do something special to make it live?'

'Yes. I have to click on this button here.'

'Go on then, click on it.'

Tabitha's eyes widened. Dare she? She glanced at Rhys, who nodded.

'What are you waiting for?' He raised an eyebrow, and she realised he was right. What *was* she waiting for?

With her heart in her mouth, she clicked on the button and instantly a pop-up box appeared informing her that the site was now live.

'Is that it?' she asked.

Rhys nodded. 'What did you expect?'

'I don't know. It's a bit of an anticlimax.'

'I could jump up and down and wave my arms in the air, if you want.' Tabitha sent him a scathing look. 'Or I could make us all a nice mug of hot cocoa?' he suggested.

She knew what she really wanted – *him* – but she was going to have to settle for cocoa.

After the drinks had been consumed and Grandad had taken himself off to bed, Rhys kissed her goodnight (which, admittedly, took a while). Then when he had gone, Tabitha couldn't resist curling up in bed with her phone and navigating to the shop's website.

Darn it, even if she did say so herself, it looked flipping brilliant!

CHAPTER 18

'Have you seen this?' Martha demanded, her face alight with laughter. She turned her phone around so Tabitha could see the screen. A video of a dog was playing, and a man's voice was dubbed over the dog's various expressions to make it seem as though the dog was doing the talking.

As Tabitha watched and listened, she began to chuckle.

'Are you on ShareStyle?' Martha asked.

'No.' She hadn't actually heard of it and guessed it must be the latest social media phenomenon.

'You should. You could put up some videos of your latest keys.'

Tabitha gave her a quizzical look, and Martha shrugged when she realised that talking about keys probably didn't have quite the same entertainment value as a funny dog video. Besides, Tabitha had a feeling that ShareStyle viewers weren't the shop's demographic.

'Are you on *any* social media?' Martha continued. 'Because I've done a search and I can't find you.'

Martha won't either, because that was one thing Tabitha had refused to budge on. There was no way she was opening herself up to that kind of pain again. She had managed perfectly well these past three years without knowing what an acquaintance had for lunch, or seeing the latest pair of shoes they'd bought, and neither did she want to read about random people's political opinions or be subjected to the wrath of keyboard warriors with nothing better to do than complain and vilify.

It was safe to say that Tabitha's experience of the social media apps she had once been a slave to, hadn't been good. Anyway, she was far too busy for that kind of time-suck. She remembered how she had lost hours going down various online rabbit holes, and as much as she found videos of talking dogs amusing, she didn't have time to watch them. Since she had reconnected with the internet, her free time had been spent skulking on the sites of various auction houses, trying to figure out how they worked and what amount she might be prepared to bid on any particular item.

Grandad sourced new stock from his network of contacts in Bath's auction rooms, and now and again people would approach him and ask if he was interested in buying an old key or two. However, Tabitha was trying to find a more regular and sustainable method of replenishing her stock, and she believed that the internet was the way forward.

Rhys didn't bother with any of the more popular social media apps either, she'd noticed, although he was part of several lively gaming forums. He currently had his arm slung loosely over the back of her chair, and his legs were sticking out in front as he relaxed into his seat. In his other hand, he held a glass of thick, dark ale.

Tabitha, Rhys, and a few others were sitting in one of the many city centre pubs. The atmosphere was light, and the conversation ebbed and flowed around her. Martha, bless her, always went out of her way to make sure Tabitha was included. Rhys and his friends had known each other for some years and had lots of shared history, so on occasion Tabitha did feel a little left out. But that was only to be expected, and she honestly didn't mind. It wasn't malicious; it was just the way of the world, and she was happy to sit back and listen, content with being in Rhys's company.

He was idly stroking the top of her arm as he chatted with Laurent about some game or another, his touch giving her a warm glow, when her phone buzzed with a message. At first, Tabitha wondered where the noise was coming from, until she realised it was coming from her pocket. Slightly alarmed, because only a handful of people had her mobile number, Tabitha squinted at the screen.

Then she let out a loud shriek, making Rhys flinch. 'It's my friend Rosalind!' she cried. 'She's had the baby! Look.' She showed him the photo accompanying the message. Rosalind was cuddling a tiny baby and was glowing with happiness. All that could be seen of the infant was a little face peeping out from the folds of a fluffy white blanket. The baby's eyes were closed, her delicate rose-bud mouth puckered in sleep.

'She was born this morning weighing seven ponds ten ounces,' Tabitha read aloud, 'and her name is Ebony-May. Isn't she cute?'

'Aw, she's gorgeous,' Martha said, and Tabitha became aware of the broody expression on the woman's face. Maybe in a few months' time, Martha and Laurent might be announcing their own new arrival.

'She's home from hospital already,' Tabitha continued. 'Gosh, they don't keep new mums in for long, do they?' Her thumbs out of practice, she slowly typed a reply, then smiled when she read Rosalind's reply.

'I'm going to visit her on Sunday,' she announced. 'I can't wait to cuddle this little one.' She returned to the mobile, scowling as she scrutinised it.

'What's up?' Rhys asked.

'The train times are annoying.'

'No problem, I'll take you,' he offered, and she gratefully accepted.

It was only later, after the evening had ended and she was alone in her bed missing Rhys's arms around her, that it struck her that she would be returning to Bristol and taking Rhys with her. It felt like a very significant step indeed.

**

In all her twenty-nine years Tabitha had never held a newborn until today. The baby felt surprisingly solid in her arms, but at the same time light and delicate, and Tabatha, balanced on the edge of Rosalind's sofa, was terrified she was going to drop the little scrap.

She was unable to tear her eyes away from the baby's serene face; every so often, the delicate, blue-veined eyelids would flutter, and the tiny mouth would purse. Ebony-May was simply adorable, and Tabitha's heartstrings were well and truly tugged.

'She must like you,' Rosalind said. 'So far, she's screamed the place down when anyone else has picked her up. My mum has felt quite put out, and Will's mother has taken it as a personal insult.' Rosalind glanced into the garden, where her fiancé and Rhys were sitting.

Rhys looked at ease, and Tabitha was pleased to see the two men getting along. For some reason, it was important to her, but she didn't know why, because it wasn't as though they would be seeing each other that often. The next time would probably be the wedding. *If* Rhys accompanied her. She hadn't mentioned that she had been invited, and she was in two minds about whether to go.

People who she hadn't seen in a long time would be there – people who knew what had happened – and the very sight of them would bring the past flooding back. But even if she did pluck up the courage to go, she would be reluctant for Rhys to go with her. What if someone said something? It would only take one comment to let the cat out of the bag, and once it was out, there would be no stuffing it back in.

She should tell him, she knew she should. It was only right that Rhys knew the truth about her past, but she couldn't face it. His opinion of her would change forever, and the thought terrified her. Although she hadn't posted those awful images herself, she still felt dirty and disgusting, and she knew the shame would never leave her. How would Rhys feel, knowing that thousands of people had seen the most intimate pictures of her? Tabitha had no doubt he would be disgusted too.

She would tell him at some point, but not yet. They were still getting to know each other, their relationship as new and as fragile as the baby she was cuddling. She would let it grow a little more, become a little stronger and more robust before she dropped that bombshell on him in the hope that maybe it could weather the storm of her telling him what Austen had done.

Tabitha took her cue to leave when the baby started fussing for a feed. Rosalind looked happy but exhausted, and Tabitha guessed she was ready for a nap. Although she would have loved to stay and cuddle Ebony-May for a couple of hours longer, she thought Rosalind had had her fill of visitors for today.

'Will's nice,' Rhys said, getting in the car.

'He seems it.' Tabitha didn't elaborate, mainly because she couldn't. She didn't know him well, as Rosalind had only just started dating him when Tabitha's life had imploded.

'How long have you and Rosalind been friends?'

'Since school.'

He started the engine and pulled away from the kerb. Tabitha had been ready to direct him to her parents' house, but he'd simply asked her for the postcode and typed it into the satnav.

She hoped he would concentrate on navigating around the city and not say anything further, but her hopes were dashed when he said, 'I've never heard you talk about any of your other friends. Just Rosalind.'

She heard the subtext – that she didn't mention Rosalind much, either. 'I kind of lost touch with everyone,' she hedged.

'When you moved to Bath?'

'Hmm.' She stared out of the passenger window, watching the damp streets slide past. It had been raining when they'd left Bath earlier this morning and it was still drizzling. The weather suited Tabitha's dismal mood. She should never have brought Rhys with her, especially since her mother had got wind that she was visiting Rosalind and had suggested she call in to see her parents, as they were in the area.

Typically, her mum had escalated it from a simple call-in-for-coffee, to a full-blown lunch. And Tabitha was nervous. She had already warned Mum to be careful what she said, and the strain of keeping the events of three years ago a secret was beginning to build. She mightn't have been responsible for Austen's actions, but she'd never truly believed she hadn't played a part in her own downfall.

Oh, for God's sake just tell him, she said to herself. Get it over with. What was the worst that could happen?

She might lose him, that's what.

Once again, she promised she would tell him. But not just as he was about to meet her parents. Now was not the best time.

***

'And this one time, she locked herself in the bathroom when we were on holiday. It was the middle of the night—'

'It was half past ten, Mum! Hardly the middle of the night,' Tabitha pointed out.

'It may as well have been, because anyone who spoke English at the office had gone home. There was only the security guard, and he didn't have a clue what your father was on about.' Her mother shook her head in mock despair. 'Trust Tabitha – she has always been accident prone.'

'The knob came off in my hand!' Tabitha protested. 'It was hardly my fault.'

'We had hired a villa on a small complex with a pool,' her mother explained to Rhys. 'Most of the properties were privately owned, only let out to guests occasionally. It would have been different if we were in a hotel with 24-hour reception.'

Rhys was smirking, and Tabitha kicked him under the table. He immediately rearranged his features into one of concern. 'How did she get out?'

'That's a tale in itself. You see, the bathroom in question was on the ground floor and it had a teeny-tiny window above the loo. Tabitha decided to squeeze through it rather than wait for someone to pick the lock, or whatever they would have to do to get her out.'

Tabitha snorted. 'In my defence, I had been in there well over an hour and Dad still hadn't managed to make the man understand that I was locked in. It could have been ages before they got the door open.'

'Kenneth wanted to break it down,' her mum explained, 'but I didn't want him arrested for criminal damage. You hear such awful things about foreign jails.'

Her dad made a dismissive noise. 'I wouldn't have been arrested. You're exaggerating. And I'm sure Turkish jails aren't as bad as all that.'

'Anyway,' her mum said, taking up the baton once more. 'Tabitha decided to try to get out of the window. However…' There was a pause for dramatic effect. 'She had forgotten she'd had a growth spurt, and she got stuck! It took the security guard, two people from a neighbouring villa who'd heard her screaming, and her father to get her out.' There were tears in her eyes and she slapped a hand on the table as she wheezed with mirth.

'Thanks for that, Mum. Can we leave it there, please? I think Rhys has heard enough stories about me. And may I add that I was only thirteen and the window was tiny.' Tabitha glared at her parents, then turned to Rhys. 'This pair didn't help. They were laughing fit to burst, and that was *before* I tried to climb out of the window. They kept making jokes about sliding food under the bathroom door if I was in there for any length of time. It had to be flat food, mind you, otherwise it wouldn't fit.'

'I'm enjoying hearing stories about you when you were a kid,' Rhys said.

He was smirking, but soon wiped the smile off his face when Tabitha said with a glower, 'I'll be sure to ask *your* mother what *you* got up to when you were a nipper. I bet she'll have a few tales to tell.'

'You'll get nothing out of her,' Rhys said.

'I bet I will.'

'Not if you don't get to meet her. If you think I'm going to sit there while she tells you about my less-than-stellar childhood moments, you're wrong.'

'I'll ask your nan. She'll tell me.'

'I'm never taking you to visit her again, so there.'

'You don't need to: I'll phone her. I'm sure she'd love a chat.'

'Has Tabitha always been this difficult?' he asked her mum.

'Oh, yes. Let me tell you about the time she—'

'Mum! Stop it!' Tabitha glared at her. 'If you don't behave, I'm leaving.'

'You came in Rhys's car,' her mother pointed out. 'You can't go until he does.'

'I'll catch a bus or get the train.'

'Good luck with that,' her dad chortled.

'No problem, I'll walk.' Tabitha stuck out her chin.

Her mum said, 'See what I mean?' She picked up her empty pudding bowl. 'I'll just clear away this lot, then I'll make the coffees. Tabitha, you can help.'

Tabitha knew better than to argue, and she got to her feet with a reluctant sigh. This was her mother's way of getting her on her own and just as Tabitha thought, as soon as the dining table had been cleared, Mum cornered her in the kitchen.

'Isn't Rhys lovely?'

'He is.'

'Are you going steady?'

Tabitha shrugged, pretending she was concentrating on stacking the dishwasher.

'Is it serious?' her mother persisted.

'I've only known him a couple of months.'

'That's not what I asked.'

'It's the only answer you're going to get.'

'Your grandad tells me the pair of you are all loved-up.'

Tabitha's mouth dropped open. 'He said *that?*'

'He tells me you're hardly out of each other's sight. Or you weren't, until the break-in.'

'Grandad ought to mind his own business,' Tabitha muttered, but there was no malice behind her words. She knew her grandfather was simply looking out for her.

'You *are* his business,' her mum pointed out. 'Just as you are mine.'

'Mum, I'm nearly thirty.'

'I don't care how old you are, you're still my daughter. I worry about you.'

'I know.'

'Is it serious?' her mum repeated.

Tabitha took her time replying. 'I love him.'

'Any fool can see that you're head over heels with him, and from the way he looks at you, I suspect he feels the same way. So what are you afraid of?'

'Losing him.'

'If you tell Rhys about Austen and he walks away, he's not worth keeping.'

'That's the thing, Mum, I don't want to find out. I want everything to carry on just the way it is.'

That was a lie, though. Tabitha *didn't* want things to stay the same. She wanted to spend every night with Rhys, but that was impossible at the moment, and might continue to be impossible for a long time to come.

Something had to give, but Tabitha didn't know what. But whatever it was, she had the feeling she wasn't going to like it.

CHAPTER 19

'It's a nested Bramah key.' Tabitha placed the key on a felt pad, and the customer bent forward to examine it. 'It's unusual and quite rare because it's a Bramah key with another Bramah key inside. I haven't been able to find out much about it, but I suspect it might have been used for a safe or a vault.' The key didn't look particularly remarkable and it certainly wasn't the fanciest one in the shop, looking more like a spring bolt than a key, but it was quite valuable.

'And this is a swivelling double bit key.' She eased a second key onto the felt. Once again, this key wasn't much to behold, but Grandad had told her he had never seen another like it and wasn't sure of its purpose. Tabitha showed the customer how the key worked, rotating the inner part of the bow through a middle shaft.

The man said, 'I like this one. Do you mind if I pick it up?'

'Of course not.'

'How much did you say it was?'

Tabitha told him. He didn't flinch, despite the high price tag.

The customer was in his forties, and from what she could gather, he was a knowledgeable and keen collector.

'How long have you been here?' he asked.

'Since 1909 – not me, the shop.'

'Really?' He peered at her over the top of his glasses. 'Why haven't I known about you before now? I've visited Bath several times over the years, but I never realised this shop was here.'

'May I ask... how *did* you find out about us?'

'Your website. My wife loves Bath, so it was no hardship to persuade her that we needed a weekend away so I could pop in and see your stock.'

'Where are you from?'

'Walsall.'

Tabitha smiled, happy to have gained a new customer. This was the first tangible proof that having a website was good for business, and she couldn't wait to share the news with Rhys and her grandad.

Elated, she closed the sale on both keys, feeling very pleased with herself.

Before he left, the man asked, 'Do you have a newsletter? I didn't see one on your website. You've got some lovely specimens, and I'd like to be kept up to date with any new ones you have in.'

'Oh, er, right. I don't have a newsletter but if you let me have your email address, I'll drop you a quick line if I get something in that I think might be of interest.'

She slid the receipt book across the counter and handed him a pen.

He wrote down his email, then said, 'I think my wife would like it here. She normally avoids these kind of shops like the plague – she can't understand my interest.' He shook his head regretfully, as though she didn't know what she was missing. 'But this is how I imagine a shop would have been in the first half of the last century. It's a real treat to visit.'

'Thank you so much. You've made my day.'

The phone rang and she picked up the receiver, smiling as he gave her a wave on his way out.

'Hello, Locke's Key Emporium,' she almost sang down the phone line.

Her greeting was met with silence.

'Hello?'

Nothing.

'I'm sorry, I can't hear you. Hello?' There was still no response, but Tabitha felt certain someone was on the other end. She had no idea why she thought it, because the line appeared to be dead, but for a split second she could have sworn she heard someone breathing.

'Hello?' she repeated cautiously, straining to listen.

Tabitha held the phone to her ear for another couple of heartbeats, before ending the call.

The phrase 'a ghost in the machine' popped into her head, and she uttered a self-conscious laugh. It was probably one of those auto-generated calls that wanted to sell her something or was phishing for her bank account details she assumed, and she promptly forgot all about it as she made a note of the not-insubstantial sale in the ledger.

Today was shaping up to be a very good day indeed.

***

Tabitha tapped the pen against her tooth as she studied the screen. She was sitting at the kitchen table with the laptop open in front of her, trying to get to grips with creating her first sales page.

Rhys had set up a template page for her, but it was down to her to photograph the relevant items and come up with a description which didn't sound as dry as the Atacama Desert. She wanted it to be factual, but she also wanted to make it compelling enough to persuade people to make a purchase.

Rhys was hovering behind her, looking at the screen over her shoulder as she typed. She had written the description out in long-hand first, and it had so many crossings out it was largely ineligible.

He put his hands on her shoulders, and she felt his warm breath on the nape of her neck as he kissed her tender skin.

'You'd better stop that right now,' she murmured, tipping her head to the side to give him better access.

'Or what?' He moved a strand of her hair and carried on kissing and nibbling.

Tabitha wriggled with pleasure. 'I'll have to stop what I'm doing and kiss you back,' she warned.

'I'd like that.'

'Yes, but kissing is *all* you'll get.'

He paused. 'I know.'

It was growing late, too late to go back to his for a couple of hours, not without risking raised eyebrows from her grandfather. Jeremy obviously knew that her relationship with Rhys was intimate, but she didn't want to rub his nose in it so she tried to be discreet.

Rhys gave up kissing her, and stroked her hair instead, his attention having turned to the webpage.

'I forgot to mention it, but that customer I was telling you about, the one who found the shop because of the website, asked if I had a newsletter. What do you think? Should I have one?'

'It's a good marketing tool,' he said. 'There's a typo, just there.' He pointed to the offending word on the screen and Tabitha corrected it. 'I suggest you collect a few email addresses first, before you go to the time and effort of writing one. You don't want to try to do too much at once.'

Tabitha slumped back, resting her head against him. 'You're right – as usual.' She let out a slow breath. 'It was so much easier when all I had to do was stand in the shop and sell a key or two.'

'Don't give me that: you *love* being in charge.'

'What if I make a pig's ear of it? Grandad's entrusting the business to me, and I don't want to be the Locke who runs it into the ground.'

'You won't. Jeremy wouldn't have signed it over to you if he didn't think you were capable. You'll do a brilliant job, and when the time comes you can hand it on to the next generation of Lockes.'

She loved that Rhys had such faith in her. 'I need a kiss.'

'Did you, or did you not, just tell me to stop kissing you?'

'I've changed my mind.'

'You'll come back to mine?'

His eyes widened, but her tone was regretful as she said, 'Not tonight.'

'Tomorrow, then?'

'We're going out with Laurent and Martha, remember?'

'Damn.' He looked so disappointed, that she had to laugh.

'I thought you wanted to go.' They had planned to visit a virtual reality room, and she knew Rhys had been looking forward to it.

'I do, but I want to take you to bed more.'

'Saturday,' she promised.

His eyes glittered. 'I'll hold you to that. How about we have a takeaway first, save you cooking?'

'That's a lovely idea but Grandad doesn't like what he calls 'foreign food.'

Rhys sat down in the chair opposite. 'I'm not so sure about that. He admitted to having sushi the other day.'

'He didn't!'

'He did, but only because one of his cronies told him it was the same as smoked salmon. He didn't discover what it was until after he had eaten it and enjoyed it.'

'Sushi, it is then,' she decided. 'But I bet he eats it with a knife and fork. He'll never eat it with his fingers.'

Rhys was about to say something when the laptop pinged, capturing his attention. 'You've got a message on your website,' he said.

Excitedly, Tabitha opened up the message box, then frowned.

'What is it?' Rhys scooted closer to read it.

The box where the sender's name should be, contained only a question mark, and the message box held several more, although the box for the email address appeared to be filled in correctly, even if the address itself was just a string of numbers and letters.

'I don't understand,' she said. 'Is it a glitch?'

'Let me see.' His fingers flashed across the keyboard, bringing up a sidebar. 'Not a glitch. Somebody either doesn't know how to fill it in, or they're messing about. I'm certain it's not a bot. Do you want me to delete it?'

'You may as well. I'm not going to reply and ask whoever it was what they meant.'

'There, deleted. Shall I make us a cup of cocoa, then I'll leave you to it.'

'That would be nice.'

How lucky was she to have such a kind, considerate, thoughtful man in her life. She didn't deserve him, and her fear was that one day he would realise it, too.

***

Tabitha glanced behind her at the camera, and a trickle of unease made the hairs on the back of her neck stand on end. It was situated at the top of the wall, near the ceiling, angled to give it a clear line of sight of the till, the card reader, and *her*.

It was like being watched all the time, and it made her uncomfortable – which wasn't surprising considering what had happened in the past, and even though Rhys had assured her that only she had access to the footage it recorded, he'd mentioned that it was backed up onto a cloud.

What concerned Tabitha was that whoever owned the cloud might also be able to view it. And although it recorded nothing more exciting than Tabitha bending over to adjust the display in the cabinet, she was nevertheless very aware that her every move was being monitored.

She was in two minds to ask Rhys to remove them, and she would have done if it wasn't for the fact that when she was upstairs in the flat, or out somewhere, she could connect to the cameras via her mobile phone, and it was comforting to see that everything in the shop and immediately outside, was as it should be.

However, she still couldn't shake the feeling that she was being watched.

Hoping she would get used to it in time, Tabitha grabbed a duster and began flicking it over the keys hanging on the hooks nearest the door. They were placed there to entice customers to come inside.

With a half an hour to go until closing time, she could run the duster over the whole shop and it would be all clean and tidy for tomorrow. Saturday was the shop's busiest day, and she wanted to hit the ground running, so to speak.

The Green was still lively she noticed, as she glanced through the window, with people using it as a cut-through to get to the abbey, and she sent up a silent thank you to her great-grandfather for opening the shop in such a prime location. Passing trade accounted for about half of their takings, although now that the website was up and running, Tabitha was hoping a significant proportion of sales would come via the online shop.

After Rhys had left yesterday evening, Tabitha had spent another couple of hours tweaking the sales page until she was happy with it. She would show it to Rhys on Sunday, and if he thought it was good to go, she would make it live, then anxiously await her first sale.

The clock chimed a quarter past the hour, and she glanced at it fondly. Its constant deep tick was comforting, even though it usually faded into the background, and often the chimes didn't register either.

Fifteen minutes to go, then she would close up.

She couldn't wait to see Rhys and was looking forward to the VR room. It would be a new experience for her. She'd had many new experiences since Rhys had walked into the shop holding his nan's tortoiseshell box. Tabitha was so thankful that she hadn't found a key to fit it immediately, because he wouldn't have had a reason to return, and she recalled how reluctant he had been to leave it with her, and how he had set up camp in the tea room opposite. She had felt him watch her through the window, ensuring his nanna's precious box didn't come to any harm.

Tabitha gazed out of the window now, remembering her first impression of him, and she was quite lost in her thoughts when she realised that she was staring across the Green and into the tea room's window.

As she did so, her gaze sharpened and she became still, her brow creasing in concentration. There was something familiar about a man sitting at one of the tables near the window. The building was in shadow, the glass reflecting the tree in the centre of the Green, but for a second, Tabitha could have sworn her ex was inside, a mug in his hands.

Her blood running cold, she blinked to clear her vision, but when she looked again, the table was empty.

Unsettled and on edge, Tabitha decided not to wait the remaining seven minutes – she would lock up now. The likelihood of a customer this late in the day was slim, and even if one did appear, her arms had broken out in goosebumps and she had a sick feeling in her stomach, so she wouldn't be in any fit state to serve them anyway.

Hurrying through the process of locking up and stowing the most valuable items in the safe, along with the day's takings, Tabitha was relieved to trot up the stairs. She would make herself and Grandad some dinner, then have a shower and get ready to go out. This evening promised to be fun.

'Tabitha? Is that you?' he called as she entered the flat.

She shook her head in mock exasperation. Who else would it be? She had told him earlier that Rhys wouldn't be joining them for dinner today. And if Grandad had cared to take a look at the laptop, he would have seen her traipsing up the stairs. It was weird to think that he could see exactly what she was up to in the shop from the comfort of his armchair, but as far as she knew, he never did.

'Yes, Grandad, it's me.'

'Can you do me a favour?' he asked, as she walked into the parlour. 'When I tried to collect my prescription from the chemist this morning, they said it wasn't ready and to call back later. I had every intention of doing so, but I dropped off to sleep for forty winks. I could fetch it in the morning, but I ran out of my tablets yesterday and haven't taken one today. They are open until six. Do you mind?'

Tabitha kissed him on his lined cheek. 'Of course I don't. I'll just grab my bag, then I'll nip out.'

'Would you like me to start dinner? What are we having?'

'Lamb chops, green beans, and cauliflower cheese. You can prepare the cauliflower if you like.'

'I can do that. By the way, that contraption has been beeping.'

That contraption was the laptop.

'I'll take a look at it later,' she promised. 'I'd better hurry if I want to catch the chemist before they shut.'

Tabitha was out of the door and hurrying across the Green in record time. She hoped she wouldn't have to wait long, as she wanted to give herself enough time to wash and dry her hair before Rhys called for her.

She scurried out of the lane and into the Green, and underneath an archway which was once the southern entrance to the abbey, her heels clicking a staccato rhythm on the old cobbles, a most satisfying sound as the echo briefly bounced on the wide stone arch overhead.

Often she would dawdle to admire it, but she didn't have time today: she had an errand to run. But as she hurried through it, she felt eyes on her once more and she hesitated, half-turning to look behind her.

A figure stood in the shadow of the plane tree in the centre of the Green. It was indistinct, but she knew instinctively that it was male and she could have sworn he was staring at her. Those damned CCTV cameras were setting her on edge and now she was imagining things, and she told herself not to be so silly. The chap was probably admiring the arch, as so many people did every day.

Tabitha kept walking. The sooner she got to the chemist, the sooner she would be home.

But as she made her way back, the box of tablets safely stowed in her bag, she slowed as she approached the archway. No one lingered underneath, and there was no one under the tree. Three teenagers were coming towards her, chattering animatedly, but there was no lone male figure to be seen. Nevertheless, her pace increased to a brisk walk as she crossed the cobbles once more and strode down the narrow lane to the rear of the shop. And as soon as she was safely inside, she hurried into the parlour to look out of the window. She even played back the video footage of the front of the shop whilst she prepared dinner, but she saw nothing out of the ordinary.

Why, then, did she continue to feel so uneasy?

CHAPTER 20

On Saturday afternoon Tabitha was surprised to see Rhys striding into the shop, holding a bag aloft and waggling his eyebrows.

'I've got the sushi,' he announced.

'You're early,' she pointed out. She still had customers in the shop and closing time wasn't for another half an hour.

He said, 'I thought I'd fetch it now so it can come up to room temperature.'

'Is that a thing?' Tabitha had always eaten hers chilled.

'That's the way it's supposed to be eaten,' he said. 'I'll go on up, shall I?'

'OK. What are we having?'

'Smoked salmon and avocado, sticky rice, cucumber maki, shrimp tempura, spicy tuna, tobiko, chilli crab...'

Tabitha laughed. 'Is that all?'

When Rhys's face fell as he said, 'Isn't it enough? I can go back and get some more,' she laughed even harder.

'I was joking. It sounds like you've got enough to feed an army.'

He took a couple of steps towards the door to the workshop then paused, whispering, 'You're going to need to keep your strength up for what I've got planned later.'

'Stop it!' she hissed. 'You'll make me blush.'

'I'm aiming to do more than make you blush.'

Tabitha's face burned as she remembered what they had done the last time she was in his bed, and she couldn't wait to do it again.

'Go on, shoo!' she cried. 'See to the sushi. I've got customers who need serving.'

Rhys blew her a kiss, then left her to it. She watched him disappear through the door and heard him climb the stairs.

Wishing she could lock up now, she turned her attention to the group of elderly gentlemen who were reminiscing over one of the more elaborate Victorian keys.

One of them said, 'I remember my grandmother having one just like that in her house. It was the key to the cellar, and she used to keep it on a hook on the wall next to the cellar door. The door was kept locked at all times, and I used to wonder what the point was, considering the key was right next to it. Then my brother told me that it wasn't locked to keep people *out*, but to keep something *in*.' He shuddered theatrically. 'I'm tempted to buy this and give it to him for his birthday. It'll serve him right for scaring me witless.'

'It's more imaginative than a pair of slippers or a bottle of cognac,' one of the other gents observed.

'I'll take it,' the first man said and, knowing it was to be a gift, Tabitha took extra care in wrapping it, using some of the lovely tissue paper with keys printed on it. She finished it off with a ribbon before handing it to her delighted customer.

The satisfaction of a job well done spread warmth through her chest. The shop had had a very good day and takings were up, she had a tasty dinner to look forward to (one that she hadn't had to cook), followed by several hours in Rhys's bed. It would be the perfect end to a good day.

Smiling to herself, Tabitha tidied away the sticky tape and ribbon, and slid the scissors into a drawer, then wrote the sale in the ledger.

She had her head bowed, totting up the sales for the week, when she heard the door open and the bell tinkle. With a friendly smile on her face, she straightened up – then let out a horrified gasp.

'*Austen!*' She felt the blood drain from her face to pool in her navy Mary Jayne's, leaving her mind numb and her legs weak.

'Tabitha, you're looking good.'

His voice made her skin crawl and loathing swept over her. She had tried so hard to forget what he looked like, what he sounded like, the way he smelt – despite not being able to forget what he had done – that to see him saunter nonchalantly up to the counter made her feel sick.

The urge to run was strong, but she fought it. She had run away from him once; she didn't intend to do it again. This was her shop. *Hers!* And the only person who would be leaving was her scumbag of an ex-boyfriend.

'Get out.' Her voice was stern, even though she was quaking inside, and he blinked in surprise. She never used to stand up for herself, and he hadn't expected her to do so now. Growing bolder, she snarled, '*Now!*'

'Oh, I don't think you want me to do that.'

'*Oh,* but I do.' Sarcasm dripped from every word, as she recognised that her fear was irrational. He had done his worst, and she was still standing. He may have broken her, but she had put herself back together, and although she still bore the mental and emotional scars of the hurt he had inflicted, they were no longer gaping red wounds. Given time, she hoped that they would become nothing more than hairline cracks.

'No, you don't.' He came to a halt in front of the counter, put both hands on it and leant across it.

He was so close, she could smell him; he wore the same aftershave he had always worn, the same scent that had invaded her nostrils the night he had filmed her naked, when she had been so trusting and vulnerable.

Bile rose into her throat and she swallowed hard. Austen was a bully, and bullies thrived on weakness. Tabitha was determined not to show him how badly his presence was affecting her.

She returned his stare, trying not to flinch. The murky grey of his eyes reminded her of ocean depths where savage slimy creatures lurked. How could she have thought they were arresting and charismatic, when she could now clearly see the blankness in them.

He was enjoying this, but maybe not as much as he had hoped, she realised, as his eyes hardened when she refused to look away.

Irrationally, she wondered whether he had his eyebrows threaded: they were remarkably well-groomed. He'd had his teeth whitened too, as his shark-like smile revealed.

She glowered at him. 'I asked you to leave. I won't ask you again.'

'What are you going to do? Throw me out?' His gaze scoured the length of her. She was no match for him physically and both of them knew it.

Abruptly he straightened up, and for a brief, hopeful moment, she thought he might leave.

No such luck.

Austen surveyed the shop and uttered a low whistle. 'Your grandad has done well for himself, hasn't he? When you told me he owned a key shop, I didn't imagine anything like this.'

Tabitha wondered whether she had subconsciously known that he couldn't be trusted, as she hadn't told him much about her parents or her grandfather. She hadn't spoken about them hardly at all. Why was that?

'I assumed he cut keys for a living in some grubby little backstreet,' Austen continued. 'But that's not the case, is it?' His gaze drifted towards the ceiling. 'It must be very convenient living above the shop.'

The blood in Tabitha's veins ran cold, making her sluggish. 'It *was* you I saw yesterday.'

His attention snapped back to her. 'Give the girl a gold star.'

'Why?'

He shrugged. 'I wanted to see for myself.'

'See what?'

The clock chimed the half hour, making her jump, but she made no move to lock up.

His eyes flickered towards it. 'Don't you find that annoying?' he asked.

'No.'

Losing interest in the clock, he continued to stare at her, and Tabitha shifted uncomfortably.

'You had me arrested,' Austen stated, his voice devoid of emotion.

He was starting to scare her, but she was determined not to let her fear show. 'You deserved it. Revenge porn is a crime.'

His bark of laughter was brittle. 'The police didn't charge me.'

'Only because I couldn't face going to court.'

'Because you knew it would be your word against mine.'

'I had no idea you were filming me,' she said, her teeth gritted, her jaw so tense that pain shot up her neck into her head.

'You were going to leave me, so I thought I'd give you a little something to remember me by – a memento, if you will. Consider it a leaving present. Everyone wants their fifteen minutes of fame, and that was yours.'

Tabitha froze. How had he known that she had been considering ending their relationship? Unless... 'You read my messages!'

'Did I?' He was smirking.

'You must have! How did you—?'

'Simple. You sleep very deeply, Tabitha.'

Pressing her lips together, Tabitha balled her hands into fists. The swine had used her fingerprint to unlock her phone while she had been asleep. Despicable.

'Can you get any lower?' she snapped, anger building, pushing aside her fear.

'Oh, I think I can. I lost my job because of you, Tabitha.'

'I lost mine, too.'

'You chose to leave. I was... how shall I put it?... *Advised* to leave.'

'I hope you're not expecting any sympathy from me.'

'An apology would be nice.'

'*An apology?!*' Tabitha spluttered. 'Are you for real? If anyone is owed an apology, it's me! After what you did—'

'Don't be such a drama queen. If you hadn't gone off the deep end, it would have blown over in a couple of days. A week at the most. Instead, you had me *arrested.*' His eyes glittered dangerously as he spat the word out.

'I wish I'd gone through with it,' she retorted. 'You should be behind bars. What are you doing here anyway?'

'Does your boyfriend know about your slutty behaviour?'

As what Austen said sunk in, the sudden spike of adrenalin was the only thing keeping Tabitha upright. Her heart stopped and the world spun. She feared she was about to pass out and she fought to stay conscious. A thud inside her chest made her cough, as her heart began to race again.

'What?' It came out as a whisper, and Austen smirked.

'I didn't think he did. After all, who would want a woman who allowed herself to be filmed in such a compromising position, and was happy for her boyfriend to post dirty pictures of her online?'

'I didn't *allow* it,' she gulped. 'And I wasn't happy. You *knew* what it would do to me.'

'As I said, it's my word against yours.'

'You hid a camera in your bedroom! I didn't even know it was there.'

His gaze shot to the camera on the wall behind the counter, then back to her. 'It hasn't put you off – you like being filmed, don't you?'

'No, I don't. Please, Austen, just go. This isn't doing either of us any good.'

'Maybe not you, but I'm having a ball.'

'What do you want?'

'I don't know.' He gazed around the shop again. 'A bit of kindness wouldn't go amiss. We were good together once, weren't we?'

Was he trying to blackmail her? Did he want paying off? Or was he deluded enough to believe they could get back together?

'How did you find me?' she demanded.

'You weren't exactly hiding, were you? Not with your photo on your website.'

Tabitha didn't think her heart could sink any further, but it managed another plunge. So much for her efforts to drag Locke's Key Emporium into the twenty-first century. Her grandad had the right idea – she should have left it in the nineteenth century, where it belonged.

Damn that burglar: if he hadn't broken in, they wouldn't have had to get an alarm system, they probably wouldn't have had broadband, and having a website would never have occurred to her. And Austen wouldn't have tracked her down.

If only Grandad had consented to his photo being on the website... But she couldn't blame him. The only person she blamed was herself, for being so gullible and falling for a shit like Austen.

Oh, and Austen himself, of course.

'Who says I've got a boyfriend?' she said, hoping he was guessing.

'Rosalind does.'

Rosalind's betrayal bit deep, and Tabitha's heart filled with fresh pain. She had led Tabitha to believe that she wasn't in contact with Austen. '*Rosalind* told you?'

'Not exactly. She told someone, who told someone else... You know how it is. I thought it might be Chinese whispers, but when I heard a key shop in Bath mentioned, I remembered you had a grandad who had a key business.' He bared his teeth at her. 'So don't try to pretend you haven't got a boyfriend, when I know you have.'

'I'm not denying it,' she replied. 'I just wondered how you knew. And yes, he knows all about those images. I told him.' She almost choked on the lie and prayed Austen hadn't noticed.

'I bet he hasn't *seen* them though, has he?' Austin eased his phone out of his trouser pocket and held it aloft.

Tabitha clutched the counter for support. 'You wouldn't dare.'

'I would, believe me.'

'But they were taken down.'

'Haven't you heard of the cloud? I can access them whenever I want. Would you like to see?'

'No!' she cried, then lowered her voice. 'Please, you can't.'

He raised his eyebrows. 'What's it worth for me not to show them to him? And F.Y.I, I don't believe he *does* know.'

'He knows,' Rhys said from behind her. His voice was soft, but there was a hard edge to it, one which Tabitha had never heard before.

'Rhys... I...' she began, then trailed off, not knowing what to say, or how to explain.

He leant against the doorframe, his arms folded, his ankles crossed. His attention was on Austen. 'Tell me, why have you still got images of Tabitha on your phone?' The melodic Welsh lilt had become more apparent, his accent stronger and more pronounced than she had ever heard it.

'They're not on my phone. I'm not that stupid. They're on the cloud. Duh.' Austen rolled his eyes, and said to her, 'Are you really shagging this yokel?' He returned his baleful gaze to Rhys. 'Get back over the bridge, mate, go play with sheep or something.'

Rhys didn't move. 'You still haven't explained why you've got images of Tabi. Obtained illegally, I might add.'

'Aw, how sweet – *Tabi*.' Austen's sneer made her cringe. But more than that, it made her want to punch him in the face.

Austen's gaze raked up and down Rhys's body, as though he were sizing him up. 'I don't have to explain anything to *you*,' he said. 'This is between me and Tabitha. It's none of your business.' He made a run-along gesture, fluttering his fingers.

Rhys slowly unfurled himself and straightened up. 'It is my business when some tosser harasses the woman I love.'

Tabitha lurched back in shock. Did Rhys just say he loved her?

Austen guffawed loudly, 'You love *her*? She's damaged goods, mate. Everyone has seen her—'

'Shut up!' Tabitha screamed. 'If you say one more word, I'm going to the police.'

'And tell them what?'

'That you are threatening to show illicit images of me without my consent. That's a crime in itself. Oh, and that you tried to blackmail me.' She lifted the receiver and dialled the first digit.

'If you call the police, those images are going live. I might as well be hung for a sheep as a lamb, eh, mate? Your girlfriend's body will be out there for everyone to see.'

Out of the corner of her eye, Tabitha saw Rhys take a step towards Austen, and she shook her head.

Slowly, deliberately, she replaced the receiver. It settled on the cradle with an audible click and Austen grinned. With measured steps, Tabitha came out from behind the counter. When she was only centimetres away from her despicable ex-boyfriend she halted. Austen's grin faltered.

For several seconds Tabitha didn't say a word, but when she finally opened her mouth her voice was reasonable, soft even, but she meant every word.

'Go ahead, do it. Post them on every site you can think of. You tried to break me once, but it didn't work. It's not going to work this time, either. You can't hurt me, Austen: not anymore.'

His triumphant grin had gone completely, replaced by malice and seething anger as he spat, 'You owe me, Tabitha, and you're going to pay.'

'I owe you nothing, you small-minded, petty, delusional little man. Now get out before I throw you out.' She risked a quick glance at Rhys. His expression was impassive.

'Hiding behind your new fella, are you? Going to get him to do your dirty work?'

Tabitha had had enough. Inhaling sharply, she shoved Austen with all her might.

He flew backwards, staggered, lost his balance, then fell to the floor, where he lay sprawled on his back, a shocked expression on his face.

Tabitha knew she shouldn't have done it, but it had felt *so* good.

Austen scrambled to his feet, brushing himself off. 'That's assault.'

'I didn't touch you,' Tabitha said innocently. 'You must have tripped over your own feet. How clumsy.'

'I'll sue.' His eyes shot to the camera. 'There's my evidence and if you delete the footage, it'll just prove you've got something to hide.'

'You really are a nasty piece of work, aren't you? Do your worst, Austen, I don't care. And if I ever see or hear from you again, I'm going to file charges, because you're not the only one who kept those images. I did, too. I took screenshots of all the sites you posted them to. If you want a criminal record, you'll have one. Now, for the last time, *leave*.'

His expression furious, Austen stalked to the door on stiff legs. 'You haven't heard the last of this,' he warned as he yanked it open.

'Stop being so dramatic. We both know this is the end of the matter.'

Austen tried to slam it behind him, but the door closed slowly, with a little tinkle of the bell. It was as though the shop was laughing at him.

With her hands on her hips, Tabitha watched him walk across the Green, and she continued to watch until he disappeared from view. It was only when she was certain he had gone, did she slump to the floor and burst into tears.

CHAPTER 21

Tabitha was only vaguely aware of Rhys locking the door because she was crying so hard, and when he dropped to his knees beside her and scooped her into his arms, she sobbed even harder.

'It's all right, he's gone,' Rhys soothed, one hand stroking her back, the other clasping her to his chest. 'I doubt if he is stupid enough to come back, but if he does, I'll deal with him.'

'I don't want you to deal with him,' she blubbered. 'I can deal with him myself.' This was her mess, her problem, and her awful ex-boyfriend. It was down to her to sort him out; she couldn't expect Rhys to do it for her, although the offer was sweet.

'So I noticed,' he said, amusement in his voice. 'He went down like a sack of spuds.'

'I shouldn't have pushed him.'

'I'm glad you did. It saved me punching him.'

'I didn't want you to get hurt.' She sniffed loudly, using the hem of her dress to wipe the tears from her face.

'Do you honestly think I would have let him hurt me?'

'He works out,' she sniffled.

'I wrestle sheep.'

Tabitha raised her head enough to sneak a peep at him. 'That's not funny.'

'It is,' Rhys insisted. 'He called me a… what was it? A yokel.'

Tabitha sat up a little straighter. Despite the wool carpet, the floor was unforgiving, and she hoped Austen had a bruised backside.

Managing a tiny smile, she said, 'You need to gen up on what a cloud is.'

'I do. I clearly have no clue about anything that isn't sheep related. What a clown.' Rhys clambered to his feet and held out a hand.

As soon as she was upright, he gathered her into an embrace. Tears threatened once more, and Tabitha gulped them back.

'There's no need to cry, Tabi. He won't bother you again – I promise.'

'I'm not crying because of him.' She heaved in a shaky breath. 'I'm crying because you told him you love me. Did you mean it, or were you just saying it for effect?'

Rhys pulled back to look her in the eye. 'I meant it. I love you.' He pressed his lips together. 'I've been wanting to tell you for ages, but I didn't want to spoil things.'

'Why would it spoil things?' She blinked as fresh tears spilled over.

'I didn't know whether you felt the same way. I was worried that if I told you I love you, I'd scare you off. I knew you had issues, so...'

'Issues?' Her laugh was bitter. 'You can say that again. How much did you hear?'

'Most of it.'

'Then you know what he did.'

'I knew anyway.'

Tabitha's eyes flew open. '*How?* Oh, no, you didn't see—'

'I didn't. I haven't been looking you up online, honest. Will told me.'

'Will?' She knew it had been a mistake to agree to Rhys going with her to see Rosalind and the baby.

Rhys continued, 'It wasn't deliberate; he assumed I already knew.'

Tabitha hung her head. 'I should have told you, but I thought you might hate me.'

'I could never hate you.'

She closed her eyes as tears leaked steadily out of the corners. She didn't seem able to stop crying. When she opened them again it was to find Rhys gazing at her, his own eyes full of love.

'He mightn't show his face again,' she said, 'but he isn't going to go away. He has still got those images.'

'Not for much longer.' Rhys released her gently and reached for his phone.

'What are you going to do?' she asked, worriedly. 'Please don't do anything that might get you into trouble.'

'*I'm* not going to do anything, but I know someone who *will*. Laurent, can you get hold of Chancer75 for me? I need a favour, but I can't ask him myself. It's better done through a third party, and you'll need to take all the usual precautions... Hell, yes, of course it's illegal! I wouldn't be asking otherwise. If it wasn't, I would do it myself. I need some images erased...' By the time the call ended, Rhys was smiling. 'They'll be gone within the hour.'

'Can your guy do that?'

'Definitely. *I* can do that, but I won't. What I *can* do though, is alter that video footage.' He jerked his chin towards the camera in the corner.

'But Austen said that if you delete it—'

Rhys scoffed, 'What does *he* know? Anyway, I'm not going to delete it, I'm going to cut and splice it.'

Wordlessly, Tabitha followed him upstairs. The laptop was on the dining table where it normally lived, the lid open, the screen showing the shop, now empty. A selection of sushi sat in the centre of the table, and three place settings had been laid. Her grandad was sitting at one of them. He had a fork in his hand and was chewing vigorously.

Tabitha had forgotten about food and she looked away, the sight of it making her tummy roll in a rather unpleasant manner.

'What took you so long?' Jeremy asked. 'I should apologise for my bad manners, but I couldn't wait. It all looks so appetising.' He popped another morsel into his mouth.

'That's OK. Last minute customer. Rhys is just going to check the internet connection because he thinks it's on the blink. He won't be long.'

'Can't it wait? I don't like eating on my own, although I suppose I'll have to get used to it.'

Distracted by watching Rhys's fingers flying over the keyboard, it took a moment for Grandad's last comment to register. 'What do you mean, *you'll have to get used to it?*'

'When I move into the complex.'

'What complex?'

He didn't answer. Instead, he said, 'You might want to go and freshen up before you eat. You've got panda eyes.'

Damn, she should have realised that her mascara would have smeared itself across her face after all the crying she'd done. 'It's dust,' she said. 'I'll wash it off later. What complex? And why would you be moving into it?'

'It's next door to the club where I go swimming. If you live in the complex, you get a discount.'

Baffled, she said, 'I'm confused.'

'I'm not. I've got eyes and ears in my head. I heard Rhys tell you he loves you. And I know you love him.'

Rhys shot her a look and his face lit up. 'You do?'

'Yes, I meant to tell you downstairs, but things were moving too fast. Hang on a minute; Grandad, *when* did you hear him say that?'

'Just now. When you were *seeing to your customer.*'

Her heart sank. 'I didn't know you'd come downstairs.' She wished he hadn't – he shouldn't have had to witness Austen's vitriol.

'I didn't. I could hear you quite clearly through that.' He pointed to the laptop.

Tabitha was appalled and she turned an accusing face towards Rhys. 'You must have left the sound on.'

'No, I didn't. It was on mute, and I didn't need to hear your ex speak to know who he was. I recognised him immediately.' When Tabitha opened her mouth to ask how, he added, 'Social media. I started with Rosalind and followed a trail of breadcrumbs until I found him. It wasn't hard.'

They both turned to Jeremy.

He was wearing a smug expression. 'The last time I was at Siegfried's office, I asked his secretary how these things worked. She showed me how to turn it on, and what she called basic stuff.'

'But you hate computers!' Tabitha cried.

'They're not so bad once you get used to them,' Grandad said, helping himself to another sushi roll. 'They have their uses. I might treat myself to one, when I move into the complex.'

Tabitha frowned. 'What's with all this talk of moving into a complex?'

'As I said, I've got eyes and ears. I can see how much you and Rhys want to be together, and I'm getting in the way. What's in this? It's rather delicious.' Jeremy held up a roll.

Rhys lifted his head enough to say, 'Chilli crab, I think,' before returning to his task.

Jeremy let out a contented sigh. 'Do you know, I might try Chinese food next. I've been told that crispy duck pancakes are quite nice.'

'Grandad! I don't want to talk about food. I want to talk about your ridiculous idea of moving. You can't leave. I won't let you.' He couldn't possibly be serious. Was he playing some kind of joke on her? If so, he could have picked a better time.

'I can and I will. I refuse to stand in the way of true love.'

'You're not. We'll work something out, won't we, Rhys?'

Jeremy placed his knife and fork neatly together on his plate and studied Tabitha over the top of his glasses. 'No need. I've worked it out for you. Rhys, are you listening, because this concerns you.'

'All done,' Rhys announced. He closed the lid of the laptop and tapped it fondly. 'What is it, Jeremy?'

'I'm going to live in a complex for retired people. I'll have my very own flat with a sitting room, a bedroom, a kitchen and a bathroom. It's got all the mod cons and I'll have a private balcony with views over the river. It's got a lift and a common room. It'll be like being back at school. We had a common room in Harrow. Several, in fact. But there isn't a dining hall in the complex, unfortunately, as the residents are expected to self-cater.'

Tabitha blew out her cheeks. 'You've got a pretty good flat here, and someone to cook dinner and do your washing and ironing.'

'You can do that for Rhys instead, if you must; but I suggest that seeing as you are a modern woman, you should insist on Rhys doing his fair share.' He gave an exasperated sigh. 'Let me be blunt – neither of you feel you can live together with me in the picture. Therefore, I am removing myself from the frame. Rhys can move in here and the pair of you can have my room, and you can convert Tabitha's bedroom into an office for him, so he can carry on working from home.'

Tabitha was astounded. 'You've got this all worked out, haven't you? What about Rhys's flat?'

'I suggest he either sells it or rents it out.'

'No.' Tabitha shook her head.

'Tough. It's happening.'

'You can't simply decide that Rhys and I will live together. We need to talk about it first. Anyway, Rhys mightn't want to.' Tabitha threw her hands in the air and grunted in disgust. 'Why are we even discussing this? Grandad, you *can't* leave. I don't *want* you to.' She sent Rhys a helpless look.

Rhys said, 'It's OK, your grandad doesn't have to go anywhere. We can carry on just the way we are.'

Tabitha had never felt so torn in her life. One half of her desperately wanted to spend all day, every day with Rhys. The other half was very conscious of the promise she had made to herself when Grandad had taken her in – that she would help run the shop and do everything around the flat.

But now Grandad felt he had to leave his home because she had fallen in love and he thought he was a gooseberry.

'Tabitha, my dear, I have made up my mind. I am going. You can come visit me every day if you wish – although I'm sure you'll soon get tired of that – but you can't stop me. There will come a point in the not-too-distant future when I'm going to need more care than you can provide, if I live long enough. The complex is that next stage. It has panic buttons in every room, doors wide enough for wheelchairs, walk-in baths... I would prefer to go in my own time and to a place of my choosing, rather than—'

'No!'

'Stop being so silly!' he barked, and Tabitha jumped. 'Anyone would think I was moving to the ends of the earth or I'm on my last legs and about to croak at any minute. Please be assured that this isn't the case. I know you won't believe me, but I've been planning this since before Rhys came along. I was just waiting for the right time. And,' he paused, 'the time is now most definitely right. You have found your wings again, darling girl; it is time for you to fly.'

***

Neither Tabitha nor Rhys had felt like rushing off to his place after they'd eaten. Rhys's appetite was just fine, but Tabitha hadn't managed more than a few mouthfuls before giving up. It was a shame, because the sushi had looked delicious. But the events of the past couple of hours had killed her appetite.

Grandad had made himself scarce by retreating to the bathroom for a long soak (in reality Tabitha suspected he wanted to give her and Rhys a chance to talk) and had left the two of them in the parlour, soft music playing in the background.

Tabitha settled onto the sofa and cuddled up against Rhys, a glass of wine in her hand. Rhys was drinking one of the stubby brown bottles of real ale she kept in the fridge for him. At one point, his phone vibrated and he checked the screen.

'It's done,' he informed her, and she knew what he meant.

Austen's images of her had disappeared and she could finally relax. It was over. Even though she didn't think Austen would have been stupid enough to pull the same stunt twice, the worry would have lingered in the back of her mind like a bad smell around an unemptied bin, and she guessed she never would have been free of it. Thank goodness for Rhys's friends.

'I'm sorry I didn't tell you before,' she began. 'I just—'

'Shh, you don't have to apologise, and you don't owe me an explanation, either.'

'I *want* to explain,' she insisted. 'It was wrong of me to keep it secret from you for so long, but the time never seemed right. It's not the kind of thing you tell people when you've just met – 'Hi, I'm Tabitha and I'm a victim of revenge porn'. And when you get to know someone better, you don't want them to think badly of you, so you feel you *can't* tell them.'

'Why would anyone think badly of you?' His thumb circled a small patch of skin on her shoulder, his touch warming her from the inside out.

'It's the shame, you see. It's quite common for victims to feel that it's their fault somehow.'

'But it *isn't* your fault.'

'I know, but it doesn't stop you from thinking you could have done something to prevent it, that you should have seen it coming, or you shouldn't have been so stupid.' She took a long swallow of wine, then balanced her drink on her thigh, her hand around the bowl of the glass. 'I kept meaning to tell you, then putting it off, until I got to the point where it was too late. I was in too deep and was terrified of losing you. I thought that if you knew, you would call time on our relationship, and I simply couldn't face it. I must have been mad! I knew you would find out eventually. It was inevitable.' She put her glass down on the floor near her feet and scooted around to face him. 'I can't believe you knew and didn't say anything.'

'I figured you would tell me in your own time, and if you didn't, it didn't matter. I love you regardless of what happened in the past.'

Wonder flowed through her. That Rhys was so accepting, made her soul hum with happiness. To think that she had spent so long fretting that he would find out, the nights she had lain awake with 'what ifs' circling through her mind like vultures, only for Rhys to be so incredibly understanding. Austen's cruelty had made such an impact on her life that she had spent the last three years hiding, but Rhys had taken it in his stride.

Tabitha offered up a silent *thank you* to the universe for sending this remarkable man to her. 'Do you realise how much I love you?' she whispered.

'I'm hoping you'll tell me.'

'You are the best thing that's happened to me. I can't imagine my life without you. I didn't want to fall in love – it was the furthest thing from my mind – but when you walked into my shop that very first time, there was something about you...'

'My devastatingly handsome good looks? My sparkling personality?'

'Don't push it.' she warned, taking his face in her hands. 'I'm trying to tell you I love you here, and all you can do is crack jokes?'

'I'm nervous.'

'Why?'

'Because I've never felt this way about anyone before.'

'Neither have I. I love you, Rhys.'

'And I love *you* more than you'll ever know.'

Tabitha had a pretty good idea of how much, and when she kissed him, she could feel the love sparkling between them, bright and full of promise for what the future might hold. Which reminded her...

'What am I going to do about Grandad?' she asked, ending the kiss by pulling slowly away.

'What do you want to do?'

'I don't want him to think he has to leave his home. When he signed everything over to me, he made me promise that he could live out his days here, or until—' She stopped, remembering what Grandad had said '*or until you find yourself a husband.*'

She couldn't tell Rhys that – it sounded like Grandad thought they were about to tie the knot. Instead, she finished with, 'Until he decides to move out.'

'Do you think he had this in mind when he said it, because I don't think your grandad does anything on a whim, or on the spur of the moment.'

'You're right, he doesn't. He considers things carefully before he makes a decision.' A thought occurred to her. 'It might be fanciful, but I think Grandad has found a new lease of life these past few weeks. He's going swimming, he's tried sushi and liked it…'

Rhys joined in. 'He's thinking about trying Chinese food. A few months ago, he would never have entertained the idea.'

'Exactly! And what about him with the laptop?'

'That's the greatest change of them all. He hates modern technology.'

'Not anymore, it seems.'

Tabitha fell silent. When she eventually spoke, she chose her words with care. 'I think I need to let Grandad go as much as he wants me to spread my wings. I wonder if my presence has been holding him back? He had been on his own for so long, doing his own thing, running the business by himself, that it must have been a shock to have his needy granddaughter descend on him. I'm not sure he knew what to do with me.'

'I think he knew exactly what to do with you: he gave you time and space to heal. And it worked. Look how far you've come. Maybe he sees himself as one of those wildlife rescuers, who nurses a bird back to health and then sets it free.'

'I thought I was a cat?' Tabitha teased gently.

'You can be whatever you want to be.'

'I want to be with you.'

'That's a given. What else do you want to be Tabicat?'

'Happy.'

'How can I make that happen?' Rhys asked, gazing deeply into her eyes.

'By never stopping loving me.'

'I'll always love you.'

'By moving in with me, here, in this flat.'

'Are you serious?'

She nodded.

'I'd like that very much...'

Tabitha got to her feet and held out a hand. 'Shall we start as we mean to go on? I want to take you to bed.'

'Will your grandad mind?'

Tabitha's heart swelled with love as she replied softly, 'No, I don't believe he will.'

CHAPTER 22

'Mum, are you sure you can manage?' Tabitha's anxiety was through the roof this morning. It hadn't helped matters that her parents hadn't arrived when they'd said they would. They hadn't been late as such, just not as *on-time* as Tabitha would have liked.

'Tabitha, stop fussing. Your dad knows what he's doing, and your grandad is on the end of the phone if we need him.'

'Good luck with that,' Tabitha muttered. After weeks of persuasion (Grandad had called it nagging), he had capitulated and allowed Tabitha to buy him a basic mobile phone. It was so basic that he could do little with it other than phone or text. He wasn't even able to take a photo, although, bizarrely, it did come with a handful of games.

However, Grandad might *own* a mobile phone, but he didn't often take it *with* him, and when he did, he insisted on turning it off 'to save the battery,' which kind of defeated the object.

Tabitha couldn't help comparing him to Pearl, who not only had the latest iPhone, she knew her way around it better than a fifteen-year-old influencer. Tabitha was forever being sent digitally enhanced photos of the old lady and her fellow residents, who seemed to have endless fun posing for the camera. They particularly liked those apps that enabled them to add cat's ears or gave them smiles like wide-mouthed frogs.

'I've put clean sheets on the bed,' Tabitha told her mother. 'And there are fresh towels in the bathroom.'

'Stop fussing, we'll be fine.'

'I'll phone every day to make sure—'

'*Tabitha! You'll do no such thing!* This is your first proper holiday for years, so enjoy it. I forbid you to think about the shop.'

You can forbid all you like, Tabitha thought; she was still going to phone. *And* she would be checking her emails and keeping an eye on any online orders. But the ultimate in 'thinking about the shop' was being able to monitor the cameras from anywhere in the world, and that included Greece. She would be able to tell at a glance whether everything was fine, or not.

Her mother huffed out an exaggerated sigh. 'The shop will still be here when you get back.'

'I should hope so!' Trying not to worry, Tabitha said, 'I've written down everything you need to know – the code for the alarm, the code for the safe, the password for the laptop...'

'I suppose you'd like us to memorise it and destroy it? Or will it self-destruct in thirty seconds?'

'You think you're so funny,' Tabitha grumbled.

'And you think you're indispensable.'

'She is,' Rhys said, walking into the parlour and giving Tabitha a careful kiss so as not to spoil her make-up. 'But I'm sure you'll do just as good a job.' He turned back to Tabitha. 'You look stunning.'

Tabitha glowed at the compliment. She had made a gargantuan effort with her appearance today – after all, the vast majority of the friends she'd once had would be at Rosalind's wedding. They probably remembered her as a snivelling, mortified mess, *if* they remembered her at all. She wanted them to see how far she'd come: she was the owner of a successful business, she lived in a gorgeous flat in the heart of a beautiful city, and she was in love with the most wonderful man in the world.

The man in question was gazing at her with love and admiration.

'You don't look too bad yourself,' she told him, thinking how sophisticated he was in his suit.

'The pair of you look lovely,' her mother interjected. 'Now, you'd better be on your way, or else you'll be late. Only the bride is allowed to be late at a wedding. Have you got your passports?'

'Mum...' Tabitha whined, sounding like a put-upon teenager. 'I'm not a kid.'

'What time is your flight?'

'Seven a.m. We're booked into a hotel near the airport, so we'll go there first to drop the cases and the car off, then head off to the wedding.'

Her mother chuckled. 'Be careful you don't drink too much today – you don't want to be flying with a hangover. Been there, done that, and regretted it.'

'I'll just go check on Dad—' Tabitha began

'Rhys, stop her. Kenneth is fine. He has stepped in for Jeremy before, so he knows what he's doing. He doesn't need Tabitha fussing around him.'

'Come on, Tabi, we'd better go. I've put the cases in the boot.'

'Check you've got your passports,' her mum repeated.

Tabitha scowled. 'Now who is doing the fussing?'

'I'm your mother, I'm allowed to fuss. Come here and give me a hug.' She opened her arms and Tabitha stepped into them, the familiar scent of Chanel wafting over her.

'Have a lovely, lovely time,' her mum said. 'Give me a ring when you get there.'

Tabitha felt Rhys prise her away, and she allowed him to bundle her down the stairs.

'Bye, Dad,' she said, as Rhys propelled her through the shop, out of the door and onto the street. 'I wanted to—' she started to say, but subsided when Rhys gave her a warning look.

'Ready?' he asked.

Tabitha shot a glance at the shop. Her mother was right, it wasn't going anywhere – unlike her. It was time to let go of the reins and spend some much-needed quality time with Rhys.

She would give him her undivided attention for the whole week she vowed, and a fizz of excitement bubbled inside her at the thought of seven days of lazing on the beach, of leisurely dips in the clear, warm waters of the Mediterranean, of eating delicious Greek food, and drinking cocktails. And seven *nights*: don't forget the nights. Or the afternoons, for that matter.

Tabitha giggled.

'What's so funny?' he asked, driving slowly away from the Green.

'Nothing, I'm just happy, that's all.'

'That's good to hear. I'm pretty happy too.' He grinned at her. 'Let's go let our hair down at this wedding, then we can jet off to the sun. I can't wait!'

Neither could Tabitha. She was so happy, she could burst. And if she had to take a bet on it, she reckoned she was even happier than Rosalind!

**

Rhys handed her a tissue. Tabitha took it and dabbed delicately at her eyes, not wanting to smear her makeup.

'I knew you would cry,' he said.

'Do you blame me? It was a lovely service, and Rosalind looked beautiful.'

'Not as beautiful as you,' he countered, and she wrinkled her nose in delight.

Then she spied one of the serving staff handing out glasses of fizz and she made a beeline for them. Grabbing two with a smile of thanks, she handed one to Rhys.

'Cheers,' she said, clinking her glass with his. 'Here's to a brilliant holiday.'

As she sipped, Tabitha studied the other guests. Many of them were relatives of the happy couple, but others she recognised and she couldn't make up her mind whether to go over and say hello.

She caught someone's eye, the woman's gaze sliding over her, before snapping back to her face. *Here we go*, Tabitha thought, as she leant towards her companion to say something. The gossip was starting already, and Tabitha steeled herself for the inevitable overt looks and comments whispered out of the sides of mouths as people recognised her and remembered.

To her consternation, Tabitha saw that the woman was threading her way through the guests, heading in her direction.

'Tabitha? I thought it was you,' she said, when she was close enough. 'It's so good to see you.'

'Hi, Daisy, it's good to see you, too.' Tabitha's tone was friendly, but inside she wanted to run away and hide.

Daisy came in for a brief hug and an air kiss. Then she asked, 'Is this your fella?' and held out a hand.

While her attention was on Rhys, Tabitha took a second to examine her.

Daisy hadn't changed a bit; she wore her hair the same way as she had done since school, and had the same lithe figure, the same confidence.

'I'm Daisy Fellows,' she said, as Rhys shook her hand. 'Tabitha and I go way back.'

'Nice to meet you.' He checked with Tabitha, 'Do you want me to make myself scarce so the two of you can have a girly catch-up?'

That was so sweet of him, but he didn't know anyone else here apart from Rosalind and Will, who were understandably occupied, mostly with having their photos taken, but also with mingling. Anyway, Tabitha wasn't sure she *wanted* to catch up.

'Can we get together later?' she asked Daisy, making a mental note to avoid her.

'You bet we can! I want to hear all about what you've been up to since I last saw you. Rosalind has filled in some of the deets, but I want to hear them from you. You're looking good, girl.'

Some of Tabitha's tension eased. 'So are you. I love that you haven't cut your hair.'

Daisy flicked her waist-length locks. 'It's my trademark,' she laughed. 'I wouldn't feel like me if I did.' Her companion, a tall guy with a beard, who could have been anywhere between thirty and fifty, signalled to her. 'Oops, I'd better get back to Simon. He doesn't know a soul, bless him, and I don't want him to think I've abandoned him.' She moved in for another quick hug, then was gone.

'She's lively,' Rhys said.

Tabitha was grinning. 'She always was.' This wasn't so bad, after all, she decided. Daisy hadn't appeared to be bothered in the slightest about what had happened to Tabitha, although Tabitha didn't have any doubt that Daisy had forgotten. Who *could* forget? But Daisy had seemed genuinely pleased to see her.

Regret that she hadn't stayed in Bristol and fronted it out, slid through her. Tabitha now understood that if she hadn't run away, the scandal would have blown over eventually. The aftermath wouldn't have been pleasant, but she realised her friends would have rallied around her if she had given them the chance.

Rhys's hand found hers and gave it a squeeze, and suddenly she knew that she wouldn't have had it any other way; because if she hadn't come to Bath, she would never have met Rhys, and life without him was unthinkable.

'I love you,' she said, tightening her grip on his hand.

'I love you, too.' The adoration in his eyes was clear for all to see, and happiness swept over her.

She had her whole life ahead of her, and hopefully this man would be by her side for every single second of it.

***

'I'm drunk,' Rosalind announced, taking another swallow of whatever was in her glass. 'I don't think I'm going to be consummating anything tonight.'

It was gone eleven o'clock and the reception was winding down. Tabitha had had a brilliant

time, eating, drinking, dancing, and connecting with old friends. She was tired, her makeup was smeared, her feet hurt (those shoes were too damned high), but she was happy.

She was also tipsy, but not as inebriated as the bride.

Tabitha and Rosalind were slumped around a table that was sticky with empty glasses and covered in crumbs from the buffet earlier. The guests had thinned out, many of the older ones and those who had children with them, having called it a night. A few die-hards were still on the dance floor, swaying to the music that had changed from foot-tapping seventies hits to slow-dance stuff.

'You look stunning,' Tabitha told her friend. 'I cried when I saw you walking down the aisle.'

'So was I! I'm so happy.'

'I can tell.'

'You and Rhys look happy, too.'

'We are.'

'I'd better have an invite to the wedding.'

'He has to ask me first.'

'*You* could always ask *him*,' Rosalind pointed out.

'I don't think so. He might say no.'

'Unlikely.' Rosalind's attention wandered over to a group of men who were standing near the bar. Will and Rhys were amongst them. 'He adores you.'

Tabitha followed her gaze and smiled. Rhys's jacket was off, his tie was nowhere to be seen, and he had unbuttoned his collar and his sleeves were rolled up, exposing his forearms. He had very nice forearms.

And she'd had too much to drink, if she was fixating on his arms.

'I'm so glad things have worked out for you, Tabs,' Rosalind said, reaching out to place her hand over Tabitha's.

'Me, too.' Her reply was heartfelt.

'I've, um, got some news about Austen, if you want to hear it.'

Tabitha stiffened. She never wanted to hear his name again, but now that Rosalind had mentioned it, Tabitha had to know. She hoped that whatever her friend was about to tell her wasn't going to ruin her night. She had been having such a good time...

'Go on,' she said warily.

Rosalind's eyes twinkled. 'He's been arrested and is in custody!'

Far from being pleased by the news, Tabitha was devastated. To think he had done the same to someone else, that he had done to her! If only she'd had the courage all those years ago, he might have been charged and prosecuted. He might even have been imprisoned. She felt so incredibly sorry for this unknown woman, as well as terribly guilty.

'Oh, no...' she murmured.

Rosalind was bewildered. 'I thought you'd be pleased,' she began, then gasped and lowered her voice. 'Don't tell me you still have feelings for him?'

'God, no! He's a toad. I'm glad he's got what he deserves, but I'm sorry another woman has had to go through what I went through.'

'What are you talking about?'

'Posting revenge porn online.'

Rosalind frowned. 'That's not what happened. He was caught embezzling money from the company he works for.'

Tabitha's relief at hearing that she wasn't to blame for another woman's heartache was overwhelming. She also felt a certain degree of satisfaction that he'd got caught. Once a shit, always a shit. He deserved whatever he got.

However, her level of satisfaction increased tenfold when Rosalind told her *how* he had been caught. After suspecting he was up to no good, the company had installed hidden cameras and had caught him in the act.

Talk about karma!

***

'Let's go for a walk on the beach before dinner,' Rhys suggested as they were preparing to go out for the evening. 'We can watch the sun go down and enjoy the sunset.' It was their second to last day in Greece, and every evening the sunsets had been spectacular.

Tabitha sprayed perfume on her wrists and throat. 'That sounds lovely.' A stroll across the warm sand, before wandering through the narrow streets until they found a restaurant they fancied, was idyllic.

Hand-in-hand they made their way down to the shore. Despite it being late October, Tabitha didn't need the cardi she had brought with her, so she draped it over her shoulder bag. During the day it was hot enough to sunbathe and swim, and in the evening the temperature was pleasantly balmy and so far this holiday they had eaten outdoors every evening. The cardi might come in handy later though, if the temperature dropped a bit.

The sun hadn't fully dipped below the horizon; a vestige of it shimmered on the sea, the sky around it glowing a brilliant shade of orange, the colour reflected in the water and rippling with the gentle rise and fall of the waves.

It was a heavenly moment, and one Tabitha would remember forever. She didn't believe it could *be* any more perfect.

Until...

Out of the blue, Rhys dropped to one knee. Tabitha, taken unawares, wondered what he was doing. Then she spotted the ring he was holding and the worried look on his face, and her heart almost leapt out of her chest.

He cleared his throat. 'Tabitha, I love you with everything I have, and I want to spend the rest of my life with you. Will you marry me?'

Joy rushed through her and she felt limp with the force of it, her heart racing so fast she thought she might faint.

'Yes, yes, I will,' she heard herself say, and saw the instant relief on his face.

With tears trickling down her cheeks, she held out her left hand. Rhys slid the ring on her finger, and got to his feet, taking her in his arms, then as one they turned to face the ocean to watch the last of the brilliant colour fade from the sky.

When the stars began to twinkle in the velvet blackness above, Tabitha's thoughts turned to the very first time she had set eyes on Rhys, because little had she known that by finding the key to his grandmother's precious tortoiseshell box, she would also find the key to her own happiness.

ABOUT THE AUTHOR

Liz Davies writes feel-good, light-hearted stories with a hefty dose of romance, a smattering of humour, and a great deal of love.

She's married to her best friend, has one grown-up daughter, and when she isn't scribbling away in the notepad she carries with her everywhere (just in case inspiration strikes), you'll find her searching for that perfect pair of shoes. She loves to cook but isn't very good at it, and loves to eat - she's much better at that! Liz also enjoys walking (preferably on the flat), cycling (also on the flat), and lots of sitting around in the garden on warm, sunny days.

She currently lives with her family in Wales, but would ideally love to buy a camper van and travel the world in it.

Milton Keynes UK
Ingram Content Group UK Ltd.
UKHW041103130224
437765UK00004B/215